PETER MCLEAN

DOMINION

A BURNED MAN NOVEL

ANGRY
ROBOT

ANGRY ROBOT
An imprint of Watkins Media Ltd

Lace Market House,
54-56 High Pavement,
Nottingham,
NG1 1HW
UK

angryrobotbooks.com
twitter.com/angryrobotbooks
He's on the throne

An Angry Robot paperback original 2016

A catalogue record for this book is available from the British Library.

ISBN 978 0 85766 611 6
Ebook ISBN 978 0 85766 613 0

Set in Meridien and Futur Rough by Epub Services.
Printed and bound in the UK by 4edge Ltd.

For Diane.
Aes Sedai of the Green Ajah
even if she doesn't know it.

CHAPTER 1

The gnomes called it Rotman, and I was starting to see why. I swung my legs over the railing and hung nervously for a moment, my feet trying to get some purchase on the crumbling concrete ledge below me.

"Come on," the gnome hissed.

I let go of the rust-eaten metal and edged to my left while the ghostly underground wind whispered in my ears. It was dark as the devil's arsehole down there, with only the dim light of the gnome's torch to see by. Somewhere above us a train hurtled through a tunnel. I had to stop for a minute and let the vibrations die away before I dared move again. There was a sheer drop on the other side of the ledge, and in the darkness I had no way of telling how far down it went. It could have been three feet or it could have been fifty. I flattened myself against the soggy wall behind me and edged sideways after the gnome. Something didn't smell very nice, and I could only hope it wasn't me.

The gnome turned to look back at me, the beam of its torch playing wildly across empty space as it moved. I caught a glimpse of the decaying skeleton of a collapsed catwalk, flaky with rust and roped with bundles of old, rotted cables

and torn insulation. Now that I could see, the drop in front
of me looked to be about twenty feet. That was at least
eighteen too many in my book.

Get a grip of yourself, Don, I told myself.

"I'm coming, I'm coming," I said, wishing it would keep
the light still.

"We're nearly across," the gnome said.

It turned abruptly again and shone the light of its torch
over a grey metal door at the end of the ledge where it
looked like the catwalk had once been attached to the wall.
I shuffled sideways as fast as I dared, blinking dust from
my eyes and trying not to think about anything. Least of
all about sheer drops onto twisted, rusty metal. That went
about as well as you'd expect, to be honest with you, and
I have to admit I'd worked up a sweat by the time the
gnome's clawed hand reached out for the door handle. I
could hear another train somewhere above, coming closer.
The door opened with a scream of rust-clogged hinges and
the gnome shuffled through. I may have shoved past it a bit,
clinging nervously to the doorframe as the train clattered
overhead and flakes of decaying concrete showered onto
my head.

"Bloody hell," I muttered.

The gnome fumbled about for a moment and then there
was light at last. Sort of, anyway. A feeble piss-yellow
glow spilled from the caged bulbs that lined the wall of
the corridor at twenty-foot intervals. The gnome turned to
look at me.

"You know, I thought you were going to be a little bit
more heroic than this," it said.

"Who the fuck told you that?"

I'm no one's idea of a hero, not by a long way I'm not.
Come to that, the thing in front of me wasn't exactly how
I'd pictured a gnome to be either. It looked sort of like a

cross between a bush baby and a giant bald molerat, if molerats were five feet tall and wearing baggy old jeans and a stained red hoodie. Its whole head looked far too pointed for comfort, with big round eyes and a twitching nose. It didn't actually have whiskers but it looked like it should have done, if you know what I mean. It was a funny looking little bugger, all things considered, somewhere in a weird place between cute and hideous. It flicked the torch off and pushed its clawed, shovel-like hands into the pockets of its hoodie.

"That's what I get for making assumptions," it said. "My mother always told me she didn't raise her daughters to go making silly assumptions, but I do seem to."

"You're a girl?" I asked it in surprise. Bit rude of me I suppose, with hindsight.

"Yes," it said. She said, I mean. She blinked at me. "Why, aren't you?"

"Er," I said. "No."

"'Course you're not," she said. "There I go again, see? When I meet something new I always just sort of assume it's female."

"Well, I'm not," I said. "And I'm someone, not something."

"'Course you are," the gnome said again. "I'd been sort of thinking of you as 'it' so far."

"Well, don't," I said, for all that I had to admit I'd been doing exactly the same thing. "Look, is it much further?"

"Yes," she said.

I sighed and ran my hands through my hair to get the bits of concrete out. They felt wet and sort of spongy. I lifted a finger to my face and sniffed. The soggy concrete smelled horrible.

"Jesus," I muttered.

"It's because of the Rotman," she said. "This is just the edges, it's a lot worse down below. You'll see."

"I can't wait."

The gnome led me down the narrow corridor. There were thick bundles of cobweb-encrusted cables running along the ceiling, puddles of stagnant water underfoot and, somehow, inexplicably, graffiti on the walls. I marvel at the determination of London's delinquent youth sometimes, I really do. How the fuck the little bastards had got down there I had no idea. The corridor ended at another rusty door which the gnome opened with one of the many keys she carried on a big jingling bunch. There was a single caged bulb on the far side, and a circular ledge around a hole in the ground. Above, the shaft ended a few feet above my head in a rough slab of unsmoothed concrete. The only other feature was the curved top of an iron ladder which was bolted to the side of the hole and extended down into the darkness. I crouched and examined the ladder carefully. Rust flaked off under my fingers and tumbled gracefully away into the darkness. That was hardly encouraging, to put it mildly.

"Really?" I asked.

The gnome nodded. "Really, hero."

"After you, then," I said.

"Depends if you want to do it in the dark," she said. "I thought you might like me to hold the torch for you."

I swallowed. Fair point.

"Right," I said. "Cheers."

I tentatively tried a foot on the ladder. It creaked, but seemed like it would hold me. I took a deep breath and trusted it with all my weight, ready to brace my back against the wall behind me to stop myself falling if something broke. I went down slowly. The gnome shone her torch down the shaft so I could at least see the rungs as I went, but that was about it. It was a shock when my feet touched down in a puddle at the bottom.

"I'm down," I called back up the shaft.

"Out of the way then," she replied.

I stepped to one side and found myself plunged into total darkness as the gnome started down the ladder. She climbed fast, but that was still far too long to stand there blind as a bat as far as I was concerned. I could hear rats skittering in the distance. At least, I sincerely *hoped* they were just rats. This deep there could be night creatures wandering around anywhere and I really didn't want to bump into one of those on their own turf.

Night creatures are horrible fucking things, and the tunnels under London are lousy with them. Picture a sort of upright alligator, with big sharp claws and far too many teeth, that can hide in shadows and make its own darkness so you don't even know it's there until it's too late. They like to rape and kill people, and they aren't fussy about what sex you are or what order they do it in either. No, I really did not want to bump into any night creatures while I was alone in the dark.

Eventually the gnome's grubby trainers splashed down into the puddle beside me and the light returned with her. She had the torch clamped between her teeth for climbing. Those teeth were chisel-shaped and raked sharply backwards, and they looked awfully strong.

"This is almost the bottom of the modern level," she said, and pushed her hood back from her head as though she was starting to feel at home.

I nodded, relieved. "Good."

"From here we go down to the old parts."

"Oh," I said. "Oh goody. That sounds like fun."

London, as you probably know, is an old city. A very, very old city. I followed the gnome down a twisting flight of concrete steps then back along what I thought was the way we had come, but now the rotting carcass of the catwalk was rather worryingly hanging above our heads. We went down yet more steps, brick ones this time that were running with water, and then into a long vaulted tunnel. Wherever we were now was Victorian by the looks of it. I began to wonder how long the batteries in her torch were good for. If the light had gone out then I think I might have had some sort of breakdown.

I kept following the gnome, watching her trainers splashing in dank puddles and the beam of her torch bobbing along in front of her. I kept closer than I really wanted to, my eyes fixed on the back of her wrinkled, hairless head.

"What's your name, anyway?" I asked after a while.

I didn't really care what her name was, but it was something to say, and I've always thought gnomic names might be long and impressive with lots of apostrophes in them.

"Janice," she said.

"Oh," I said, feeling rather disappointed. "I'm Don Drake."

"I know," she said, and that was the end of the conversation for another ten minutes. It was a bit of a letdown as these things go.

We finally stopped at a place where the crumbling Victorian brickwork of the tunnel wall had been roughly hammered out into an open arch. There was another tunnel on the other side, this one sloping down and looking almost natural. Janice stepped through and turned to face me. She showed me her big strong teeth in what I can only assume was meant to be a smile. If it was meant to be a reassuring one it failed dismally.

"We're home," she said.

I followed her through the arch and my shoulder brushed lightly against the brickwork as I went. The brick seemed to sag and wilt against my coat, and a great rancid clump of it broke away and oozed down my sleeve. It stank like month-old meat left out in a damp room. I gagged and shook it off.

"It's getting worse, isn't it?" I said.

"I told you it did," she said. "Watch what you touch."

"So this Rotman of yours has been here?" I asked her.

She shook her head. "No, it's not *that* bad. You'll know when you're somewhere it's actually been. This is just the... I don't know, the edges of its effect, I suppose. You're the wizard, you tell me."

I felt like telling her I wasn't a sodding wizard, for one thing, but that seemed like a fairly fine distinction to be making right then. I *am* a magician though. A diabolist, to be precise.

"So have you ever seen it?" I asked her instead. "This Rotman, I mean."

"No," she said. "No, but Alice has. Come on, I'll introduce you."

She led me down the tunnel and into a sort of roundish chamber with a low ceiling and various other tunnels leading off from it, some sloping up slightly and others going further down. They all looked uncomfortably like burrows. There was furniture after a fashion, a table that rose from the ground like some sort of natural rock mesa with benches around it, all of one piece with the floor. That must have taken some serious carving, I thought. It took me a few moments to realise that I could see far more than the torch was illuminating.

"I can see," I said.

"Oh good," she said, and turned the torch off. "Batteries cost money."

Now that the electric light was gone, I realised the walls of the tunnels or burrows or whatever they were seemed to be giving off a pinkish light of their own. I looked at

Janice's big, clawed hands, and I thought about burrowing animals and bioluminescent secretions. I decided I had absolutely no interest in finding out exactly *what* made the light. None whatsoever, but I was glad of it all the same.

"So," I said after a moment, "you were going to introduce me to this Alice of yours."

"Yeah," Janice said, and shuffled her feet. "Look, about Alice… she saw the Rotman, like I said. And the Rotman saw her. Only from a distance, of course, and she ran like a rat to get away, but…"

"But?"

"Well, you've seen what the Rotman's doing to the warren."

"Ah," I said. I had a nasty feeling I knew where this was going.

"Poor Alice," said Janice. "Try not to stare, OK?"

Alice was in a small chamber by herself, and staring was the last thing I wanted to do. She was curled up on a sort of shelf-like bed that looked to have been carved directly out of the side of the burrow, with a thin grey blanket half covering her naked body. She was quite obviously dead, the body pretty far gone to putrefaction. It smelled indescribably vile in there.

"Hello Alice," Janice said.

The rotting corpse lifted its head and smiled weakly. "Hi Jan."

"Jesus," I whispered.

I couldn't believe the poor little thing was still alive. Her skin was a mottled greenish blue, with black rotted holes in some places and pus oozing from others, her bones visible in some of the deep fissures in her flesh.

"This is Don. He's here to help," Janice said. "Tell him about the Rotman."

Alice turned her huge, blind white eyes towards me. Putrid milky fluid leaked from them and trickled down her cheeks.

She giggled.

CHAPTER 2

Maybe I ought to take a little step back for a minute. My name is Don Drake. I once killed a five year-old child and was forgiven by a real live angel. No, I'm not a lunatic, I'm a diabolist. Admittedly, it's a pretty fine line between the two sometimes.

Anyway, all that was last year. It was a Sunday in spring now in the haunted wilds of South London, and I had a client. The old boy was sitting in my office across the desk from me in his grey nylon coat, wearing his National Health glasses and his grey trousers and beige shirt and beige cardigan. Exactly at what age do people go colourblind anyway?

"I'm an old man, Mr Drake," he said, as though that wasn't blindingly obvious. "I'm an old man, and I'm terrified of my wife. She has dementia, you see."

He certainly looked old, sitting nervously on the edge of the chair across the desk from me. He looked to be eighty if he was a day, and poor. He looked very poor, and that's never a good sign. I'm expensive.

"Um, OK," I said

"Oh, I'm not scared of her because of that," he went on. "She can't help it, bless her. No, I'm scared of her because of what she was before she got that way. I'm scared because now... well, now she can't control it. I've been lying to our children about her their whole lives, but now..."

"Yes?"

"I don't think I can cover up for her any longer. I've already had to stop our grandchildren from seeing her. It ain't safe for them any more."

"I see," I said, for all that I didn't. "What, um, what exactly is it you think I can do to help, Mr Page?"

"Well," he said, "I heard you were a... well, I don't know what you call it. Like my wife I suppose, but a man. It says 'Don Drake, Hieromancer' on your door but I'm afraid I don't know what that means. A warlock, is it?"

Ah. It's like that, is it? And no, no I wasn't a fucking warlock. Of course, I wasn't really a hieromancer either, but advertising yourself as a diabolist isn't exactly what you'd call a good idea. What a diabolist does, in case you didn't know, is summon demons. That's the strict definition anyway. What a diabolist does in reality is summon demons and send them out to kill people, for money. Certain people, not very nice people admittedly, will pay a hell of a lot of money to get you to set a demon on someone.

That's what I do. Well, that's what I *did*, anyway. Things had got a bit complicated since the whole "forgiven by a real live angel" thing. I wasn't making that bit up, trust me. I sighed and pushed my fingers back through my hair. I needed a haircut, but then I usually did.

"I'm not exactly a warlock, no," I said. "Look, I'm really not sure how you think I can help you."

"Oh," he said.

He looked crushed, and old, and very, very scared. Now I don't do charity. I'm expensive, like I said, and this wasn't exactly my usual line of work anyway. I'm not really in the "helping people" side of the business. My focus had always been more on the "killing people" aspect of things, after all. I'm basically a hitman, once you strip all the magic and mumbo jumbo away. I mean, I don't shoot people or whatever, but I *do* use magic to do pretty much the same thing. There isn't a hell of a lot of difference at the end of the day. Not that I did that any more, not after what had happened last year. I was about to shake my head in a final refusal when he started to cry.

Oh, for God's sake…

He was about the same age my dad would have been if he had still been alive. Admittedly my dad had been a violent, abusive shit of an alcoholic, but all the same I didn't want to watch him cry.

"Look," I said again. "What exactly is it you want me to do?"

"I want you to help me," he said. "With my wife, I mean. I… well, I'm not trying to tell you how to do your job, Mr Drake. Perhaps if you came and saw her for yourself you'd… I don't know. I'm sure you'd know the best way to… to do what needs doing."

His faith in me was touching, and entirely misplaced.

"I suppose I could–"

"Yes?" He looked up hopefully, the tears glistening on the seamed cheeks behind his glasses.

I supposed I could *what*, exactly? What the fuck was I thinking?

I was thinking that maybe I could try not to be such a shit all the time, if I'm perfectly honest about it. Besides, helping someone for once might cheer Trixie up a bit. I had enough money to be going on with for now so perhaps a bit of pro bono wouldn't kill me just this once.

"All right," I said. "I mean, this isn't the sort of thing I usually do so I can't make any promises, you understand?"

"Of course," he said. "No promises."

"All right," I said again. "Let me have your address and I'll come over tonight."

"Thank you Mr Drake. Thank you so much!"

He gave me his details and left. He looked overjoyed.

Trixie very much didn't, when I told her about it.

"You said you'd do *what*?" she snapped at me. "What on earth for?"

Angels, huh? They're the very souls of sympathy sometimes.

"He cried," I admitted.

"Oh that's just pathetic," Trixie said, and turned back to the window.

Remember that real live angel I mentioned? Yeah, that was Trixie. She was sitting at my kitchen table, smoking a long black cigarette and staring listlessly out into the yard behind Mr Chowdhury's grocery shop downstairs. She hadn't really done a great deal of anything else for several months now, not since her glorious performance at Wormwood's club. On the whole I think being my guardian angel was boring her shitless.

Of course, she wasn't really *my* guardian angel at all. Trixie, or Meselandrarasatrixiel to give her the full honours she was due, was the guardian of the Burned Man on the direct order of her Dominion. That was something like a royal decree from what I could work out, certainly not something a simple soldier like her could argue with, however much she'd rather have just gone home. The Dominion was her boss, her commanding officer in the Heavenly Host, but it was much more than that too. She had tried to explain it to me once, but we had hit problems with the language barrier and I still wasn't too clear how it worked. What it said went, I had got that much. All the same, I could tell she wasn't happy about it.

Of course, that wasn't the only problem. She wasn't over Adam and that's all there was to it.

She looked as gorgeous as ever, sitting there in a pair of tight jeans and a plain white blouse, her long blonde hair hanging loose over one shoulder as she smoked her awful Russian cigarette. There were three dead ones crushed out in the ashtray already, their crumpled gold butts and mashed black stems making them look like so many dead scarab beetles. At least she'd finally got the hang of opening the window when she was smoking. That was something, I supposed. I coughed anyway as I put the kettle on.

"Want one?"

She shrugged and blew smoke out of the window into the gloom of South London on a damp spring afternoon. "Not particularly," she said.

I shook my head and poured water onto cheap instant coffee. I had to admit she was starting to do my head in for all that I loved her, she really was. She was still sleeping in my bed for one thing, and I still wasn't sleeping in it with her. Look, I'll be honest, I really wanted to shag her. She was *so* gorgeous she almost took your breath away, you know what I mean? I suppose it stood to reason that she would be, being an angel and all that.

It wasn't like that though, with her. I mean, it was for me, but sexy as she might be, she somehow managed to be weirdly sexless as well. I really couldn't see her going for it. Not just with me I mean – there are more than enough *human* women who don't want to sleep with me, ta very much. I haven't got any illusions on that score. No, I mean in general. I just didn't think sex was something she went in for.

Ah, but then there was Adam. I knew she was more than a little bit in love with the fallen angel who called himself

Adam. Oh yeah, we were old mates, Adam and me, if "old mates" was some sort of euphemism for "bitter enemies". I had a nasty feeling she could go in for it with him all right. Unrequited love is a bitch, I tell you. Not that she had the faintest idea how I felt about her, I knew. I'd never got up the nerve to tell her and I couldn't see that changing any time soon, to be perfectly honest.

"Damn!" I yelped as hot brown water slopped over the edge of my cup and onto my hand.

"Stop pouring when it's full, Don," she said, without turning away from the window.

I sighed and looked at her, my trained magician's gaze able to see her aura clearly outlined against the window. She had never gone back to hiding it, that was something, I supposed. It made it a lot easier to keep an eye on her. In all honesty, sometimes I felt like I was looking after her and not the other way around.

Angelic auras are a beautiful golden colour, in case you didn't know, or they should be anyway. Trixie's, well, wasn't exactly like that. When I'd first met her she had been masking it with a dazzling white light and back then I hadn't known any better. By the time I'd found out she was faking, she wasn't in good shape. Trixie *wasn't* a fallen angel, she was very clear on that point, but by her own admission she had certainly slipped a bit. She had slipped more than a bit last year, if you asked me. Last year she had still been fighting the Furies, and she had gone to some rather extreme measures in the end that had involved her trying to steal the Burned Man from me.

Of course, that had been exactly what the Burned Man wanted her to do and it hadn't ended well, and Trixie had very nearly fallen for good. She would have done, in fact, if it hadn't been for the intervention of her Dominion. Even now there were greenish rotten patches in her golden aura, and a few remaining black traces of corruption. Oh yes, she still had Adam on her mind all right.

Still, all that aside, things were looking up on the whole. Trixie had well and truly put Wormwood in his place, and the Burned Man had never been so well behaved since its foiled escape attempt and a close encounter with the Dominion that could quite possibly have smashed it to atoms. Well maybe, anyway.

I still wasn't too clear on who would have won that fight if it had come right down to it, but my money was on the Dominion. The Burned Man was an archdemon, sure, but a Dominion is something like a general in the Heavenly Host. If you know anything at all about angels, you'll understand that makes it a double hard bastard by anyone's standards.

I mopped up the spilled coffee and went to stand beside Trixie at the window. There was a mangy old ginger tom walking along the top of the wall at the back of the yard downstairs where Mrs Chowdhury was busy hanging her washing out. The old lady clapped her hands at it and the cat startled, turning enough for me to see that half its face was scar tissue and it was missing an eye. It jumped down off the wall and out of sight.

"Horrible-looking cat," I said, for want of anything else to say.

Trixie ignored me. Down in the yard Mr Chowdhury came out of the back of the shop, leading one of his grandsons by the hand. The boy was about four or five years old, and he came to visit them every weekend. Every time I saw him I felt a vicious stab of guilt.

Vincent and Danny McRoth had had a grandson about that age and I had killed him. Not on purpose of course, but my screamers had torn him to bloody rags all the same. I must admit I *had* killed Vincent and Danny on purpose, to pay off a debt to Wormwood. The boy had just been there when he shouldn't have been, that was all.

I knew that made no difference whatsoever.

They say time heals all wounds, but then *they* talk a lot of shit in general. It had been nearly five months now and that wound wasn't showing any signs of healing, forgiveness or not. When I least expected it, the memory of his face would suddenly swim up behind my eyes and I'd have to remember it all over again. The only thing worse than remembering would have been forgetting. Forgetting is denial, and a denial of that magnitude would send anyone round the bend. Well it would me, anyway. I'm no gangster like Gold Steevie, to take that sort of thing in my stride and just move on. I may have been forgiven, but I knew I would never forget him.

Looking back on it I was probably nursing a nice little case of undiagnosed post-traumatic stress disorder, but there you go. Whatever, I didn't want to watch that little boy outside playing with his grandparents.

"I'm going to see what the Burned Man has to say about this little bit of business," I said. "Coming?"

"No I'm not," Trixie said. "I may have to be that horrible thing's guardian but that doesn't mean I want to have to look at it."

I knew she was going to say that, of course. Trixie hadn't set foot in my workroom since last year, not since her horribly ill-advised attempt to steal the Burned Man from me. We were over that now of course, or at least I sincerely hoped we were, so I kept trying. Trixie and the Burned Man were the two most important people in my life since I lost Debbie and it would have been nice if they had been able to at least tolerate each other, especially as we all lived under the same very small roof together. Well, I say "people" but you know what I mean. They might have been a half-fallen angel and an imprisoned archdemon, but they were still the closest thing I had to a family. That pretty much summed up my life at the time.

I shrugged and left her to it, and went to speak to the Burned Man.

"Afternoon," I said, as I pushed the workroom door open.

"Blondie stood me up again then has she?" it sneered.

The Burned Man was a nine-inch tall fetish that stood on the ancient oak altar at the far end of the room, and it contained the imprisoned soul of one of the most powerful archdemons in all of Hell. It was chained to the surface by tiny iron manacles around its wrists and ankles, and its whole ugly naked little body was blackened and blistered, the skin cracked open in places to show the livid, weeping red burns beneath. It was a bloody horrible little thing, and it was always hungry.

"You know she has," I said. "Peckish?"

"Is a bear Catholic?"

I sighed and crossed the room, stepping over the grand summoning circle that was carefully inscribed into the hardwood floor. This was where the work got done. The real work that is, summoning and sending demons, not helping little old men with batty wives. For free, at that. What the hell had I been thinking?

I knelt down in front of the altar and unbuttoned my shirt. The Burned Man lunged forwards and sank its nasty needle-like teeth into the meat beside my nipple, gurgling contentedly to itself as it started to slurp on my blood. I sighed and looked down at myself. My chest was more scar than not these days. You'd think I'd be used to it by now but it still hurt like a fucking bastard.

"So what's up?" it asked when it had finally had enough.

I winced and dabbed the smear of blood off my chest with a tissue.

"We've got a little job," I said. "Don't get excited, it's not exactly the usual this time."

"Why are we doing it then?" it asked me. "Shitloads of cash, I trust."

"Why don't you let me worry about the business side of things?"

"Because we'd go broke in a month," it said. "Even the bank of Blondie can't be fucking bottomless."

I shrugged. Trixie always seemed to have money when I wanted some, and if it stopped me working she was happy to give it to me. Trixie *really* didn't approve of my line of work, to put it mildly. All the same, the Burned Man was right, of course. I couldn't count on that forever. Besides, a man has to have some pride. Which made doing a job for free seem even stupider, now that I thought about it. I cleared my throat.

"Look," I said. "There was this little old man, and he's got a problem."

"And shitloads of cash?" the Burned Man asked hopefully.

"I doubt it," I admitted.

"Pillock," it said. "Sometimes I wonder about you Drake, I really do."

"Whatever, we're doing it," I said.

I was still holding out a thin hope that Trixie might come around to the idea and cheer up a bit, maybe even join in, although I had to admit that was starting to look a tad unlikely.

"So what's this ancient pauper's problem then, apart from being old and poor?"

I sighed and told it what the old chap had told me. The Burned Man frowned up at me.

"She's some sort of witch then, is she, this batty old dear?"

"Yeah, it sounds like it," I said. "I'll have to go and see I suppose."

"I suppose you will," it said. "I'm not a sodding oracle, I don't know what we need to do until you can properly tell me what's what."

"Right," I said.

I got up and left it to whatever it did when I wasn't there. I shudder to think, to be honest.

CHAPTER 3

I went down to Big Dave's café next door for dinner first. Trixie hadn't wanted to join me there either, although as I looked at the greasy plate of lukewarm bacon pie and soggy chips in front of me, I had to admit I didn't really blame her. Big Dave ran a proper old-fashioned café, not one of those poncey places that were starting to take over the neighbourhood. None of that artisanal coffee and your food served on a roofing tile bollocks here, thanks very much. That said, the place was a bit crap if I'm honest about it.

Big Dave was his usual jolly self though, and he must have told me at least five times that if I'd fallen out with Trixie he'd gladly take her off my hands for a small fee. I forced myself to banter along with him whilst trying not to think about how many pieces Trixie would have cut him into if she'd heard that. And me as well, probably. The highlight of the meal was seeing the ugly ginger cat from Mrs Chowdhury's yard almost get hit by a bus as it ran across the busy road outside.

Big Dave's wasn't exactly the sort of place where you linger after eating so I was back outside by half six and in a taxi ten minutes later. We crawled through the stagnant ooze of the London traffic until it eventually pulled up outside the address the old chap had given me.

I looked out at the place with a sinking feeling in my guts that wasn't just down to Big Dave's cooking. The house was in a grotty row of shabby old terraces, but predictably enough his was the grottiest one in the street. The tiny front garden was overgrown with dead weeds, and the windows were so filthy it was a wonder there weren't more weeds growing on them as well. The grim tower blocks of a sink estate loomed over the rooftops a couple of streets away. I sighed and paid the cabbie.

"Cheers mate," I said as I got out, trying to muster an enthusiasm I didn't feel.

It was nearly dark but I couldn't see any lights on in the house. If this turned out to have been some sort of elaborate windup I wasn't going to be best pleased. I walked past the overflowing wheelie bin and looked for a doorbell, almost falling over a mangy ginger cat as it dashed between my legs. I frowned after it. Nah, it couldn't have been the same one. There didn't seem to be a bell, so I rapped on the front door with my knuckles, and rattled the letterbox for good measure. A moment later the front room light came on and I heard footsteps shuffling towards me behind the door.

"Who is it?" the old boy called out.

"Mr Page? It's Don Drake," I said. "You came to see me this afternoon."

The door opened and he peered out at me through his plastic-framed glasses.

"Oh yes, yes, hello Mr Drake," he said.

"Call me Don," I said.

"Oh, oh all right. I'm Charlie, then."

He ushered me inside and closed the door behind me. The house was chilly and quiet, and smelled of damp and boiled cabbage. I could hear a clock ticking somewhere in the back but that was all. The front room looked like one of those formal sitting rooms people used to have in the 1930s, a dusty sofa no one ever sat on and a fireplace that was always cold. Kept for a "best" that never came. And for funerals, of course. For laying out the dead. What a cheerful thought that wasn't.

"Come through, come through," Charlie said.

I followed him through the door at the bottom of the stairs and into the back room, the parlour or whatever you'd have called it. Honestly, I don't think this place had been done out since it was built. There was a three-bar electric fire with one miserable bar glowing like a half-dead salamander, and a big ugly wooden clock on the mantle above it. Above that hung a faded print of the Queen in a cheap frame. The print looked like it was from maybe forty years ago, perhaps a souvenir from the Silver Jubilee.

Two shabby armchairs were pulled up next to the fire and a couple of dining chairs stood against one wall, and that was it. The too-small rug was threadbare and surrounded by splintery looking floorboards.

I could tell that this was going to be about as pro fucking bono as work got.

Charlie lowered himself into one armchair and waved vaguely at the other one. He wasn't wearing his nylon coat any more, but other than that he still looked the same as he had that morning. He didn't offer me a cup of tea or anything, I noticed. Still, I hate tea anyway and I couldn't imagine he had anything approaching drinkable coffee in the grotty little kitchen that led off the parlour. I sat down. The clock was ticking loud enough to give me a headache.

"So," I said. "Um, Mrs Page?"

"Oh yes, yes, bless her," Charlie said. "Ever so sad, Mr Drake, but it's got to be done."

"It's Don," I said again. "I was hoping I could see her. I

need to get some idea of what I'm dealing with, you see."

"Oh, yes, well," he said.

He looked me up and down, peering oddly at my suit. I might not be a fashion icon exactly but I was a damn sight better dressed than him so I wasn't quite sure exactly what his problem was.

"What?" I had to ask eventually.

"I mean, have you brought... something? It must be quite small, if you have."

"Well no," I said. "Not yet. I mean, I don't even know what sort of working I'll need to do until I've seen her."

"But I thought..." he started. "I mean to say, I heard you, well, that you..."

The penny dropped with a thoroughly unpleasant clang.

"Mr Page," I said, "I'm not killing your wife for you."

The old bugger had been trying to see where I was hiding the gun I didn't own, I was sure he was. He licked his lips with a nervous, wet-looking tongue.

"I'm sorry, I thought that's what you did," he said.

Oh for fucksake, how had I ever got myself into this?

"I'm a magician," I said, "not a murderer."

Well of course that wasn't strictly true, by which I suppose I mean it was technically a straightout lie. I *am* a killer, but I kill gangsters and terrorists and black magicians, for other gangsters and terrorists and black magicians. Now and again I'll do a job for some other people too, people I've always suspected work for the government, but that was beside the point. I'm not in the business of bumping off sweet little old ladies and that was all there was to it.

What about innocent little boys? the nagging voice of guilt whispered in the back of my head. I told it to shut up.

"Oh," said Charlie. "I'm terribly sorry if I've wasted your time but... well, I'm really at my wits' end. I didn't know what else to do, you see. I can hardly take her to the doctor, can I?"

I couldn't really see why not, but I was there now and he was getting that pathetic look about him like he'd had in my office that afternoon. I didn't want to have to watch him cry all over again.

"Look," I said, "just let me have a look at her. I'm sure I can think of something."

Charlie sighed and nodded, and got to his feet. He led me up the creaking stairs.

"I keep her in the back bedroom," he said.

He opened the door for me and I stepped inside.

Mrs Page was indeed little and old, a tiny birdlike woman in a heavy cotton nightgown sitting up in bed propped up on three pillows, but she didn't look very sweet. She was almost bald for one thing, her remaining thin white hair sticking out in odd directions, and there was a long string of thick drool hanging out of the corner of her mouth. I had just opened my mouth to say something when a metal bedpan lifted off the floor all by itself.

The bedpan hovered in the air for a moment then hurtled violently towards my head.

I ducked back just in time and it slammed into the wall where I had been standing, hitting hard enough to take a big chunk out of the faded wallpaper and leave a crater in the plaster. Mrs Page shrieked like a banshee and the door cracked straight down the middle with a bang.

I started to understand why Charlie Page couldn't take her to the doctor's like a normal person.

CHAPTER 4

I left pretty sharpish after that. I told Charlie again that I'd think of something and get back to him, but he didn't look too hopeful. I didn't really blame him, to be honest.

I must admit I hadn't given much thought to how I was going to get home again when I sent the taxi on its merry way. Charlie's neighbourhood was too far off the beaten track to find any cruising cabs so I ended up having to catch a bus, of all things. The only thing I like less than the bus is walking. I sat on the upstairs deck with my hands stuffed in my coat pockets, staring out of the dark window and waiting for it to be over. I heard a shrill burst of laughter, two young girls hurrying up the stairs behind me.

"…see that bleedin' cat trying to get on the bus?"

"Innit, I'm so tweeting that!"

I like cats about as much as I like buses, and giggly teenage girls aren't much higher up my list of enjoyable things.

I got home eventually and found Trixie had already gone to bed. My bed. The sofabed she'd bought me to replace my old couch was comfy enough I supposed, but sleeping in my office every night was starting to get a bit old now. I looked round the office and sighed. The wall at the far end was a slightly different colour to the rest, where last year I'd had to dig a bullet out of it and repaint it to cover the stain left by the brains of a very unpleasant man who had tried to torture me to death. Oh yes, this room held so many happy memories for me, it was the ideal place to sleep every fucking night.

I made myself a coffee and took it through to the workroom.

"What's up, smiler?" the Burned Man asked me.

"Do you have to sound so cheerful?" I said. "Stupid old fart."

"I might be old, but I'm not fucking stupid," it snapped.

"Not you, I mean Charlie Page," I said. "That old boy I told you about, remember? The one with the batty wife?"

"Oh yeah, the one with no fucking money," it said. "What about him?"

"He thought I was just going to do her in for him," I said.

The Burned Man shrugged. "It'd be easiest," it said. "Summon up a vorehound and send it round to see her, chomp chomp, job done. You get to collect your no fucking money and we can forget the whole stupid business."

"If we sent a vorehound I think she'd eat it," I said.

That made it look up. "Oh yeah? Why's that then?"

"She's a telekine at the very least, maybe more, and I'm not sure it's just dementia that's wrong with her. She looked batshit crazy to me."

"Telekines are bloody dangerous," it admitted. "What'd she throw at you, a chair or something?"

"A bedpan," I said.

The Burned Man snorted laughter. "How very fucking apt," it said.

"Oh shut up. We need to do something about her, but I'm not just bumping her off. She can't help it, after all."

"Maybe she can and doesn't want to?"

I shook my head. "Nah. She needs a doctor, but we'll have to calm her down first before anyone can see her. I need some way to block her energy and stop her throwing things at people's heads."

"That's doable," the Burned Man said. "I can make an amulet that will do that, but I'll need some bits and pieces. You'll have to go and see Wormwood."

"Well that's always a pleasure," I said. I thought about the sofabed, and the closed door of my bedroom. "Oh fuck it, I might as well do it now. I could use a drink before I turn in anyway."

I rustled up another taxi and rode it to Wormwood's club. That bloody one-eyed cat had been on the pavement outside again when I left, prowling up and down and making the place look even untidier than usual. The whole left side of its face around the missing eye was a horrible mass of greyish scar tissue. It probably had fleas, too. Horrible thing. I got in the taxi and forgot about it as we drove.

The cab pulled up at the kerb and I walked into the alley, trailing one hand absently along the graffiti-covered brickwork as I went. It was starting to rain, and I could hear a siren dopplering mournfully in the distance. Somewhere a cat yowled and someone shouted something at someone else, too far away for me to hear the words. The alley smelled of stale urine and fresh puke.

I remembered watching Aleto the Unresting slaughter a devourer right there in that alley. I shuddered at the memory. I had been to bed with her after all, and look how that had turned out. That had been the last shag I'd had, come to think of it. There ought to be a plaque up on the wall or something, I thought, one of those round blue ones they put up for tourists that say things like "Queen Victoria slept here, 1865", that sort of thing. Something like "Don Drake finally realised he has shit taste in women, 2014".

I don't know, since Debbie had left me for good, maybe just not shagging Trixie for evermore was my best bet. I sighed and headed for the door.

Wormwood's club isn't open to the general public, of course. It isn't even *visible* to the general public, come to that. You can't see it and if you didn't know it was there, you'd never find it. I, on the other hand, had been there enough times before to know exactly where it was.

I walked through the glamour that covered the front door, feeling the illusion twist around me like a cold, sticky spider's web. I stepped into the plush little bar on the other side and looked around. Connie was looming at the bottom of the stairs in his giant tuxedo, his horns almost brushing the ceiling.

"Evening, big lad," I said, giving him a cheery wave.

"Don!" he grinned. "I haven't seen you in ages!"

I can't help but like Connie. He's Wormwood's minder and a nine foot-tall hulking brute of a demon. He's bald as a coot and I'm not joking about the horns, but for all that he'd given me more than one good kicking in the past, I have to admit he's one of the most affable people I've ever met.

It was only about ten o'clock and the club itself wasn't open yet, the thick red velvet rope still pulled across the bottom of the stairs behind where Connie was standing. The downstairs bar had maybe fifteen people in it, and they were mostly humans this early in the night. There was no one I recognised from the actual club, and I didn't usually hang around in the bar. That was for mugs, by and large – anyone worth knowing had enough clout to get themselves invited upstairs where the gambling and the dealmaking got done. I vaguely remembered seeing a few of the faces before, but there was no one I really knew to speak to other than Connie himself. I got myself a beer and wandered over to chat to him.

"How've you been?" I asked him.

"Can't complain," he said. "I look after Mr Wormwood and he sees me all right, you know how it is. What about you – are you still seeing the Lady?"

I could hear the capital letter in his voice, and I knew he meant Trixie. She'd made quite an impression on everyone the first time she'd been here.

"Yeah," I said. "Well you know, not 'seeing' exactly. We're friends."

"Me and Tasha are 'friends' now," he said, giving me a slow wink that he probably thought was subtle.

Tasha was one of the waitresses from the club upstairs, a pretty little demon with a cute tail. I'd quite fancied her myself at one point to be honest, but she was no Trixie. I sighed. No one was, that was the bloody problem.

"Good for you, mate," I said, and reached up to clap him on the shoulder. That seemed like the sort of thing he'd like. "Is the boss about?"

Connie gave me a slightly dubious look. "She's not with you, is she? The Lady, that is. I mean, you're welcome Don, 'course you are, but Mr Wormwood isn't too keen on her, I'm afraid."

No I bet he isn't.

"Nah, it's just me, mate."

"All right then," Connie said. "As it's just you. Go on, I'll let you up early. Mr Wormwood won't mind."

He lifted the rope up for me and I ducked under it and went on up.

Wormwood was sitting in an armchair under the window, wearing an expensive-looking black suit. He was reading the *Financial Times* and smoking. He looked up as I came in, and from the look on his face I think he *did* mind actually but there you go. That was just his tough shit as far as I was concerned.

"Evening, Wormwood," I said.

"We ain't open yet," he said. "But as it's you, have a seat. Have a drink. It *is* just you, I take it?"

"Yeah," I said, helping myself to a chair and a generous single malt from the bottle on the table beside him.

Wormwood did keep good whisky, I had to give him that much, I supposed. He was otherwise bloody horrible. He was short and sallow and grey and greasy, unshaven and unwashed and he stank of cigarettes and misery. Other people's misery, to be fair. Wormwood was probably on the list of the top hundred richest people in London, or he would have been if he'd officially existed. Archdemons don't, of course, but that didn't seem to stop him living in Mayfair and being chauffeured around in a bloody great Rolls Royce. Lucky for him he at least looked like a human, albeit a particularly ugly one.

"Good, good," he said, visibly relaxing. "What can I do for you then? Cards?"

"Ingredients," I said.

Ever since Debbie had left me under rather unpleasant circumstances I'd been without an alchemist, but Wormwood knew everyone. He was also terrified of Trixie, which was bloody handy. She had made him agree to keep me supplied with whatever bits and pieces I needed, and at a knockdown price too. I knew it was the cheap prices that really hurt Wormwood. He was a child of Mammon after all, and easily the most avaricious person I've ever met.

"Oh, right," he said. "What do you need then?"

"A vial of tincture of mercury, a lodestone, two live toads and a hexring," I said, reciting the shopping list the Burned

Man had given me.

Wormwood pulled a face. I think he did, anyway. With a face like his it was hard to tell.

"A hexring ain't going to be cheap, even with our little arrangement," he said. "I mean, *really* not cheap."

"I don't want to hear that, Wormwood," I said. "You promised Trixie that–"

"No no no," he interrupted. "Let's not get into another unfortunate misunderstanding here. I mean yeah, 'course, if you need a hexring I can get it for you. Said I would, didn't I? Thing is though Drake, I could do with a little favour myself. I was thinking we could work something out on the price is all. You help me out and I'll do it below cost."

I squinted at him through the choking haze of cheap cigarette smoke. It always seemed strange to me that someone as rich as Wormwood didn't smoke a better brand, but I suppose that was how he got to be so rich. He really didn't like to actually *spend* his money, and I knew the words "below cost" must be almost causing him physical pain.

"Oh yeah? That doesn't sound like you, Wormwood."

I knew it was killing him to have to ask nicely. Wormwood was used to having people like me under his thumb, not the other way around. Of course he was only being nice to me because he was shit scared of Trixie, but that suited me just fine. Right now the boot was firmly on my foot and I intended to keep it that way.

"Yeah well," he said. "I owe some people a small favour, and they've just called it in."

"People?" I echoed. That didn't sound too likely to me. "Actual people?"

"Gnomes," he corrected himself.

I snorted. "Seriously?"

"If you're thinking of jolly little fuckers sitting around a pond with white beards and fishing rods you can fucking think again," he snapped. "These are *proper* gnomes. Earth elementals, you understand me?"

"Why the hell do you owe *them* a favour?" I asked. I didn't really care, but he was squirming and seeing Wormwood squirm never got old.

"They told me things, once. Things I needed to know at the time. They know all sorts of things, the gnomes do."

"I suppose they know how to dig holes," I said. "Can't imagine it's much more than that."

"That's because you've got the imagination of a dead dog," Wormwood snapped. "They know things all right. Deep things."

"Deep bleedin' holes," I sniggered. "Oh all right, whatever, I'm only winding you up. The gnomes told you a Jackanory and now they want a little favour in return, I get the picture. And you want me to do it for you. I don't suppose there's any chance you could just pay them off?"

Wormwood shook his head.

"They work in favours, not money," he said. "So I'm asking you to go down there and do them a favour from me in return. They're a bit like the Chinese like that, all about the relationship. You ever done business with the Chinese, Drake?"

I winced as I thought about a particularly nasty Triad guy I'd worked for once and could quite happily not ever see again in my life. I nodded. Now, I don't know how much you know about doing business with the Chinese, but I'm going to take a guess at not much. They have this thing called *guanxi*, which is a bit like networking and business relationships, but more so. It's all very cultural and traditional and whatnot, but it pretty much comes down to "scratch my back and I'll scratch yours". If the gnomes were going to be like that, this could be interesting. Interesting in the Chinese sense.

"That hexring had better be free for this, Wormwood, and you'll still owe me one."

"It will be," he said. "Thanks Don."

I nearly fell out of my seat. I don't think I've ever heard Wormwood say thanks before, or call me by my first name for that matter. With hindsight, that's when I should have started to smell a rat.

"Right," I said. "Right, well. Looks like we've got a deal then."

He nodded. "Good. I need to make some calls, set it up. Hang around, have a drink. We'll be opening in a few minutes anyway. Play some cards if you want. Roulette, whatever."

I leaned back in my chair and poured myself another whisky while he shuffled off to his office. People started to trickle into the club after about half an hour, by which time I was starting to feel comfortably tipsy. Whisky always tastes better when it's someone else's, especially when it's as good as the stuff Wormwood served. I didn't feel like playing cards that night and I'm shit at roulette, so I just sat and drank whisky and leafed through Wormwood's newspaper until he eventually came back.

"Have your jabs and pack your passport, you're going north of the river," he told me. "One of the gnomes will meet you down the Tube. They're down the Northern Line, in the deep tunnels. Be at Bank on the DLR concourse at nine sharp tomorrow night. That's the deepest of the lot."

I noticed his left eye twitch as he said it. I nodded. I'm not exactly a Tube nerd, but even I knew that. The Docklands Light Railway platforms at Bank were a good hundred and thirty feet underground and they led to proper bored tunnels rather than the cut-and-cover that makes up most of the subterranean parts of the London Underground. That shit freaks some people out, I knew.

"Not a fan of the Tube then, Wormwood?"

"No I bleedin' ain't," he said. "Underground. I don't like it. Very thin Veils down there. Too bleedin' thin."

Well, that was worth remembering. I hadn't known *that*, I have to admit. About the Veils being thinner underground *or* about Wormwood not liking it down there. Both of those things were well worth knowing as far as I was concerned.

The Veils, in case you didn't know, are the things that keep the dimensions apart. When people like us talk about Veils we mostly mean the ones between Earth and Hell, but I suppose there are others too. Either way they're ridiculously old and vitally important, and in some places they're starting to wear a bit thin. Places like London, and Edinburgh, and some of the other spooky old cities around the world too I don't doubt. I wouldn't really know, I'm not exactly what you'd call well-travelled.

Don't ask me what they really are or how they work because I haven't got a bloody clue, but the general opinion of people cleverer than me is that the Veils are alive somehow. I must admit that thought sort of creeps me out, which means I try not to think about it.

"Right," I said. I swallowed the last of my whisky and rather reluctantly put the glass down on the table between us. "I'd better be off then. Night, Wormwood."

I was there on time the next evening, despite almost falling over that sodding cat on my way out of the front door again. I could have kicked that fucking thing, I really could. I got a cab to the station and caught an overground to London Bridge then rode the Tube into Bank with five minutes to spare. I'm not a big fan of trains as it goes, but a cab all the way into central London seemed a bit extravagant at the time. Fuck knows why, looking back on it. I still hadn't quite got the hang of living off Trixie at that point. I knew it didn't bother her, but I have to admit it still sort of bothered me.

The gnome was waiting for me on the platform, hunched against the tiled wall and trying to look inconspicuous. It was a wizened little thing in baggy old jeans and a stained red hoodie, the hood pulled right forward over its eyes. It had its hands stuffed deep into its pockets.

"You must be the wizard," it said by way of introduction. "Come on then, this way."

It led me down a side corridor and had a furtive look around before it fished in the pocket of its hoodie and produced a big jingling bunch of keys. It used one to open a grey metal door marked with the Transport for London logo and a stern sign that read "Strictly No Admittance. Unauthorised Persons Will Be Prosecuted".

The gnome held the door open for me and locked it carefully behind us again, then ushered me down a cramped corridor lit by overhead neon tubes and lined with bundles of neatly caged cables. It ended in another door marked "High Voltage: Danger of Death". The gnome unlocked it with a different key, then we were heading down a spiral metal staircase. The gnome rifled through its keys and opened a further series of industrial doors as we went, each of them covered in increasingly hostile-looking warning signs. I wasn't too sure what a yellow triangle with a picture of a black lightning bolt and "Danger 22kV" written under it meant, but it didn't look very bloody welcoming, that was for damn sure.

The gnome locked each door carefully again behind us as we went, always going down. We were well below the deepest tracks now, down in the bowels of London somewhere between the Tube and the sewers.

"So," the gnome said after a while, "you're the hero who's

going to save us from the Rotman, then."

I stared at it.

"You what?" I said.

And that's how I came to be far too far underground with the gnomes of the earth, looking for something called the Rotman.

CHAPTER 5

"Tell him about the Rotman," Janice said.

Alice turned her weeping blind eyes towards me and giggled.

"Have you ever seen a travelling cat?" Alice asked me. "Wherever you are, that's where it's at."

It was just a bit of nonsense doggerel, I'm sure, but it made me think all the same. How many times had I seen that horrible one-eyed ginger tom now, and in how many places? That, now that I actually thought about it, was a bit odd. Not as bloody odd as poor rotting Alice, I grant you, but odd none the less.

"Oh hush with that," Janice said. "The Rotman, Alice."

"I can see his tusks," Alice said, although from the look of her eyes I doubted she had seen anything for a good while. "They glisten with bile, and his eyes glow like fire."

She lapsed back onto her soggy blanket, breath wheezing in her throat. If that was all we were going to get out of her, it wasn't very helpful to say the least.

"Where did you see him?" I asked, after a moment.

"Below," Alice whispered. "In the deep warren. I ran away."

Dear God, it goes deeper than this? What a cheerful thought that wasn't.

"'Course you did, Alice," said Janice. "It's all right. I would have run too."

She hadn't run fast enough though, had she, poor little Alice? I wondered just how much exposure to the Rotman it had taken to turn her into the gangrenous horror that lay on the cot in front of us. I had a nasty suspicion it probably hadn't been a hell of a lot. Bloody Wormwood, I'd skin him alive for getting me into this. Well, obviously I'd ask Trixie to do it for me, but you know what I mean.

Alice lay there wheezing, her breath gradually slowing to the rhythm of sleep. Janice touched my arm with her claws and steered me back into the chamber with the carved table and benches.

"How long has she been like that?" I asked her.

"A couple of weeks," Janice said. "It wasn't so bad to start with. Mother treated her with root and rhyme, but she just kept getting worse. I don't think she's got very much longer."

I looked at Janice's ugly, pointed little face and my heart went out to her.

"She's your sister, isn't she?" I asked her.

Janice nodded. "Yes," she said.

I reached out and put a hand gently on her shoulder. She stiffened for a moment, then just sort of sagged weakly against me and started to cry. She cried almost silently, trembling and giving out the occasional wet sniffle. I held her awkwardly for a few minutes until she got herself under control and pulled away.

"We ought to go on," she said. "You'll want to see the matriarch, I'm sure."

I wasn't all that sure I did to be perfectly honest, but I supposed it would have been rude to say so. I let Janice lead me down another tunnel, sloping downwards and curving around on itself until I was sure we must be pretty much underneath the place we had started from. The ground felt spongy underfoot, and when I turned to look behind me I could see that our footprints were gradually filling up with an oily looking liquid. Given that I was fairly sure the tunnels were cut through solid rock, just the sight of footprints wasn't a good sign. God only knew what the wet stuff was.

"Don't touch the walls or anything," Janice said, when she saw what I was looking at. "The warren is starting to get infected now."

She led me down another tunnel and we finally started to see some more gnomes. I'm sorry but they really *do* all look the same. Now I'm sure that's wildly unfair and they would probably say the same thing about us, but at the time that doesn't actually help. If they had all been dressed the same as Janice I'd have lost her in a heartbeat, but luckily it seemed she had dressed up specially to venture out into the Tube station. The others wore a motley collection of, I suspected, whatever they had found discarded in the Tube, or nothing at all apart from footwear. There was a pair of jeans here, a jacket or a sweater there, but even the naked ones were all wearing shoes or boots or trainers of some sort. That didn't do much for my confidence in the state of the ground underfoot. Their clothes were obviously for protection not for warmth or reasons of modesty.

"We don't wear clothes normally," Janice said, as if she'd read my thoughts. "But that stuff that oozes out of the rock burns if you get it on your skin for too long."

"Oh," I said. "Right."

I tried to remember what the soles of my shoes were made of, and couldn't. I hoped it was something fairly robust. The last thing I wanted was burned feet – I had to climb all the way back up out of here at some point, after all.

Janice led me through an opening and into a big, low chamber, and there she was.

"Don, this is the matriarch," she said.

"Um," I said. "Evening."

This chamber was a lot more impressive than the rest of the warren had been so far, that was for sure. The light was brighter in here for one thing, enough for me to see that the walls were covered in carvings. Some were bas reliefs showing gnomes at work, tunnelling and carving and... well, I'm not too sure *what* they were doing in some of them. Gnome things, I supposed. I dare say I wouldn't have understood even if someone had explained it to me, which they didn't. The rest were intricate three-dimensional geometric designs of the sort that made me think of advanced mathematics. I knew damn well I wouldn't understand those.

At the far end of the room, under a large carved pattern of interlocking cubes, was a raised dais. On top of it, all one part with it as far as I could see in fact, stood a throne. There was a gnome sitting up there. She stood up and I looked at her tiny little bald ratty face, extra wizened even by gnome standards and creased with deep lines around her big eyes. She was wearing a shiny purple raincoat of the sort that had been fashionable with a certain kind of faux-bohemian Notting Hill housewife a few years ago, the fabric hanging from her in folds that made it look like a robe. There were a few other gnomes milling about in the room, watching us.

"This is the hero?" the matriarch asked.

"Well," said Janice, awkwardly, "sort of. I mean, I think so, Highness."

"Look, I think there might have been some sort of misunderstanding," I said. "I don't know who you think I am exactly but–"

"We made a pact with an archdemon, long ago," the matriarch of the gnomes cut in. "The lord Wormwood came to us for the Words of Unbinding, and we gave them to him. In return, when the rhyme of prophecy turned and our hour of need came upon us, he promised to send us the hero who would deliver us. That hour has come, and so must come the hero."

"That's all well and good," I said, picturing Wormwood roasting over a slow fire, "but I think–"

"That would be you," she interrupted me again. "You will stop the one my children call the Rotman."

I frowned at that. This creature obviously knew things, just as Wormwood had said. I wasn't quite sure what Words of Unbinding were, but I'd have bet good money they were something to do with how Wormwood had escaped from whoever had summoned him in the first place, and how he had managed to remain on Earth ever since. This was more than a *small favour* he owed the gnomes, the lying little git.

Still, like I said, she obviously knew a few things.

"That's what the girls call it, yeah," I said. "I'd be more interested to hear what *you* call it, Highness."

"I call it what it is," she said. "I call it by its name. I call it Bianakith."

"Bianakith?" echoed the Burned Man. "Oh fuck me, that's not good."

"No it bloody isn't," I said, turning the book around in my hands to hold the page where the Burned Man could see it. "Look, it's right here in the *Testament of Solomon*. Blah blah 'demon of decomposition and disease; he layeth waste to houses and causeth flesh to decay and all that which is similar.' Oh fucking joy. Oh yeah, and this bit here – 'doth torment his victims by making their bodies waste away and their flesh unto rot, even though they be still living.' Poor little Alice, old Solomon wasn't kidding about that part."

"Who the fuck is Alice?"

"A gnome I met," I said. "What was left of her, anyway. She saw the Rotman, this Bianakith, and apparently it saw her too. Just for a moment and not up close and she legged it sharpish, and she still looks unto a fucking month-old corpse."

"Shame," said the Burned Man in a tone that meant it couldn't care less. "Anyway, do you really think I don't know this shit? You've got an old bloody book, whoopee for you. I *know* this cunt, Drake. Me and Bianakith are from the same fucking neighbourhood, you know what I mean?"

Shit, I supposed they were at that.

"So fill me in," I said.

The Burned Man shrugged. "To be fair your book's pretty much got the gist of it," it admitted. "Bianakith is plague walking. It's the Wasteland on legs, you understand me? Anything this fucker comes near will die horribly, or corrode or rot or fall apart. Your little Alice never stood a fucking chance. I mean, it's thick as shit and twice as ugly, but you don't want to get anywhere near it, get it?"

"Jesus," I muttered.

What a lovely fucking thought that wasn't.

"Still, it's not really our problem, is it?" the Burned Man said. "Just tell Wormwood to go fuck himself or you'll set Blondie on him. Job done."

I sighed and put the book down. Sometimes I let myself forget exactly what the Burned Man was but it was usually quick enough to remind me, one way or another.

"It's not really that simple," I said.

"Sounds it to me," it said.

It wasn't though. I hadn't stayed any longer with the matriarch of the gnomes than I'd had to, and shortly after my audience was over I had let Janice guide me back to the surface. It was the early hours of the morning by then and all the Tube stations were shut, so we ended up finally poking our heads above ground out of a manhole cover near St Paul's. Finding a cab to take me home had been fun and games, what with how I smelled by then, and it was getting light by the time I got in and started rooting through my books. One thing I had noticed on our long, smelly climb back up to civilisation was just how far and how badly the rot was spreading.

"You haven't been listening," I told the Burned Man. "It's rotting down there, you understand me? Everything that central London stands on top of is rotting and crumbling and basically trying to turn into rancid soup. How long do you think it's going to be until things start to fall into the ground?"

"Ah," it said. "Fuck, you might have a bit of a point there. That wouldn't be good. The Veils are so bloody thin underground that I dread to think what might start shoving its way through if those thin bits weren't buried any more."

I rubbed my temples in frustration. That wasn't really what I'd been getting at, obviously, but then the Burned Man didn't think like you or me. Or like anything human for that matter. The potential for tens of thousands of deaths obviously hadn't even crossed its mind. That or it simply didn't care, one or the other.

"Yeah that too," I said. "Fuck knows what we're going to do about it though. The bloody gnomes seem to think I'm some sort of fucking foretold hero who's going to kick the Rotman's arse and save them all."

The Burned Man snorted with laughter at that. "You?" it sneered. "A hero?"

"Yeah, exactly," I said, although I could almost have taken offence at that. "Not going to happen. Though I can't say I much fancy trying to summon and bind this thing either."

"Well, for one that would be a spectacularly messy way to commit suicide," the Burned Man said, "and for another it's not even possible, you pillock. You can't summon something that's already on Earth, remember?"

It shook its chains bitterly at that, and stifled a small cough.

Of course you can't, I thought. I knew that, now that I thought about it. That was the whole principle that kept the Burned Man itself safely out of harm's way and stuck in the fetish on my altar – while it was there, in a fixed place on Earth, it couldn't be summoned anywhere else by anyone else so it could never escape the way Wormwood apparently had. Its whole original escape plan had revolved around getting free of that fetish, after all.

"Yeah, good point," I said. "Sorry, it's been a long day. I need a shower and some kip."

"You need a shower, I'll give you that much," it said. "You fucking stink."

"Thanks pal," I muttered. "More to the point though, what are we going to do about this? Come on, you're usually full of bright ideas."

"Usually, but not right now," the Burned Man admitted. "I mean, like I said, I *know* Bianakith and I'm afraid it's way beyond anything you can summon and send against it. What with your pussy limits on ingredients it is, anyway. I'll have to give this one a bit of thought."

Summoning doesn't run on wishful thinking, sadly. Every real working needs to be powered by something, and the best source of magical power is always lifeblood. I use toads, usually. Partly because it's traditional and partly because toads are so bloody horrible I don't feel guilty about it. Occasionally I might need something a bit bigger, a goat for example, but only for what I would regard as the really big shit. The Burned Man's view of my "pussy limits" amounted to my refusal to carry out human sacrifice, just for the record. It's a lovely little thing, it really is.

"Well have a good hard think about it," I said. "It's been on the rampage down there for weeks at least, I dare say it'll keep another day or two. Meantime I've still got old Mrs Page to sort out. I'll squeeze the hexring and whatnot out of Wormwood tonight so at least we can get that done."

"Whatever," it said, quite obviously not interested in a job that wasn't going to pay a penny.

"Anyway, I'm going to clean up and go to bed."

I left it to it and headed for the bathroom, noticing as I went that it was daylight outside now. I often end up practically nocturnal when I'm working, up all night and snatching what sleep I can get during the day. Unfortunately Trixie didn't seem to work the same way. The bathroom door was locked and I could hear the shower running.

"For fucksake," I muttered as I went to make a coffee instead.

She came out wrapped in my good white towel about five minutes later and cornered me in the kitchen.

"You didn't come home last night," she said, then looked at me and wrinkled her nose at the smell. "Don, what on earth have you been *doing* all night?"

So I told her all about it, trying hard not to think about how she wasn't wearing anything except that towel and failing miserably. She sat at the table and lit a cigarette, and listened.

"Oh dear," she said when I was done.

She crossed her legs, nearly giving me a heart attack as the towel started to come open.

"Trixie for pity's sake please put some clothes on," I said, forcing myself to stare out of the window instead of at her.

"Oh," she said. "Oh, if you like. Back in a minute."

I glared at the yard downstairs, where that fucking hideous cat was sitting there licking its balls bold as brass in a sunny patch under the clothes line. What had Alice said?

Something about a travelling cat always being wherever you are, and what the fuck even was a travelling cat anyway? Oh, what did it matter – she was obviously bananas, poor little thing.

Trixie came back in wearing a jumper and jeans.

"Better?" she asked. It was, but only a bit if I'm honest. "Now then, how much do you know about Bianakith?"

"Only what was in the book, and the Burned Man backed it up," I said. "The Burned Man didn't seem too keen on it, that's for sure."

"I'm not surprised," she said. "This is an archdemon, Don, not something that could have slipped through by itself however thin the Veils are down there. Which means someone must have summoned it on purpose. Someone very powerful deliberately brought it through, and they must have had a good reason for doing that."

"To wipe out the gnomes?" I wondered, thinking out loud.

Trixie shrugged. "Possibly," she said, "but I can't imagine why. Elementals keep themselves to themselves on the whole. They're not known for bothering people who don't bother them first."

"Well, whatever the reason, I need to do something about it," I said. "Janice is counting on me, for one thing. They all are. Besides which, I'm not having the middle of London and everyone in it falling into a sodding great hole in the ground."

"Well do you or your horrible little friend have any ideas of exactly *what* to do about it?"

"No," I admitted. "Not yet, anyway. Anything *I* could send against it would get eaten alive. I don't suppose…"

"So would I, I'm afraid," Trixie said, crushing that hope before I could even voice it. "I'm just one soldier after all, and Bianakith is a bit out of my league. I mean obviously I could kill it, but not without ending up like your poor friend Alice and I can't say I fancy that very much."

Damn. There went that idea then. I sipped my coffee and watched the cat saunter along the wall downstairs like it owned the place.

"Is there any way we can ask for help?" I said after a moment.

"Help?"

"From, you know, Upstairs," I said. "From your Dominion, maybe."

"Hmmm," Trixie said. "I don't know. I can try, but I don't know what the answer will be."

"Well give it a go if you can, please," I said. "It can only say no. Look, I need a shower and some sleep then I've got that other business to sort out, once I've given Wormwood a piece of my mind."

"Oh yes, your pet charity case," Trixie said with a wry smile. "Have fun."

CHAPTER 6

"Hero?" I shouted in his face. "Fucking hero?! Are you out of your tiny fucking mind?"

"Steady on now Don," Connie said, looming suddenly at my side.

Wormwood waved him back and lit yet another cigarette.

"Sorry about that," he said. "You were the best I could come up with in a pinch."

"You do know what's fucking down there, don't you?"

"Not really," he said, "and I don't really care. I promised them a champion and they got you. I never promised them you'd be any bloody use."

I coughed his smoke out of my face and sat back in the chair with a scowl. It was late afternoon and we were in his office off the downstairs bar. His secretary really hadn't wanted to let me see him, but I had insisted.

"I want that hexring," I said. "And the rest of it. Now, and for free."

"Maybe I ain't got it now," he said.

"Maybe I'll treat Trixie to a night out later," I countered. "We could have a lovely time here. A few drinks, a nice little game of cards, send Wormwood screaming back to

Hell, that sort of thing."

"All right, all right, keep your fucking panties on," he grumbled.

He unlocked the top drawer of his desk and took out a flat black case. He turned it around on the scrolled leather top of the desk and flipped it open to show me what was inside. The hexring lay on a bed of crimson velvet. It was a six-sided band of glistening black stone about the size of a fat wedding ring, inscribed all over with tiny swirling lines in patterns that seemed to move if you looked at them for too long.

"Get his other crap would you, Connie?"

Connie came back while I was still admiring the hexring. It really was rather beautiful, in a nausea-inducing sort of way. Connie was carrying a canvas bag that was wriggling slightly. A croak floated out of it.

"Toads," he said proudly. "And, um. The other stuff."

"Thanks, Con," I said as I took it off him. I put the hexring back in its case and slipped it into the inside pocket of my jacket. "Right, well. That'll do for starters, but you still owe me, Wormwood. You owe me fucking big time for all this bollocks. And I want your direct line, too. I'm not too keen on your secretary, and she seems to hate me for some reason."

"Can't fucking think why," Wormwood muttered, but he passed me a business card anyway.

I smiled when I saw it had his personal mobile number printed on it. He glowered and opened the *Financial Times* with a flourish.

"You done?" he asked. "I'm a busy man."

I left him to it and hung around the closed bar while Connie called me a taxi back home.

Trixie was gone when I got in, hopefully off to commune with her Dominion somewhere. She had told me she needed peace and quiet for that, by which I knew she meant she didn't want to be under the same roof as the Burned Man while she was doing it. I can't say I really blamed her, all things considered. I had no idea where she had gone but for some reason I had a mad vision of her standing on the dome of St Paul's Cathedral, arms outstretched to the heavens and her flaming sword in her hand while a single sunbeam blazed down and made her hair shine like spun gold. The poetic effect was only slightly spoiled by me picturing her wearing that towel while she was doing it, but there you go. Can't have everything can you?

I took the bag through to the workroom and dumped it on the floor, and showed the hexring to the Burned Man.

"This do you?" I asked it.

It nodded approvingly. "Perfect," it said. "Now go sort those toads and get a little paintbrush, there's a good lad."

I gutted the toads in the kitchen sink and mixed their blood with the tincture of mercury while the Burned Man did whatever it was doing with the lodestone. Then it was just a matter of applying the blood and mercury mixture to the fine lines in the hexring while it sat atop the lodestone on the altar in front of the Burned Man. The hexring drank the mixture greedily, absorbing every drop until it was all gone. Not all magic has to be overly complicated if you've got the right bits and pieces. And an imprisoned archdemon to help you out, admittedly.

"That'll do the trick," the Burned Man said.

I phoned Charlie Page and told him I'd be over about nine.

After the last time, I had the sense to tell the taxi driver to wait for me. I didn't expect this to take too long and I was buggered if I was getting the bus home again. Charlie opened the door wearing his usual combination of grey and beige, and looking as forlorn as ever. And poor. He still looked very poor too. I sighed.

"Thank you for coming back," he said. "I wasn't sure you would."

"I said I would, didn't I?" I said, as I followed him into his miserable little house.

"I'd have been in so much trouble if you hadn't," he said. Funny thing to say really, but I didn't give it much thought at the time. "Have you got what you need?"

I patted my pocket with the hexring in it.

"Yeah," I said.

"What are you going to do, if you don't mind me asking?"

I took the ring out and showed it to him.

"This is what you might call a magic ring, for want of a better word for it," I explained. "I just need to put it on her finger and she'll be fine. No more throwing things and breaking stuff, no more screaming, not so long as she keeps the ring on. Then you can get her to a doctor like normal people do, all right?"

"That sounds… wonderful," he said. He ushered me up the stairs ahead of him. "Go on up, you know the way. I've made sure she hasn't got any bedpans to throw at you this time."

I opened her bedroom door while Charlie was still climbing the stairs.

Six knives were hovering in the air over the bed.

Six long, wicked carving knives with gleaming sharp blades turned in the air as one to face me. Mrs Page screamed with hatred and they flew at me in a blizzard of steel.

I hurled myself backwards and crashed through the door behind me, the one into the front bedroom. Charlie's bedroom. I hit the floor with a thump as three of the knives whizzed over my head and slammed into the wall. They stuck there quivering from the sheer force they had been thrown with. The others smashed straight through the front window and shot out into the dark street. I heard an engine start, and a squeal of tyres outside. There went my ride home then.

As I pulled myself up onto my knees I saw the altar under the window. The table was draped in a black cloth, with black candles on it and an inverted cross for the altarpiece. And on the walls, scrawled over and over again in Charlie Page's spidery old man's handwriting, filling every inch of space, two words repeated endlessly. *Adam says. Adam says.*

I spun round to find Charlie coming at me with another knife in his hand. This one was a sharp ritual dagger, the sort of thing *I* use. He didn't look anything like as old and frail now, and he certainly didn't look like he was crying any more.

"Adam says!" he screamed, as he plunged the knife down at me.

I rolled out of the way just in time, starting to panic. I know he was only a little old man but anyone's dangerous with a knife in their hand, and one thing I'm not is a fighter. I never have been. Fights scare the shit out of me, to be perfectly honest about it. I don't even know *how* to fight.

Charlie stumbled past me in his haste and I flailed at him with one outstretched hand. I managed to grab his ankle, more by luck than judgment, and yanked. I only half-tripped him but he lost his balance and slipped, and I snatched at the trailing hem of his cardigan and pulled him all the way down. He thumped onto the floor beside me and lost his grip on the dagger. He was quick as a snake though and he was on top of me before I knew what was happening, clawing at my face with an unnatural strength. His lips drew back from his yellow teeth in a grimace of hatred.

"Adam says!" he bellowed at me, spraying spittle in my face.

There was no way he should have been that strong. I could feel the magic in him, some spell driving him beyond his limits. No skinny old geezer had any right to be that strong and I knew he wouldn't be able to keep it up for long, spell or no spell, but at this rate he was going to kill me before it wore off. I was going to have to do something drastic.

I got an elbow under his chin and shoved, wrestling with him in an unskilled, schoolboy sort of way until I managed to get hold of his hand. I pressed up on his scrawny throat with my forearm to keep him from biting me and fumbled in my pocket with my free hand until I found what I needed. He was still hissing and spitting when I rammed the hexring onto his finger. All the magical strength went out of him at once as the hexring did its work. He sagged limply on top of me, gasping.

I punched him in the face as hard as I could. I know, I know, he was a poor little old man and all that, but for fucksake!

He flopped over onto his back on the floor, unconscious. I sat up with a wince, cradling my hand against my stomach. Fuck, that had hurt. I left him there and went back into Mrs Page's room. I was careful, but I didn't think she'd be dangerous any more.

I was right. She was quite dead, poor old love, and looked like she had been for a good long while. I touched her cheek and found she was ice cold. I sighed.

What did that evil old bastard do to you, sweetheart?

I gently took one of the pillows from under her head and laid her down, closing her eyes with my fingertips. I carried the pillow back into the front room where Charlie was still out cold, and stood looking down at him for a moment.

Then I knelt down beside him and pressed the pillow firmly over his face.

No, I'm not in the business of bumping off sweet little old ladies, but murderous devil-worshipers? Yeah, those I'll kill. I held the pillow down until I was sure he had stopped breathing, then took the hexring off him and slipped it back into my pocket. That might come in handy again another time.

I let myself out.

CHAPTER 7

Of course, my taxi had scarpered as soon as it started raining blades outside. Just like I had thought. I couldn't say I blamed him really, but it was a pain in the arse all the same. I walked for a couple of streets until I hunted down a pub to sulk in.

The pub stood in the bleak shadow of the tower blocks and was called the Goat's Head, of all things, and it didn't look any more welcoming than the rest of the neighbourhood. It had a flat roof for one thing, and that's never a good sign in an estate pub. There was a small crowd of sullen-looking smokers loitering around the front door. Tracksuits and hoodies seemed to be the order of the day, I noticed. My suit drew a few hostile looks but no one actually said anything as I walked through the miasma of cigarette smoke and pushed the door open. They probably thought I was a copper, looking back on it. That was a fucking laugh after what I had just done.

The place was the sort of dump you only seem to get in deprived residential areas. There was a pool table with its cloth ripped in two places and a cluster of broken lights hanging over it. The three garishly flashing fruit machines lined up against the wall seemed to be competing with the overhead neon strip lights to see which one could give me a headache first, and the TV over the bar was showing football. Fuck but I hate football. The place's only saving grace was that it was half empty. It was a dump but it had booze, and that was all that really mattered right then.

The landlord had one of those faces people round these parts call "lived in", which was a sort of friendly euphemism for "scarred like a butcher's block". What a charming place this wasn't. I bought myself a pint and a whisky chaser and wormed my way behind a table in the corner. I felt a strong urge to have a wall at my back, and not just because of the locals.

Adam says. Fucking hell.

I must admit I was feeling more than a bit shaky. For one thing, I hadn't killed anyone with my own hands for a bloody long time, but I can't say I would lose any sleep over Charlie Page after what he had done to that poor old lady. I wondered if she really had been his wife. Anything was possible I supposed, although I doubted it. Reanimating the corpse of your own wife and turning it into a weapon was a bit much even for a Satanist, surely? Still, that was neither here nor there, really.

Adam says.

I should have known that smarmy fucker wouldn't leave me alone forever.

I necked my whisky and looked round the depressing pub. Just then one of the tracksuit wearers got a big payout on the fruit machine he had been playing. The coins rattled and clattered into the tray in a long stream. He scooped them up and turned gleefully towards the bar, and I caught sight of his face for the first time.

Well fuck me, that was a turn up for the books. I got up and followed him, and leaned my elbows on the bar next to him.

"Hello, Weasel," I said quietly.

He nearly jumped out of his skin, the poor bastard. Harry the Weasel was an unfortunate little bloke in his early thirties, no more than five foot six and already half bald, with a droopy lower lip and a lazy eye that made him look thick.

He wasn't, though.

"Mr Drake," he said, gaping at me.

"What are you doing in this godforsaken shithole, Weasel?" I asked him.

"This is my local, Mr Drake," he said. ""And if you don't mind, in here could you maybe just call me Harry?"

I looked at him for a moment

"Nah," I said. "You'll always be Weasel to me. I'll have a large scotch, ta."

"Yes, Mr Drake," he muttered.

He took his pint from the slab-faced landlord and reluctantly bought me a double whisky as well. Well, he was in the money wasn't he? And I knew why.

"I hope you're not overdoing that, Weasel," I said. "People will notice. People will notice, and then you'll get your head kicked in."

"Yes, Mr Drake," he said again, looking mournfully into his pint.

I had a feeling that had probably already happened somewhere. You had to be careful about using my little trick with probability. It's not that powerful, not enough to win the lottery or cheat Wormwood at Fates sadly, but it works well enough to tickle a fruit machine when you need to. The key point there is *need* to, not every bloody time you go to the pub. That's how people get suspicious, and no one wants that.

"Step into my office for a minute," I said, ushering him over to my table. I wriggled back onto the bench with the wall behind me and pointed at the chair across from me. He sat down and sipped his pint. He looked nervous, but then he usually did. "That little trick I taught you isn't for every day, Weasel. You do know that, right?"

He nodded. For all that you'd never guess it in a million years from looking at him, Harry the Weasel was a magician. Not a very good one, admittedly, but he had his uses. I hadn't seen him for well over a year, and if he lived round here I supposed that was no wonder. This wasn't the sort of neighbourhood I went to if I could help it. A few years back though he'd been pestering me no end, wanting to become my apprentice. Now obviously I had never let him anywhere near the Burned Man or anything that really mattered, but I *had* taught him a few things, and my little trick with probability had been one of them. Perhaps that hadn't been entirely wise but people like to see tangible results, you know what I mean? It's up to them if they abuse them and get themselves in the shit. Anyway, it wasn't hurting me, and it had been a good way to keep him pretty much permanently in my debt.

"I need a little favour, Weasel," I said.

"Thought you might," he said.

"Have you been hearing anything recently about a bloke called Adam?"

Weasel's lazy eye twitched. Now for all that Weasel was horrible, he knew pretty much everyone else who was horrible too, and in South London that was a fucking lot of people. Pick any petty criminal – low-level gangsters, street-corner dealers and junkies, burglars and toms, rent boys and cheap magicians, Weasel either knew them or he knew someone who did. That made him bloody useful sometimes.

"Adam?" he asked. "Lots of people are called Adam, Mr Drake."

He gulped his beer and stared down at the sticky table. I

knew he was scared of me, that was how it was supposed to be, but I was starting to get a nasty feeling he might be scared of that name, too.

"Yeah they are, Weasel, but lots of people aren't like *this* Adam, are they?"

"No, Mr Drake," he muttered.

"Look at me, Weasel," I said. He reluctantly lifted his head and met my eye. I gave him a little prod with my Will. "Tell me about Adam."

"I dunno really," he said. "There's been some people talking, that's all. You know, the Black Mass crowd. I don't like them, Mr Drake."

"I don't think anyone does," I said. "What have they been talking *about* exactly?"

"Someone called Adam, and what he's been telling them. I don't think…" He lowered his voice to a whisper and leaned forwards so I could hear him. "I don't think he's human, Mr Drake. I think he's… he's a *demon*."

"Hmmm," I said. I knew exactly what Adam was, but there was no need for Weasel to know that. "And what *has* he been telling them, do you think?"

"I dunno, Mr Drake," he said, "but they're all listening to him. When Adam says do something, they do it."

Adam says. There it was again. This tasted bad, even worse than the horrible cheap whisky I was drinking.

"Yeah, I bet they do," I muttered.

"Look, Mr Drake," Weasel said. "I've been thinking. I mean, I help you out, don't I?"

"When I can find you," I said. "Where the fuck have you been, anyway?"

Weasel coughed. "The Scrubs," he admitted. "I done twelve months."

I didn't ask what for. That would have been very rude in these sort of circles, in case you didn't know.

"Oh, right," I said instead.

"Only got out a couple of weeks ago," he went on. He leaned forwards again, his voice dropping to a nervous whisper. "I've been meaning to call you, actually, Mr Drake. I had a lot of time to think, when I was inside. I wanna learn off you. Properly learn, I mean."

Oh fucking hell, do you?

"Oh yeah?"

"Yeah. I mean, I've got me books and that but... it ain't the same as when you taught me them bits and pieces."

Of course it wasn't – magic isn't for everyone. Some people simply have no intuitive ability at all and there's not a lot you can do about that. Magic isn't painting by numbers. Harry the Weasel had a bit of spark about him, hard though that might be to believe, but not a lot. Not enough for me to be able to teach him anything that really mattered, anyway.

"A grimoire ain't a cook book, Weasel," I told him. "It's not a matter of 'this plus that plus the other equals Weasel gets laid', it doesn't work like that."

"I know," he said. "I know, but I'm trying, Mr Drake. I'm really trying. I've got hold of a copy of the Goetia now, you know."

Oh God, that'll end well.

The Goetia is the first book of the ancient grimoire *Lemegeton Clavicula Salomonis*, or *The Lesser Key of Solomon the King*, in case you didn't know. It's basically a manual for summoning demons, and it's the last thing on earth someone like Harry the Weasel should be allowed anywhere near.

"Knock yourself out," I said. "Go ahead and call up a demon, tell it I sent you if you want. Just don't be surprised when it turns round and bites your fucking face off."

Weasel gulped down the rest of his pint and wiped sweaty palms on the thighs of his already greasy-looking tracksuit.

"That's what I'm scared of," he said. "That's why I want

you to help me, Mr Drake."

"Yeah well, we'll see," I said. "Let me think about it."

I really wasn't in the market for an apprentice, and even if I had been, I can't say Harry the Weasel would have been at the top of the list of prospective candidates. Or even *on* the list, for that matter. All the same, if I could dangle the chance of it in front of him for a bit he might make himself useful.

"Thanks, Mr Drake," he said.

"While I'm thinking about it, I want to know everything you hear about Adam. Every word of it," I told him. I pushed my empty glass across the table towards him. "It's still your round, by the way."

I have to admit I was more than a bit pissed when I got home, and I crashed on the sofabed in my office without speaking to Trixie. Stupid of me, looking back on it. When I woke up the next morning I found her sitting at my desk, smoking a cigarette and staring at me.

"It wouldn't come," she said, her voice strangely flat.

"What?" I said blearily, sitting up in the tangled mess I'd made of my bedding.

"My Dominion," she said. "I called and I called and I prayed and called and cried and screamed and it wouldn't *come*, Don."

I blinked and noticed for the first time how red her eyes looked. She really did look like she'd been crying, and I'd just come home drunk and passed out without even talking to her.

Jesus wept, and I wondered why she didn't fancy me?

"Oh God, Trixie, I'm sorry," I said.

"Yes," she said, whatever that was supposed to mean.

I sighed and pulled a sheet around me as I got up.

"I'm going to grab a shower and get dressed," I said, "then we'll talk."

I shut myself in the bathroom and sat down on the bog. I scrubbed my hands over my face, trying to wake up enough to think. I had been going to tell her about what I'd found at Charlie Page's house, about Adam and what Harry the Weasel had told me. Now I wasn't so sure that was a good idea. It appeared her Dominion had stood her up yesterday and she had obviously got herself in a bit of a state over that. Was bringing Adam up now really such a good idea, what with how fragile her sanity still was after last year? I sighed. It really wasn't, was it? Oh well, it would just have to keep then.

I did the morning shit-shower-and-shave routine and got dressed, and when I came back I found she had made coffee for us both and was sitting behind my desk again.

"I've been thinking," she said.

"Oh?"

I took my coffee and wandered over to the window with it.

"Something must be wrong," she said. "*Upstairs* I mean, as you so succinctly put it. My Dominion has never ignored me before."

"Well isn't there a chain of command or something?" I asked her. "You told me once before it works like the army, so aren't you supposed to go through your sergeant first? Your archangel or whoever it would be."

"In general, yes," she said, "but I'm a bit of a special case."

Why doesn't that surprise me?

"Oh, right," I said.

"My original assignment with the Furies was given to me by my Dominion in person, so I'm a... well, we have a word for it, but I don't know how you'd phrase it in English exactly. I work directly for that Dominion, outside of the usual structures."

"Like a knight errant?" I ventured. "A sort of paladin?"

I'm sorry, I used to play Dungeons and Dragons when I was at university. Try not to hold it against me.

"Yes, yes, something like that, I suppose," she said. "Anyway, again to try and put it into your words, the Dominion is my immediate commanding officer. I've communed with it many times in the past without a problem."

I looked at her, and I could still see the thin black tendrils of corruption that streaked her aura. I'd have to phrase this one a bit delicately.

"Have you communed with it since you, you know... slipped a bit?"

Trixie put her cup down and gave me a hard stare. "*I'm* not the problem here, Don."

"All right, all right," I said. She was emphatic enough that I didn't want to argue about it, but I wasn't completely sure I believed her all the same. That, and she hadn't actually answered the question, I noticed. "In which case, what is?"

"I don't know," she said. "That's why I think there must be something going on."

"Upstairs?"

"Well I suppose so, yes, although I have no idea what. It's no good, Don, we need the Dominion's help if we're going to deal with Bianakith. If it won't answer my call you'll have to summon it."

I almost choked on my coffee.

"*What?*"

"You did it before," she said.

"No, I didn't," I said. "Summoning is making something manifest against its will. I never summoned your Dominion. I wouldn't know where to start with that, or if it's even remotely possible for that matter. What I did was more like... I don't know. I begged it to come, and it did. It *chose* to come Trixie, I didn't make it."

You summoned Adam once though, didn't you? a little voice in my head reminded me. Yeah I had, but I had no idea how I'd done that either, and no particular desire to attempt it ever again. How I'd got away with that I still didn't really know.

She sat in thoughtful silence for a moment, fiddling with her cigarette case.

"Not many magicians can do what you do, can they Don?" she asked suddenly.

"No," I said. "Thankfully."

Summoning and sending is bloody difficult, not to mention monstrously dangerous, that's how come I can charge so much for it. Hell, *I* can't do it without the Burned Man. *You summoned Adam without the Burned Man though, didn't you?* Yeah, but I was trying not to think about that. Shut up, little voice in my head. Just shut the fuck up.

"But lots of magicians commune with demons and spirits, don't they? Or they say they do, anyway. How do they do that?"

"Ah, that's different," I said. "Talking to something is a damn sight easier than making it physically manifest."

"Yes, but *how*?"

"Invocation or evocation," I said. "Invocation's the sort of thing Papa Armand does, where you invite something to come into your mind and body and speak through you. I'm not a fan, personally. I mean, I can do it, but… it's different for him of course, with his loa. That's a religious thing in Vodou, and anyway, they're not like the sorts of things I deal with."

"Oh," she said, and smiled. "How is dear Armand?"

"He's fine," I said. "His usual self, you know how he is."

For some reason Trixie had taken quite a shine to the eccentric old Houngan who seemed to have inexplicably taken me under his wing. Probably because he was so impossibly charming, and almost ridiculously polite to her.

"So what *would* you do?" Trixie asked, catching me off guard. "Evocation then? That's what, exactly?"

"Part of the Goetic grimoire tradition," I said, starting to lecture now I had a willing audience for once. "The magician causes the spirit to appear in a triangle of art before the circle, usually in a mirror or a crystal, where he can speak with it and... Trixie?"

"Mmmm?"

"Did you just play me?"

She smiled and lit another cigarette. "Perhaps a little bit," she said. "When can we do it?"

So much for my lecture. This wasn't academic interest she was showing, obviously.

"It's still not that simple," I said. "Not with something as powerful as a Dominion it isn't, anyway. Evocation might not be as rude as flat out summoning but it's still not a polite invitation exactly. It needs a bit of oomph behind it. A *lot* of oomph for a Dominion, I expect. We'll need to talk this through with the Burned Man."

"You can do that," she said. "I'm not going in there."

"You'll have to sooner or later if you want to do this," I said. "That's where the circle is."

Trixie pulled a sour face that said she hadn't thought of that, which was some small consolation for the way she had just deftly wrapped me round her little finger. Women, huh? I left her to her smoke and went to speak to the Burned Man.

"Let me get this straight," it said, after I had explained the idea. "You want me to evoke that thing that manifested like a fucking nuke going off and tore Aleto the Unresting into charred mincemeat just by fucking *speaking to her?* Are you out of your tiny cunting *mind*, Drake?"

I think it's fair to say the Burned Man wasn't completely on board with the plan.

"I'm not talking about trying to fucking summon it, I haven't got a death wish," I said. "Just an evocation, that's all."

"That's *all?* Have you got even the faintest idea what this fucking thing is?"

I wasn't sure I really had, to be perfectly honest about it. I tried to remember how Trixie had explained the hierarchy to me. Angels to Archangels to Principalities to Dominions, that was it. Then something called a Throne I think, I couldn't remember how it went after that and I was sure it didn't really matter anyway. I had a feeling a Dominion was as close as a mortal could get to meeting God Himself and still come out alive. Well, *hopefully* come out alive.

"I know it's dangerous but we haven't got a lot of choice. Trixie needs to speak to it about Bianakith and–"

"Oh, *Trixie* needs, I see. And Blondie gets whatever Blondie wants around here, doesn't she?"

Oh for fucksake, seriously? It was *jealous*? I decided to try some ego stroking, that usually worked.

"Look, you'll be right here with me," I said. "You're an archdemon for fucks sake. An archdemon so powerful that *you* were the one Oisin chose, right? Back in Tir Na Nog, when he first bound you into that fetish. He chose *you*, above all the archdemons of Hell. You can stand against a Dominion, can't you?"

"'Course I bloody can," it said, and showed me a nasty grin. "The question is, can *you?*"

"I'll just have to," I said. "What are we going to need to make this work?"

"Yeah, that's going to be a problem. You remember that angel's skull you didn't win from Wormwood?"

"Oh fuck me, how could I forget it?" I said.

"Well, we need that. Or another one like it, I don't care, but an angel's skull is what we need."

"Wonderful," I said. I could still remember how much that bloody thing had turned out to be worth. "All right, leave that with me. Anything else?"

"Nah, not for an evocation," it said. "You don't need blood for that, just the focus. Get me that skull and slap together a triangle of art and I'm sure I can rustle you up five minutes of earache from a Dominion."

Get me that skull, just like that.

Fucking hell.

CHAPTER 8

"Fancy a night out?" I asked Trixie.

"I'm sorry?"

"I need to pay Wormwood a visit, and I'm really going to need you along this time," I explained. "We need to persuade him to lend us his angel's skull, and I don't think me asking nicely is going to cut it somehow."

Trixie smiled. "Oh, I'll ask him extra nicely, don't you worry."

I'd sort of been counting on that, truth be told, so that was a bit of good news for once.

We made a proper night of it, me in my best suit and Trixie in a stunning black evening dress she'd rustled up from somewhere while I wasn't looking. I *still* had no idea how she did that. After dinner in a nice restaurant and a couple of cocktails afterwards we took a cab to Wormwood's club. It was gone midnight by then, well past opening time, and the bar was crowded. Connie was in his usual spot at the bottom of the stairs where he was making sure only those who were on the list of invited guests made their way up to the actual club proper. We made our way over to him, narrowly avoiding being jostled by a big, smiling ginger-haired bloke wearing an eyepatch with a nasty scar around it. Something about that guy jogged at my memory but then Connie saw us and his face fell in obvious dismay, and I forgot all about it.

"Evening, Con," I said.

"All right, Don," he said. "Good evening, ma'am."

"Hello," said Trixie. "It's Constantinos, isn't it?"

Connie looked flustered that she had remembered his name, bless him, and I couldn't help but smile at that.

"No bother, Con," I said. "We're just having a night out. Thought I might play some cards."

"Oh," he said. "Righto."

"And have a little chat with Wormwood, if he's about."

"Mr Wormwood has been unavoidably detained on important business," Connie said, pronouncing the words carefully as though he'd been taught them specially for just this occasion. Which he probably had been, to be fair. "Means he's not here."

"What a pity," said Trixie.

"Ah well, just cards it is then," I said.

I offered Trixie my arm and we went up the stairs together. I chanced a quick look back and saw Connie talking urgently into his phone. Funny that. Not as funny as the mental image of Wormwood scurrying across the club like a frightened rat and barricading himself in his office, admittedly, but funny all the same.

The club itself wasn't particularly busy yet but it was warm and comfortingly dark and smoky, the way a proper club should be. I could hear soft music playing and the clink of glasses, the rattle of dice on the craps table and the clatter of the roulette wheel. I could feel my gambling muscle starting to twitch. I snagged us a couple of glasses of champagne from a passing waiter and nodded towards the far corner.

"That's his office door," I said. "Twenty quid says he's

hiding under the desk."

Trixie smiled and sipped her drink.

"I'll go and have a little chat with him," she said. "Try not to lose too much money while I'm gone."

She sauntered off with her champagne glass in one hand and a long black cigarette in the other, giving Audrey Hepburn lessons in how it was done. I watched her for a moment, and sighed wistfully. It was no good, was it? It just wasn't going to happen. I went to look for a game of cards.

It didn't take long to find one, to be fair. There was a bloke I didn't recognise sitting at a table by himself, the two decks laid out in front of him ready for Fates. I eyed the cards, the thick deck for the suits and the slimmer one of major arcana which were the trumps in the game, and I felt my gambling muscle twitch again. Trixie had told me not to lose too much money but she never told me not to play at all. I think she probably knew me better than that by then anyway. I went and sat down opposite the geezer.

He looked up at me with eyes that glowed with a reddish light in the gloom of the club. Now normally that wouldn't exactly be a good sign but Wormwood's is that sort of place, in case you hadn't gathered by now. You get all sorts in there. Other than the eyes he looked human. He was wearing a smart suit and he had a long, sharp silver ring on each finger of both hands.

"Evening," I said.

"I don't believe I've had the pleasure," he said.

"Don Drake."

"Hmmm," he said. "Call me Antonio."

If he was Italian I was from fucking Mars, but whatever. You didn't ask questions about who or what people were, not in Wormwood's you didn't anyway. That just wasn't polite. A quick squint at his aura was enough to tell me he definitely wasn't human. No human has a dark red aura.

Interesting bloke, our Antonio.

"Fancy a few hands?" I asked him, and he nodded.

I glanced up at the hovering croupier.

"Go on then, mate," I said. "Set us up."

Customers never get to deal the cards at Wormwood's place. They're very firm about that, which is a pain in the arse. I'm good with cards if I say so myself, but when I can't cheat, my luck isn't always quite so impressive. The croupier reached between us to cut the two decks then began to deal the minor arcana, the suits. I picked my hand up and fanned the cards, looking over them at this Antonio geezer. His eyes glowed back at me as he did the same thing. Nothing showed on his face, nothing at all.

My hand was a piece of shit. A ten of swords was the best card I had, and nothing went together at all. I tossed a useless two of cups face down on the table, and my opponent also chucked a card down.

"Card," I said, and he nodded.

The croupier dished us each out another card from the minor arcana. The way Fates is played, you have to decide on your suits before you draw your trump and once you have, you can't change it. That's the Fate part of the game. I slid the card towards me and up into my fan. Ten of pentacles. That was more fucking like it. I threw in another useless card, and again the bloke opposite me did the same. I got something equally useless back. Still, a pair of tens wasn't too bad, and a decent trump could still make it a winning hand. It would have to do.

"Stand," I said.

Antonio changed yet another card, then he was done as well.

"Trumps," the croupier announced.

He picked up the slim deck of major arcana and gave it a flamboyant shuffle, then dealt us each a card. I looked down at mine and had to try hard not to smile. I had drawn Judgment. Judgment is the twentieth trump so it scores one from maximum, or two from maximum depending if you're playing Fool high or low. The house rule at Wormwood's was Fool low, making it score nothing at all. Wormwood didn't suffer fools gladly, after all. Anyway, that meant I had just turned a mediocre hand into a bloody good one.

"Fifty," I said.

Ol' Red Eyes nodded.

"And raise you fifty," he said.

We went back and forth till we got to five hundred, then he shook his head.

"Call," he said.

He had a pair of sixes and the Lovers so that was him well and truly beat. I grinned as the croupier noted my win in his tablet against Antonio's account. No one plays with anything so vulgar as cash or even chips in Wormwood's club. Unless artefacts are being gambled for, everything is on account, with the assumption that anyone able to even get in there is going to be good for it. That had bitten me in the arse once before, admittedly, but there you go.

"Another hand?" I asked.

Antonio nodded.

"I want to win my money back," he said.

I bet you do, I thought, my gambling muscle going into spasm now. I was starting to feel like this guy might have "easy mark" written all over him, despite his less than welcoming appearance. Looking scary doesn't mean you can play cards for shit, after all.

The croupier dealt again, and again I ended up with a reasonable if not brilliant hand.

"Stand," I said, after swapping out a couple of cards.

I lifted my trump and slid it into my fan, carefully keeping my face smooth. Judgment again. I see...

"Fifty," I started.

Antonio called me at five hundred again, and again I had him.

"You drew the same trump twice in a row," he observed.

"Yup," I said. "Looks that way."

"Hmmm," he said. "Again."

Now, you have to understand that Fates isn't just about gambling. The Tarot has its own power, and all of Wormwood's croupiers are highly skilled with it. They're all psychic too – no one *ever* cheats in Wormwood's club, with the possible exception of Wormwood himself. The croupiers would know it straight away. Anyway, the point is, Fates is as much about divination as it is about the money that changes hands over it. The last time I'd had a string of the same trump in Fates it had been the Tower, the card that commonly meant danger, crisis and destruction, and my life had gone quite rapidly to shit in a sack almost immediately afterwards. I was starting to wonder about this.

We played again, and this time I managed to get myself a nice eight-high flush. Not bad at all. Antonio was looking intensely at me over his cards.

"Trumps," he said.

The croupier dealt, and I slowly edged mine up off the table. To be honest I already sort of knew what I was going to get, and I was right. I slid Judgment into my fan and swallowed. Someone was definitely trying to tell me something here, but I shuddered to think who.

"Hundred," I said, keen to get this over with now.

"Raise you two hundred," Antonio said.

I looked down at my cards, at Judgment looking back at me. We played with the classic Rider Waite deck at Wormwood's. The image for Judgment in that deck is the Archangel Gabriel looming out of the sky at the end of the world, in case you didn't know. The Day of Judgment. I wasn't finding that very comforting right then, for all that I was about to take this bloke yet again. I found myself losing interest in the game all of a sudden.

I called him, and tossed my cards down on the table. He snarled and leaned forward over the table towards me, his eyes blazing red.

"I don't believe it," he hissed. "Three times? You're a cheat!"

I leaned back in my chair and let the croupier take care of it. Cheating is a very serious accusation anywhere, but *especially* in here where everyone should know it was flat-out impossible. That was a direct insult to both Wormwood's security and to the competence of his croupiers. Not a wise thing to say, on either count.

"I assure you the gentleman is *not* cheating," the croupier said.

He reached out and put his hand over Antonio's face. His fingers grew like many-jointed spines, popping out extra knuckles and stretching and elongating until they had enclosed Antonio's entire head in a nightmarish cage of flesh and bone. The croupier squeezed and Antonio went rigid in his seat, his glowing red eyes suddenly bulging in their sockets. A hiss of wordless pain escaped his lips and I realised he was seconds away from having his skull crushed to pulp.

"You will be leaving the club now, sir," the croupier said, "and you will be settling your account before you go. You will not ever be coming back."

A moment later another three of Wormwood's people appeared beside him and took Antonio by the arms. The croupier let him go and his enormous hand gradually shrank back to normal size, all the extra knuckles cracking disgustingly as they retracted.

"Please accept the apologies of the house, Mr Drake,"

he said. "I will make an adjustment to your account to recompense you for the inconvenience."

"Yeah, thanks," I said, staring queasily at the guy's hand.

I swallowed. That was just nasty. I got up and left the card table as Antonio was escorted firmly away.

I can't even play cards in peace these days.

"Don-boy Drake," said a voice at my elbow. The thick Haitian accent was unmistakable. That and no one else has ever called me that. "Long time no see!"

I turned and grinned at him. "Hello Papa," I said.

Papa Armand was very old and very black and very handsome. He was wearing a tuxedo tonight, with his trademark silk top hat tipped at a rakish angle and a thin white silk scarf draped around his narrow shoulders. Diamond signet rings glittered on his fingers as he lifted a glass of rum to his lips and drank.

"Your health, Don-boy," he said. "I see you brought Madame Zanj Bèl to smile on us tonight."

He always called her that. As far as I could work out it was Haitian Creole for "beautiful angel". She certainly didn't seem to mind, anyway.

"Yeah," I said. "She's just having a little chat with Wormwood but I'm sure she'll want to see you too."

"Fine lookin' woman right there, Don-boy," he said, although he knew *exactly* what she was. "Mighty fine lookin' woman."

"She certainly is that," I agreed.

"Mighty dangerous, too."

"Yeah, that too," I said, and sighed again.

"Could be dangerous for *you*, I'm thinking, you pick the wrong side. She could fuck you up, that one." The old goat was forever flirting with Trixie, but under all that I knew he took her very seriously indeed. "Come now, throw some dice with Papa."

He lit a cigar and led me across the club to a craps table that wasn't being used, where he shooed the croupier away with a dismissive flick of his hand. Papa Armand was almost as rich as Wormwood and seemed to be able to pretty much do as he pleased here. He reached into the inside pocket of his tuxedo and pulled out a handful of polished bones.

"Chicken bone," he said. "Ver' traditional."

He tossed the bones onto the green felt and stirred them thoughtfully with one finger. The diamonds in his rings caught the light and sparkled hypnotically. He pushed one bone over another and chuckled. He had a wonderful laugh, dark and rich as molasses.

"Drawin' vévés on the craps table, how the world change," he said, and laughed again. "Can you see Papa Legba leaning on his cane, Don-boy? Can you smell the smoke of his ol' corncob pipe? You stand at the crossroads wit' Papa Legba, Don-boy, while the Houses draw up for war 'round you. Which way you goin' walk?"

I was starting to feel a bit lightheaded. Papa Armand blew cigar smoke in my face, thickly scented with rum. For a moment I thought I really could see the loa of the crossroads standing where Papa Armand was, the image of a battered straw hat wavering in and out at the edge of sight in place of his silk topper. Legba had the stem of his pipe between his teeth and a kindly smile on his face that made me feel... welcome.

"That's quite enough of that, Armand dear," Trixie said.

I blinked, and as suddenly as that the image was gone.

"*Bon aswè, Zanj Bèl,*" he said, and laughed again.

He bowed low and kissed her hand.

"Armand, you're incorrigible," she said, but she was smiling too. "Don, I'm pleased to say our host has graciously agreed to lend us the thing which we asked to borrow."

"Graciously?" I asked.

"Well," she conceded, "perhaps not. But he has agreed, which is all that really matters."

"Who could refuse Madame Zanj Bèl any request?" Papa Armand murmured.

I left Papa Armand flirting outrageously with Trixie and went to find another drink. Wormwood was still nowhere in sight and I couldn't help wondering if Trixie had left him whimpering in the corner of his office. I did hope so, the little git. I rounded myself up a whisky and turned away from the waiter to find myself face to face with a handsome woman in her mid-fifties. She flicked open an extravagant peacock feather fan and wafted it slowly up and down in front of her face, looking at me over the top of it. I remembered her then – I didn't know who she was but I'd seen her there last year, the night Trixie had well and truly put Wormwood in his place. The woman had been having a heated argument with Papa Armand that night.

"Mr Drake," she said, her voice low and flavoured with an American accent, from somewhere in the South. "You haven't been paying any mind to that fool of a Houngan I hope?"

I tried on my most disarming smile. "He's harmless," I said, although I knew he really wasn't.

"He is not, and you know it," she said. So much for my disarming smile. "He's crazy, and he's dangerous."

"Look," I said, "sorry, but I don't think we've been introduced. You seem to know my name but I'm afraid, um…"

"They call me Miss Marie," she said, and gave me a flirtatious smile. "Just Marie to you, honey."

"Right," I said, feeling a bit awkward.

I offered my hand and she shook it, and gave it just a little bit too much of a squeeze before she let go. I have to admit I'm not used to being flirted with. It was weird, and I couldn't help thinking that I'd really rather she didn't. *That* was how bad I had it for Trixie, I have to admit.

"About that old fool," she said, leaning close enough for me to smell her expensive French perfume. "I have to say, Mr Drake, you could do a lot better. If you're feeling the need for a teacher, well, I'm sure I could show you a few things."

I was sure she could, but that was hardly the point. The point at that precise moment was that one of her breasts was resting on my arm, and she didn't seem to be inclined to move any time soon. It really was making me feel a bit uncomfortable.

"Call me Don," I felt obliged to say. "And I think I can pick my own friends, ta. I'm a big boy."

She laughed at that, covering her mouth with her fan as she did so. At least she moved away a bit to do it, that was something I supposed.

"Oh I'm sure you are and I'm sure you can," she said, "but can you pick your own side? He's leading you by the nose like a hog to market, and you're going the wrong way."

"Oh yeah? How's that then?"

"I've seen you around, and I've heard things," she said. "The way you speak to Wormwood, for one. That isn't normal, honey. A mortal speaking to an archdemon like that, shoving him around. That's the sort of thing that gets a man noticed, and that kind of notice isn't always good, if you take my meaning."

I wasn't sure that I did, but I didn't get the chance to ask her to explain.

"Is everything all right, Don?" Trixie asked from beside me.

"Yeah," I said. "Yeah, I'm good."

Marie tipped her head to one side and looked Trixie slowly and unsubtly up and down.

"Mmmm," she purred. "Well hello there."

I have to say she looked a lot more interested in Trixie than she had in me, which was a bit of a relief. It was also quite funny, in all honesty.

Trixie blinked at her in obvious confusion, and it was an effort not to laugh. For all that Trixie was death walking when she wanted to be, she could still be endearingly naive in other ways. The thought that Miss Marie was attracted to her would never even have entered her head, I was sure.

"Hello," she said. "Do I know you?"

"Why, would you like to?" the woman asked.

"No she would not," Papa said, appearing on my other side in a cloud of cigar smoke. "No one want to know you, old whore."

"Haven't you died of the goddamn clap yet?" she asked. "I was *trying* to talk to this gentleman here, and this lovely lady."

"No one want to know you, no one want to talk to you," Papa snapped. "Maybe you forget what I told you, Marie. You're not welcome here, in my eyes."

"Erm," I said, "we should probably go. Goodnight Papa."

"Go well, Don-boy," he said. "*Orevwa, Zanj Bèl*. I will dream of you."

Trixie smiled and we left him to his argument.

"Who was she?" Trixie asked, as we made our way down the stairs.

"You know, I have no idea," I said. "Probably no one."

CHAPTER 9

The skull was delivered to my office the next afternoon.

I opened the door to see one of Wormwood's boys standing there, a reasonably humanlooking one wearing a plain black suit. Human-looking apart from the spines growing out of his neck, anyway. I was fairly sure he was one of the waiters who had helped to sling Antonio out of the club last night, but I couldn't have sworn to it. He had a big aluminium flight case in his hand, and over his shoulder I could see Wormwood's huge black Rolls Royce idling at the side of the road. The tinted front window rolled down and Connie nodded at me from his position wedged in behind the wheel.

"Hi, Con," I said, giving him a wave.

"This is for you, Mr Drake," the probably-waiter said.

He passed me the case. It was surprisingly light for the size of it.

"Cheers," I said. "Tell his nibs thanks for me."

The waiter or whatever he was nodded and got into the back of the Roller without another word. I watched it slide smoothly into the traffic, shaking my head at Wormwood's awful, naff *WW 1* registration plate. I saw one or two heads turn to watch the car go past. Connie had driven it round to mine once before, but all the same you didn't exactly see a lot of those around here. I went in and shut the door before anyone thought to notice me.

I carried the flight case up the stairs and set it on my desk. Trixie pulled a face when I opened it.

"I hate the thought of that thing," she said. "It shouldn't be here on Earth, being traded back and forth by…"

"People like me?" I asked when she trailed off.

I lifted the skull carefully out of the cut foam lining of the case and held it up to admire it. The bone was obviously very old, yellowed with age and smoothly polished as though by the passage of thousands of worshipful, avaricious hands. Perhaps it had been, at that. I suppose I could see where she was coming from, but all the same, that was a bit rude.

"You know what I mean," she said. "It's not right."

"It's what we needed," I said. "You didn't object last night."

"I wasn't looking at it last night," she said.

Fair point, I supposed. I put the skull back in the case and closed the lid.

"Look," I said, "we don't have to do this if you don't want to."

"I don't want to," she said, "but I have to. We need to speak to my Dominion about Bianakith, and just as importantly I need to know why it ignored me yesterday."

"Trixie," I said, choosing my words extremely carefully, "if it doesn't want to speak to you for some reason, for *whatever* reason, then it might not be best pleased when we do this. You do realise that, yeah?"

She sighed and flicked her hair out of her face. She was wearing it loose today, and she looked absolutely gorgeous.

"I suppose so, but it can't be helped," she said. "If I anger it, then so be it. It's only the results that matter."

Yeah, that was my Trixie. The ends justified the means, every single sodding time. She had far more in common with the Burned Man than either of them would ever have been prepared to admit. I glanced sideways at her, taking in the wavering black tendrils in her aura. I didn't *think* there were any more of them than usual, but I wouldn't have bet on it. There certainly weren't any less, that was for sure.

I sighed and went through to the workroom to see about my triangle of art. I hadn't done an evocation in donkey's years but I had a circular black mirror already, tucked away in a cupboard in case I ever needed it, so it was simply a matter of constructing the triangle itself around it. Not a difficult job really, you just need a few bits of wood. You inscribe one God-name per side – Tetragrammaton, Primeumaton, Anaphaxeton – facing outwards, then the letters MI – CHA – EL set within them facing inwards and running in the other direction; place the mirror in the middle and you're golden. One triangle of art, ta very much. That was the easy bit.

I set the mirror in the middle of the triangle and stood it up in front of the grand summoning circle, then lit tall white candles at each of the cardinal points of the pentacle while the Burned Man watched me with a sceptical look on its nasty little face.

"You sure about this?" it asked me.

"Honestly? No. Fuck, I don't know mate. It needs doing though."

"Blondie needs it doing, you mean," it corrected. "Is she at least going to grace us with her presence for this?"

"She'd better, or I'm not doing it," I said. "Fucked if I'm facing that thing without her."

To be honest I was really rather starting to hope she had stood me up. I would rather have faced Bianakith alone than have to hear that Dominion again. At least, at the time I thought I would. Turned out I was wrong, but there you go.

Trixie came in a moment later with the flight case in her hand. So much for that hope then. It looked like I was doing it.

"You look good enough to eat as usual, Blondie," the Burned Man said. I had a nasty suspicion it meant it literally.

Trixie ignored it. "How does this work?" she asked.

"Well," I said, and realised I couldn't remember. It's amazing how much you forget over the years. It's my age, I'm sure it is. "Um, well."

"Oh for fucksake," the Burned Man snapped. "Put the skull in the north cardinal of the circle, in front of the altar. Set the triangle up behind the skull, *outside* the circle, mind. You two stand *in* the circle. It's not fucking rocket surgery, Drake, and we have done this before, you know. Any number of Billy No-Nuts occultists can do this."

"Not with a fucking Dominion they can't," I muttered, but I did as it said anyway.

Truth be told the last time I had done an evocation I was still a spotty oik in university back when the Burned Man was training me. Once you can do real live summoning it seems a bit pointless really, but then I'd never expected to need to commune with anything too fucking dangerous to even attempt to summon. This was going to be fun. Not.

"I don't suppose there's any chance you know its true name?" I asked Trixie.

"Of course I do," she said.

She was standing in the circle next to me now. The circle was only really drawn out for one and that meant she was standing very close to me indeed, which wasn't exactly helping me concentrate on the task at hand. All the same, she could try the patience of a diabolist sometimes.

"And it's... what?"

"Oh," she said. "Oh, well it's not really a word as such. I don't know how I'd tell you – it's more of a... I don't know how you'd put it. A vibration, I suppose."

"Well vibrate it then, Blondie," the Burned Man said. "I'll do the rest, seeing as fucknut here seems to have forgotten his baby lessons."

I scowled at it, but it was right. A bloody long time had passed since we'd last done this, and I'd had other things on my mind. Trixie began to hum an alien note deep in her throat and a vision of the child swam suddenly up in front of me, the bloody holes where his eyes had been. I'd had so *much* on my mind over the years. There was that Russian mobster, torn to pieces by my vorehounds on the morning of his daughter's wedding. The Giardi family, shredded by my screamers. Harry the Hat, nailed to the wall of his warehouse by a talonwraith. The child, bleeding beside his grandmother's corpse. Danny McRoth had fought like a cornered bear to save that kid but I'd killed her all the same and then my screamers had taken the boy too. I'd tried to stop them, and I had failed miserably. The child died because of me. I killed him. Me. The child, the child, the child...

"It's coming," the Burned Man said.

Dear God, the guilt was killing me. I remembered taking Ally home and fucking her when I should have been with Debbie. I remembered that government job, a pack of vorehounds slaughtering their way through an Iraqi village in the middle of the night. I remembered Nicky Sparks, ripped open and splattered all over the back room of his snooker hall. I could feel tears on my cheeks, a hot burning in the back of my nose that meant I was close to sobbing like a fucking baby. The child, the child, the child...

Oh yeah, it was coming all right. Judgment was coming. *Damn those cards.*

Judgment again. There was no escaping it this time. It was coming for *me*. Justice was coming.

Judgment.

Dominion!

The black mirror flared with sudden light, making me throw a hand across my eyes. I felt Trixie stiffen beside me, heard the sharp intake of her breath.

Now, an evocation is supposed to be an astral experience, which means it mostly happens in your head. Which a lot of the time basically means you're kidding yourself and making it up.

Not this time.

A voice bellowed out of the mirror, making the room shake around us.

"Who dares?" it demanded. "Who dares disturb a Dominion of the Word?"

"Meselandrarasatrixiel," Trixie said, and I noticed the nervous tremble in her voice. "I call you, Dominion, as I called to you yesterday."

"You have your instructions, Meselandrarasatrixiel," it thundered. "The task is given, the work will be done. It is not for you to question us in this."

I felt a sudden need to kneel. This wasn't quite like last time, with the Furies. That time the Dominion had actually manifested, and kneeling hadn't been fucking optional. In fact, just the force of its presence had flattened me to the ground, leaving me grovelling on my face while it thundered and roared unseen behind me. It wasn't *quite* that bad this time, but all the same I was overwhelmed.

Something was different though.

Last time I had felt an all-encompassing awe, the presence of a Divine too powerful, too perfect to withstand. This time I felt fear, pure and simple. A deep, instinctual fear. Maybe it was just because of what the Burned Man had said about the dangers of evoking a Dominion, but I wasn't sure. It felt more dangerous this time even though it wasn't even really there. I fell to my knees, shielding my eyes from the blazing light that was scorching out of the mirror like a nuclear chain reaction.

"I beg for guidance," Trixie said. "Bianakith walks the earth once more. I need to stop it, but I lack the strength."

"Bianakith is not your concern," the Dominion rumbled, its voice dipping fractionally below the pain threshold. "The Word moves as the Word Wills."

"The elementals of the deep Earth are dying," Trixie said. "The ground rots, and the thinnest of Veils are exposed. We cannot just ignore–"

"Silence!" the Dominion roared. "Your task is given, Meselandrarasatrixiel. Guard the Burned Man on Earth. Carry out your task and *do not* question us again!"

I glanced up at Trixie, at the black threads and greenish rotten patches in her aura, and I wondered. She hadn't fallen, we were all quite clear on that point, but she had most definitely slipped a bit. All the same, I found myself wondering if a Dominion had an aura and if so, what this one's looked like. Something was wrong.

"But Dominion, I–"

The triangle of art exploded.

The blaze of light blinded me for a moment, and the noise was so shattering it passed beyond agony into utter silence. An impossible wave of pressure threw me off my knees, shards of broken black glass pattering noiselessly onto the hardwood floor around me as though in slow motion. I dug my fingers into my eyes and gasped, trying to clear my vision.

Trixie was sprawled on the floor half in and half out of the circle, and I was lying almost on top of her. I shook my head and took a ragged breath, and reluctantly got off her. She was saying something, or at least her lips were moving, but all I could hear was a shrill whine. She frowned for a moment then reached out and touched my forehead with her fingertip, and my hearing came back.

"...something wrong," she said.

"You fucking think?"

"It's Bianakith of all things, Don, the very essence of corruption. I can't believe this is part of the Word's plan. I just... I just can't. My Dominion has never spoken to me like that before. So harsh, so dismissive, like I was nothing."

I got up, leaving her sitting on the floor. She pulled her knees up and folded her arms across them, and put her head down. I suddenly realised how scared she looked. I supposed it was understandable. Her whole foundation had just been pretty much ripped out from under her. If her Dominion was lying to her, then... I don't know. Then, what? What the fuck had really just happened?

"That could have gone a little bit better than it did," the Burned Man said.

"No shit, Sherlock," I said. "Thoughts?"

"You're a prick?" it suggested. "I did tell you this was a fucking stupid idea."

It had, to be fair.

"I can't," Trixie said. "I can't be in here with that thing."

She got up and stalked out, shutting the door firmly behind her.

"Well, that's us told then innit?" the Burned Man said.

"Look, mate," I said, "could you maybe try and be a bit less of a cunt to her?"

"Don't see why I should," it said. "She fucking stole me, remember?"

"You wanted her to!" I shouted at it. "You were fucking banking on it, weren't you?"

The Burned Man coughed and scowled at me. It couldn't talk about freedom and it could never ask to be free, those were two of the primary tenets governing its original binding, but all the same we both knew how badly it wanted out of that fetish.

"I think," it said after a moment, "that Dominion wasn't being exactly straight with our Blondie."

"I think you're right," I said. "Which scares the crap out of me, to be perfectly honest. If something like *that* isn't playing with a straight bat then... what? For fucksake, what's going on?"

"Choose a side, your hoodoo daddy keeps telling you," the Burned Man said. "Which side is that fucking thing on?"

"I don't know," I said. "I don't even know what the sides *are*, and that's the most worrying thing of all."

Once upon a time when I was a young occultist, before I met the Burned Man, it would have been obvious. You had angels and the forces of Heaven on one side and the demons of Hell on the other, and that was that. But I had an enslaved archdemon and a murderous angel on my side, and I'd done a deal and then fallen out with Lucifer and been almost killed by a Dominion that was now trying to tell us another archdemon was doing the Lord's work. I closed my eyes and scrubbed my hands over my face, the stubble rough against my palms. Why was nothing simple any more?

I didn't know, but I knew a man who would.

At least, I sincerely *hoped* he would.

CHAPTER 10

Papa Armand lived in a Knightsbridge penthouse that had to be worth eight figures even in today's market. I had never been there before, and the doorman looked a bit dubious when I showed up, but after a short phone call upstairs he was all fawning politeness as he showed me to the lift. No, I didn't tip the patronising bastard. I didn't even know if I was supposed to, to be perfectly honest. This wasn't exactly the sort of place I was used to visiting.

Papa opened his door wearing an outrageous black silk kimono patterned all over with golden dragons. His bald head gleamed in the light and his big black feet were bare on the pure white hall carpet. The diamonds on his fingers shone like stars.

"Hello Papa," I said, bowing my head respectfully.

"Don-boy Drake," he said with a grin. "Good to see you!"

I had called first of course, so he knew I was coming, but he still looked pleased and surprised to see me standing me at his door. He ushered me inside, and I felt a pang of self-consciousness. I had known he was rich, but this was bloody ridiculous. I took my shoes off without being asked and padded after him into an acre of white-carpeted living room. Almost one entire wall was made of smoked glass, with a stunning view out over Kensington Gardens and the Serpentine to Hyde Park. A flight of solid walnut floating stairs drifted artistically up one wall to the second floor, and there was a tall blonde who looked barely eighteen draped equally artistically over a white leather sofa under the window. She was wearing a satin copy of Papa's kimono, albeit several feet shorter, her long bare legs providing an unwelcome distraction.

"Papa, *qui est-ce*?" she asked.

"*En Anglais, chérie*," he said. "Don-boy not good with languages."

He laughed, the rich molasses and rum sound of his voice warming the cold monochrome tones of the room.

"Oh," she said, and swung her bare feet onto the carpet. "Hello, Don-boy."

Her accent spoke of private schools in Switzerland and stately homes in the countryside, of old money and distant connections to the Royal Family. She was very posh and very pretty and far, far too young, but she was no Trixie. No one was, as far as I was concerned. I cleared my throat.

"Just Don is fine," I said. "Hi."

"I'm Jocasta," she said, in her cut-glass accent.

Of course she was.

"Pleased to meet you," I said, feeling increasingly awkward as she yawned and stretched.

"I'm going back to bed," she announced. "Don't be too long Papa, I'll get lonely."

"Papa got to talk some business just now," he said, without looking at her. "Have a bath, watch some TV. There coke in the nightstand, case you get bored. Go 'way."

She blew him a sulky kiss and strolled leisurely up the stairs in her ridiculously short kimono, making no attempt to hide her bare bottom. I shook my head in bewilderment and looked at Papa Armand.

"Papa, I need your advice," I said.

"It make my heart sing that you come to me for advice, Don-boy," he said. "I starting think Madame Zanj Bèl your whole life these days."

"No," I said. "No, not all of it. You know I respect you, Papa."

He chuckled and touched a shiny gloss black cabinet. It unfolded like some magic trick of futuristic furniture origami, splitting and spreading and extruding a fully stocked cocktail bar. For fucksake, how much must a cupboard like that cost, and where would you get one even if you had the money? I tell you, Papa Armand lived in a whole different world to me.

"Have a drink with Papa, Don-boy," he said. "Then we talk."

It was all of half past ten in the morning but you know, when in Rome and all that. I couldn't have refused Papa Armand anything right then.

"Thank you Papa," I said. "I'll have a whisky, please."

Papa's whisky was even better than Wormwood's, and again I winced at the mental image of what it must have cost. He wasn't stingy with it either, sloshing it generously into a heavy crystal tumbler. He poured a rum for himself and touched a button on a remote control. The huge smoked-glass wall split smoothly down the middle and slid open to give access to a lavish balcony complete with heavy lead planters full of mature shrubs, and an antique white wrought-iron table and chairs. The dull roar of traffic seemed far away beneath us, the humdrum bustle and noise of London muted by a wall of sheer money.

Perhaps the Burned Man had a point after all – maybe I really *had* been wasting my talent all these years. I mean, if Papa Armand could have all this then why the fuck couldn't I? I worked for cheap gangsters like the Russian and Gold Steevie, who themselves could only dream about this sort of wealth. I remembered the Burned Man telling me once how pathetic that was, how it was those twats who should have been afraid of me, how they should have been kissing my handmade shoes in Monte Carlo by now. Fuck me, but I was doing something wrong somewhere, that was for sure.

Papa settled into a chair and I took the one across the wrought-iron table from him, setting my glass down carefully. It was cool but sunny, and the view across the park was magnificent. Papa reached into the sleeve of his kimono and produced a gold cigar case and lighter. He offered me one, but smoking has never been my thing. I shook my head and sat patiently while he got his going.

"So," he said after a moment, "what on your mind, Don-boy?"

I cleared my throat again. I wasn't really sure where to begin, and for all that I liked and respected Papa Armand I had never been too sure how much I could trust him. He knew what I did, but he didn't know I had the Burned Man, that much was certain. No one knew about that except Trixie. *And Adam*, a voice whispered in my head. *Adam knows.*

Adam says.

Yeah well, I'd burn that bridge when I came to it.

I looked at Papa Armand. He gave me a fatherly smile, and I made my decision.

"Papa, I need to trust you with something," I said.

He nodded in silence and sipped his rum. I don't know about you but I take a lot more reassurance from someone who just keeps quiet and listens than from people who'll interrupt you to tell you how trustworthy they are. Anyone who feels the need to tell you that they're honest usually isn't, in my experience.

"You've told me several times I need to choose a path," I went on. "Well, what are these paths I need to choose between, exactly?"

Papa Armand shrugged and blew cigar smoke into the crisp air.

"The safe path and the dangerous," he said. "The choice between making and breaking, between healing and hurting."

"So... which is the right one?"

He threw his head back and laughed. "Oh, I like you Don-boy," he said. "You always know nothing as simple as it look first time."

No it never is, is it?

"Bianakith is loose," I said. "You know what that is?"

Papa Armand nodded slowly. "Bad shit," he said, immediately awarding himself the understatement of the day award. "*Where* it loose?"

I held his eye and pointed at the floor beneath our feet. "Right there," I said.

"Kaka," he muttered, and swallowed his rum. "Madame Zanj Bèl was made to kill demons, Don-boy. That what she *for*. Turn her loose against this thing and let her write bloody slaughter."

"Yeah, she's not keen," I said. "Not even a little bit. To be honest, I think Bianakith is a bit more than even she can handle on her own. She says she can kill it and maybe she could, but I think its rot aura would do for her all the same. I met a gnome who'd seen it, and... yeah. Well, yeah, it wasn't pretty, if you know what I mean."

He frowned. "So what she want do, la Zanj Bèl?"

"We evoked her Dominion for help," I said. "That... Shit. That didn't go well either."

Papa Armand gave me a quizzical look.

"Her Dominion?"

So I told him.

I sat there on his balcony looking at his fifteen million-quid view drinking his grand a bottle whisky and I told him all about Trixie and Alice and about the Dominion, and then I told him about the Burned Man.

That, looking back on it, was when everything went to fuck.

"Well well Don-boy," he chuckled when I was done. "I always knew you were more than met the eye, eh? The Burned Man, Don-boy? That some heavyweight shit you carrying right there."

"Yeah, well," I said, feeling faintly embarrassed. "You know how it is."

"No I *don't* know how it is," Papa Armand shot back at me. He put his glass of rum down on the table and leaned forward to fix me with a hard stare. "This some *serious* shit you got there, white boy."

"I know, Papa," I said.

"Papa," he echoed me. "Yeah, I told you call me Papa. Would I have done that if I'd known what you had, Don-boy?"

I shrugged. "I dunno, would you?"

Armand was a Houngan, a Vodou priest in the Haitian tradition. Him giving me permission to call him Papa was tacit acknowledgment that he had taken me on as a spiritual pupil. It sounded like he might be having second thoughts about that just now.

"I dunno neither." He kept that hard, flinty gaze on me for a moment longer, then lifted his glass and laughed. "Guédé laughing at me now, Don-boy," he said, and clinked his glass against mine. "Fuck it. You my boy."

I grinned and raised my own glass in a toast. "Fuck it," I repeated. "What's the worst that can happen?"

CHAPTER 11

Oh boy, those famous last words again. Papa Armand had known exactly what to do, of course. I suppose that's why he was a multimillionaire and I wasn't. I stood in front of the Burned Man and outlined Papa Armand's plan to it.

"So basically, in a nutshell, you need me to keep Bianakith's rot aura down while Blondie slaughters it for you," it said.

"That's about the size of it," I said. "The only thing that can suppress an archdemon's aura is another archdemon, according to Papa Armand. I can't see Wormwood coming down to play into the gnomes' warrens with me somehow, so that leaves you."

The Burned Man shrugged and rattled its chains at me with a sarcastic look on its ugly little face.

"I ain't exactly fucking portable," it said.

"Nope," I said, "but I explained that to Papa and he's got a plan."

"'Course he has," the Burned Man said. "I haven't even met this smug cunt and I hate him already."

"Fuck off and just listen for a minute," I said. "I can make a talisman out of you, yeah? An ouanga, he called it. Something I can carry down into the warrens with your essence in it that will protect me and Trixie from the rot while she gets all avenging angel at Bianakith."

"Oh can you now?" the Burned Man said. "You ain't great with talismans, as I recall."

It was true, I wasn't, and that had bitten me badly last year. All the same, I'd been learning. Some of the books Papa had lent me over the last few months had been most educational.

"I've got a bit of an idea," I said. "I reckon a blade of unmaking ought to hold you long enough to put this wanker in its place."

The Burned Man snorted.

"You'd need a weapon of unholy power to make one of those," it said, "something forged in the very depths of Hell. Where the fuck are you going to get something like that?"

I nodded at the cupboard in the corner.

"Third drawer down," I said.

"You what?"

"Ally's dagger, remember that? I kept it."

It blinked at me in surprise, then a slow grin spread across its face.

"Sometimes you amaze me, Drake," it said. "Not often, granted, but sometimes."

That dagger was certainly of unholy power, there was no argument about that. Adam had given it to Ally – or, to give her her proper name, Aleto the Unresting, the leader of the Furies. I had seen her use it to channel demonic lightning at her command, and call up hellfire from the ground. If anything could contain the power of the Burned Man it was that thing.

Trixie was a hell of a lot less supportive of the plan, all things considered. And that was *without* me explaining exactly what I had in mind, or mentioning the dagger.

I hadn't quite told her that I still had it for one thing, by which I mean I had flat out lied to her and told her it had been destroyed along with Ally herself. I knew I was going to have to phrase that one very carefully indeed when it eventually came up.

"I have to guard that horrible thing, Don," she said, rather waspishly I thought. "It's supposed to stay trapped in its awful little fetish, you know that. You remember the... difficulties we had, when we almost let it free."

When you stole it, you mean, I thought. *When you almost fell, and nearly allowed it to break free and lay waste to the land. Those the* difficulties *do you mean, Trixie?*

I didn't say any of that though, much as I might have liked to. She looked sour today, more so than usual, and I didn't want to wind her up. I had to admit I was still scared of Trixie for all that I was hopelessly in love with her. I was glad she had stopped hiding her aura, but I couldn't help seeing those rotten patches in it, and the black streaks that told their own tale of just how close she had come to falling altogether. There wasn't any sign of them getting any better, either, and I wasn't sure why not.

"I know, I know," I said, "but I'm all out of ideas of how else we can do this without us both ending up like poor little Alice. Papa said this was the only way to get close to Bianakith and still stand a fighting chance."

"You get me to it without me rotting and it's dead," Trixie said. "No fighting chance about it. I can take that thing."

She is proud, a little voice whispered in my head. *Just like the Burned Man is proud.* Once again I told that little voice to shut the fuck up. I didn't want to hear it.

"'Course you can," I said, with a levity I didn't feel. "It's the whole not rotting part that's going to be the tricky bit. Papa's way makes sense, Trixie."

"But we'd be letting it out," she said.

"Out of the fetish, maybe," I agreed carefully, "but that doesn't mean setting it free. Bound in the fetish or bound in… something else, something portable, it's still bound. Don't worry Trixie, I know what I'm doing."

Have I mentioned famous last words at all?

Trixie sighed and looked at me. "There's nothing else we can do?"

"Not that I know of," I said. "I had hoped your Dominion would have a better answer but… yeah. We know how that went."

"Yes," said Trixie. She lit a cigarette and blew smoke into the air, then frowned at me with her mouth set in a hard line. "I've been thinking about that."

I bet you have.

Like Sisyphus pushing his rock uphill for all eternity, Trixie had originally been doomed to battle the Furies on Earth forever. When the greater threat of her falling to Adam – and of the Burned Man breaking free for that matter – had started to look like it might actually happen, the Dominion had appeared and put things right. It had destroyed the Furies out of hand without any great appearance of effort, and straightaway had given Trixie another makework assignment – to babysit the Burned Man. That kept her stuck here on Earth just as indefinitely as fighting the Furies had, and for no better reason. I couldn't help thinking that someone Upstairs really didn't want her going home, and I was starting to give more and more thought as to why that might be.

"How are you going to do it?" she said at last, cutting off my train of thought.

I shrugged. "I'll make a magical container, a sort of talisman," I said. "Kind of the same sort of thing that Wellington Phoenix kept his devourers in, but instead of enchanting it with a live summoning I can imbue it with the essence of the Burned Man instead. That way we get to bring a real live archdemon with us, like Papa said, and it can keep Bianakith's aura suppressed while you do your thing. It's not like I'll actually be summoning it, just having it with us will be enough to do the trick."

"And Armand is sure this will work?"

"He's sure," I said. "Trust me, Trixie."

She mashed her cigarette out in the ashtray and gave me a long look, but eventually she sighed and nodded.

"All right," she said. "I trust you."

Famous last words. I'm telling you, nothing good ever comes of them.

This one needed a *lot* of stuff, of course. It meant a phone call to Wormwood on his personal number and then a long wait, but eventually everything arrived. I knew it was going to be expensive, deal or no deal, but I'd worry about that later. I still had his angel's skull after all, so I had a few negotiating options.

I expect the sight of a live goat being led out of the back of a van and up the stairs to my office probably turned a few heads on the high street, but it was dark by then and most of the locals were used to me by now. Sort of, anyway. I dragged the goat and the suitcase full of other bits and pieces into my workroom and shut the door behind me. Ally's dagger was lying on the altar in front of the Burned Man.

"You didn't tell her, did you?" it said at once.

Damn, but that little fucker could read me like a book sometimes.

"I told her most of it," I said. "I'm making a container with you in it, and just having that in my pocket will stop Bianakith's aura from touching her. That much is true, well true-ish anyway, and that much will have to do."

It nodded down at the wickedly curved black blade in front of it. "So what's this for then, you prick?"

"Insurance," I said.

A blade of unmaking is a bit special, in case you didn't know. Which I'm guessing you didn't, all things considered. Things like this are where the legends of runeswords come from, I'm sure they are. You need, as the Burned Man had said, a weapon of unholy power to make a blade of unmaking. Something forged in the very depths of Hell, and that's just for starters. Then you need the soul of a demon to enchant into it. Not just any demon either – no one ever made a runesword out of a vorehound, know what I mean? No, this was proper grownup magic, archdemons or nothing. Excalibur had been a blade of unmaking for certain, and Beowulf's Hrunting too if I'm any judge.

Of course Hrunting had turned on Beowulf in the end, but then if magic was easy, every fucker would be doing it.

"Insurance?" it echoed me. "Oh dear oh dear, are you finally starting to doubt Blondie's unstoppable awesomeness?"

"Everyone has their limits," I said, "and she's only one soldier, as she's said herself. I mean, I *hope* she can do it. I'm sure she *can* do it, as long as you keep up your end of the deal. But it can't hurt to have something up my sleeve, can it? You know, just in case something goes pear-shaped, and if it does, a container talisman won't cut it. If I really have to, I need to be able to bring you out to play. It can't hurt."

"Oh no, no, it can't hurt at all," the Burned Man said. "I ain't arguing mate, just taking the piss a bit. Come on, you've got to let me have a little bit of fun now and again."

It rattled its chains in an attempt to look sorry for itself, and grinned at me. Of course with hindsight I really should have smelled the rat by then.

But I didn't.

"Yeah, yeah, poor hard done by little you," I said instead. "Come on you wanker, let's get this done."

The goat made a bloody mess, literally, and none of the other things we needed for this were entirely pleasant either, but eventually the work got done. It was late by then, one or two in the morning, and I found myself wondering if Trixie was waiting up to see the results of my hard work or if she had got bored and gone to bed by now. My bed.

Oh, who was I kidding? Of course she had gone to bed.

I sighed and wiped my hands on a towel that was already sticky and red. The dagger glistened in the candlelight, soaked in blood and mercury and... other fluids, some of them mine. I'm not going into that. Magic isn't all fast cars and yachts, I'm telling you. I just wish *some* of it was, but there we were.

"You ready then?" I asked the Burned Man.

"Ready," it said.

So we did it.

I pressed the tip of the enchanted dagger into the Burned Man's tiny blackened chest, just enough to make a small incision. The blade quivered with power as the poisonous black aura that always surrounded the fetish gradually shrank away to nothing. The fetish slumped lifeless in its chains, but I could feel the dagger throbbing slowly in my hand. I shuddered and withdrew the blade. I needed a drink. Oh fuck me, did I ever need a drink.

Trixie *was* waiting up, as it turned out, although by then I had convinced myself she wouldn't be. I came out of the workroom still holding the dagger. That, I have to admit, was not an entirely clever move.

She stared at the dagger in my hand. Ally's dagger. The dagger that Adam had given Aleto the Unresting to kill Trixie with as part of his ultimate betrayal of the pair of them.

Trixie hissed like a scalded cat.

"You... Don, you lied to me," she said.

"Trixie, look..." I started, but it was far too late for bullshit and I knew it.

"You lied to me," she said again, her voice turning cold.

"Look, I'm sorry," I said. "Things were confused as all hell back then. I found Ally's dagger afterwards, and, well, you know, I kinda thought it might come in handy so I just, you know, sort of hung onto it, and then, well, I mean..."

"I explicitly asked you what happened to that," she said, "and you very clearly said that it had been destroyed. I remember you saying that to me, Don."

"Yeah, I did," I confessed. "I just... Look, you weren't really yourself right then, Trixie. I thought it might be best if, well, I mean, in the state of mind you were in..."

She was so angry the black threads in her aura were moving, twisting and growing before my eyes. She wasn't really herself *now* either, that was for fucking sure. She caught me looking at her and her aura flared blinding white as she slammed down the shutters and went back to hiding it.

"How *dare* you judge me!" she screamed.

She lashed out and backhanded me across the face hard enough to fling me to the floor and halfway across the room. I hit the side of my desk with a crunch and slowly raised a hand to my bloody mouth.

I hate to admit it, but I remembered this. Not *quite* like this of course, not this way around anyway, but the memories of a childhood I didn't tend to dwell on suddenly came flooding back. I remembered my dad coming home on a payday Friday night, drunk as a lord with one grievance or another on his mind and just me and my mum to take it out on. I was only a little lad then, of course – he did us both a favour and died of a heart attack when I was ten – but I still remember my poor mum putting herself between him and me, time and time again. And more often than not she ended up like this, on the floor with a bloody mouth.

Oh, fucking hell.

"Now look what you made me do," Trixie said.

Look what you made me do. Dad always used to say that to Mum, afterwards. Like it somehow wasn't his fault.

Cunt.

"I'm sorry, Trixie," I said, and I meant it.

I know, I know, but... no actually I *don't* know. She frightened the life out of me sometimes but I *loved* her, you know what I mean? For a moment there I actually felt like it *was* my fault, for upsetting her. Stupid of me I know, but there we are. I couldn't help wondering if my mum had felt the same way all those years ago.

"Oh Don," she gasped suddenly. "Oh Thrones, I'm so sorry!"

She knelt at my side and reached out towards me. I couldn't help flinching just a little bit.

Bloody hell...

"Oh don't," she said. "Oh Don, please don't be afraid of me. I'm so sorry. I don't know what I was thinking. It'll never happen again, you have to believe me. Here, let me get that for you."

She lightly touched my split lips and I felt a warm tingle as the wound healed.

"There," she said, "all better now."

My mouth was, but... really? All better now? I wasn't so sure of that. I may have mentioned it before but when I was a student I wasn't really a big drinker, and the memory of my dad was most of the reason why not. Of course, Professor Davidson and the Burned Man had soon changed that between them, but there you are. Shit happens and life goes on, I suppose. Just like it would now.

Trixie's aura blazed a brilliant white lie that mocked her soothing words. I thought about that aura, and again I wondered what her Dominion's own aura looked like by now. There was some sort of bond between them, I knew that much. Some connection beyond just a soldier and her commander. If Trixie's Dominion was slipping, would that affect her too? I had a nasty feeling that it might.

"Thank you," I muttered.

She hugged me, and for a moment there it really *was* all better. She had never done that before, and I liked it. I liked it a lot, and it was enough to make me stop thinking about auras. All the same, I didn't like being hit one little bit.

She helped me to my feet and I bent cautiously to pick up the dagger. She gave it a hard stare and I wanted to flinch again but I forced myself not to.

"We need this, Trixie," I said. "I know you don't like it, and I'm sorry that I lied to you, but this is what I had to use for the talisman. It's the only thing I had that was strong enough to contain the Burned Man."

Yeah, I do know that I was still lying to her now. Sometimes a little lie is better than a painful explanation, you know what I mean? And when I say "better" of course I mean "easier", but there you are.

"I understand," she said. "I'm going to bed now."

She lingered in the doorway for a moment and I half let myself wonder if that was some sort of a question, possibly even an invitation. *Idiot.* Of course it wasn't.

"Right," I said. "Night then."

"Yes," she said, "it is."

She closed the door behind her.

I sat down behind my desk with a weary sigh and put the dagger down in front of me. I looked at it, and I thought about my mum, and I started to cry.

I took the whisky out of the drawer.

CHAPTER 12

The next morning I called Wormwood to set up the meet with the gnomes, and again it was set for the evening. Janice obviously didn't like to come out during the day, which I suppose wasn't surprising really. I spent the day getting over my hangover and catching up on the laundry and doing some grocery shopping and all the other shit it's too easy to forget about when life gets hectic. Basically I was staying as far out of Trixie's way as I could get, if I'm honest about it. The atmosphere between us was a little strained, to put it fucking mildly.

All the same, that evening Trixie and I met Janice on the platform at Bank. I was wearing the thickest boots I owned and an old coat I didn't mind having to burn later. Trixie had dressed down in jeans and low-heeled boots with a sweater and leather jacket, but she still shone like a star. I had been half-expecting her to turn up in the same sort of combat armour she had worn to face Wellington Phoenix's devourers, but apparently not this time. She was certainly confident, I had to give her that. Maybe a bit *too* confident, considering what we were on our way to face. Janice looked up at her from the shadows of her hood and wuffled her pointed little nose.

"Who's this?" she asked me.

"This is Trixie," I said. "Trixie, this is Janice."

"Honour be to the gnomes of the deep Earth," Trixie said. "Honour be to the guardians of the watchtowers of the north."

Gnomes are Earth elementals, and the watchtowers of the north represent the cardinal point of the compass governing Earth in the traditional four-element system. *I* knew that of course, but I must admit I was a bit surprised that Trixie did. Janice looked pleased though, and more than a little bit flushed and embarrassed. There really was something about our Trixie that appealed to everyone.

"Thank you," she said, shuffling her feet. "You're with the hero, then?"

"Janice," I said, "she *is* the hero. The real one, I mean."

"Oh," said Janice. "Good. Well, we ought to get below."

I nodded and let her lead us both the way she and I had gone before. I was prepared this time and had brought a bloody great big torch of my own, one of those police issue Maglites that take six D cells and could double up as a warhammer in a pinch. I had the dagger thrust through my belt, under my coat. Trixie hadn't brought anything and didn't seem to need it. All the same I was still scared crossing the ledge by the ruined catwalk, while Trixie didn't appear to be remotely bothered by either the drop or the darkness. If anything it was even worse than last time, and the concrete was now spongy and wet under my boots. It smelled absolutely vile down there.

Janice led us all the way down through the Victorian levels and into the warrens of the gnomes, and still I hadn't asked. The warren was still glowing with its own light, so I turned my torch off to save the batteries and stuffed it awkwardly into the biggest pocket in my coat. We were all the way down to the first round chamber by the time I plucked up the courage to speak.

"Um, how's Alice?" I asked.

Janice seemed to hunch into her hoodie, and for a moment she didn't say anything. I heard a choked sniffle and almost wished I hadn't asked.

"She's gone," she said at last. "But thank you for asking. I appreciate it. I'm... glad you didn't forget her."

I nodded. I supposed there was that, if nothing else. I reached out and squeezed Janice's shoulder. Poor Alice. Trixie gave me a quizzical look but I ignored her. She obviously *hadn't* remembered her, and that pissed me off far more than it should have done. Trixie hadn't even met her, after all, so why would she remember a name from a brief conversation we'd had several days ago?

Am I being reasonable, or am I making excuses for her? I touched my lip and winced. It didn't hurt of course, but only because she had healed me afterwards. If she hadn't, it would have been a throbbing purple mess today, I knew that much.

Mum had always made excuses for Dad, afterwards, but then Dad had been a violent bully. Trixie wasn't that. She was strong and powerful and yet so fragile it was like she was made of spun glass, so brittle one crack could destroy her. Again I found myself wondering exactly which of us was looking after the other one.

"Come on," Janice said. "This way."

"Are we going to see the matriarch again?" I asked, but Janice shook her head.

"Her Highness is barricaded in the nest with all my sisters," she said. "It's too dangerous to be out in the warrens now."

"You are," Trixie pointed out.

Janice shrugged. "Someone had to guide you," she said. "I volunteered."

"Thank you," I said, and I meant it.

She was a brave little thing, I had to give her that. Janice led us deeper into the warren, into curving tunnels that dripped with rotten corruption. We went deeper and deeper, through more tunnels dug through the bedrock far beneath the city. They were rotten to the core, the rock itself turning to putrid slime. Hideous fungal growths sprouted like cancer from the walls and the ceiling, and the floor was awash with something horribly reminiscent of bile. It was getting gradually darker, too, as though even the glow of the walls was starting to fail the deeper we went.

It suddenly occurred to me that Janice probably wasn't expecting to survive this trip.

"Stay close to me," I said to her. "I've got something with me, some magic. It will stop the taint reaching us but you have to stay close, OK?"

"Oh," she said. "I understand. Thank you."

Bless her, poor little thing. She almost clung to me after that, and I realised just how scared she must have been.

"I can feel something," Trixie said suddenly. "I think we're close."

She reached out and twisted her right hand through a figure-of-eight movement, and the air shimmered as her sword appeared. Damn, but I *had* to learn how she did that. She lifted the gleaming steel blade in her hands and it burst into flames.

"Angelus Mortis!" Janice gasped.

"Yeah," I said, and lowered my voice to a whisper I was confident only she could hear. "Sort of, anyway, but not exactly. Just stay close to me, Janice, and whatever you do don't get in her way."

We advanced slowly, keeping behind Trixie as she led the way with her blazing sword held before her. It was the only light we had now that the bioluminescence of the warrens seemed to have been killed by the all-pervading decay. I heard something growl in the darkness ahead, a distant rumble of sheer malice.

Janice grabbed my arm and pulled me up short.

"Wait," she begged. "We can't get any nearer!"

"We have to," I said. "I have to keep Trixie close as well, I'm afraid. We all have to go."

Janice nodded miserably and cowered against me as I followed Trixie. She was terrified, bless her, and who wouldn't have been, but she did it anyway. Brave little thing, as I said.

I dug the torch out of my pocket and flicked it on. The light washed over Trixie, standing in her guard position with the burning sword held motionless in front of her. Beyond her the cavern stretched out and up, looking half natural and half dug like the warrens. However it had originated, it was now a seeping horror of corruption, dripping and reeking. In the shadows at the far edge of the torch's beam something was moving.

It approached slowly, a monstrous figure with the misshapen body of a man and the head of a gigantic wild boar. It was easily nine feet tall, even stooped as it was, and the hump on its muscular back bristled with stiff hair. It was carrying a great hammer on a shaft six feet long, the head a lump of solid iron the size of a breezeblock. It growled again, poison dripping from its foot-long razor sharp tusks as it put its head down and glowered at Trixie with burning red eyes.

This was Bianakith, I knew. This was the Rotman.

Bianakith is plague walking, I remembered the Burned Man telling me. *Anything this fucker comes near will die horribly.*

I could only pray that this was going to work.

I could feel the dagger quivering against my stomach as the Burned Man's aura battled with Bianakith's. I knew the Burned Man would win that one. In its true form the Burned

Man was appallingly powerful, and now I had given it the opportunity to demonstrate that power directly, rather than through the limitations of summoning. I knew it wouldn't let me down, if only because it wanted to show off. I knew Trixie could feel it too. She took a confident step forwards, her sword never wavering from its strict guard position.

"Come on, you filthy thing," she said. "Come and dance."

Bianakith roared and charged, its hammer raised. Trixie met it in a blaze of fire, her sword leaving burning streaks in the air as she cut high then low, her blade clanging from the hammer's shaft. Bianakith took a swing that would have broken her in half if it had connected, but Trixie pivoted gracefully out of the hammer's descending arc and struck back. Bianakith had an enormous advantage in reach with its much bigger weapon, and it must have been four times her weight at least, but she danced around it like a steel ballerina. Fuck me, but she was truly a master swordswoman, even I could see that.

Bianakith roared and swung again and she spun, her footwork dazzlingly perfect as she swept her blade up and across the monster's humped back in what should have been a killing stroke.

Should being the operative word. Bianakith shrugged her off and turned again, bellowing. I edged closer, almost dragging Janice along with me. I had to keep Trixie inside the Burned Man's protective aura, and I had no idea how big that was. It might have been a good fucking idea to have asked it beforehand, thinking about it. You've got to love hindsight.

Trixie's sword looped and cut again, droplets of molten flame spattering across the rotten ground in its wake. Bianakith turned the blade on the shaft of its hammer and brought the head round to smack Trixie in the chest. It was only a short blow, without the monster's full weight behind it, but still Trixie grunted and staggered back a couple of steps, obviously hurt. The hammer arced up and over and smashed down towards her head.

I gasped, but she threw herself aside just in time, tucking and rolling on one shoulder with the sword still in her hands. The hammer crashed into the ground and threw up a great gout of foul liquid from the putrid rock underfoot. Trixie sprang to her feet and spun, always attacking, her flaming sword already cutting savagely for Bianakith's head. It ducked and twisted away, but still the blade slashed its shoulder open almost to the bone. Again though it shrugged off the hurt, the wounds only seeming to make it angrier. It spun the huge hammer as though it weighed nothing and rammed the end of the shaft into Trixie's stomach like a spear, taking her off her feet.

"Trixie!" I yelled.

"Be quiet," she shouted at me as she regained her feet. "I'm working!"

She leapt clean over Bianakith's next swing and cut for its head but somehow Bianakith parried with the hammer, catching her blade right under the huge block of iron. It moved a lot faster than it looked like it had any right to be able to. It forced her blade downwards then suddenly closed on her, roaring. Trixie kicked its forward knee hard enough to take a car door off its hinges. It staggered and she wrenched her sword up and around with incredible strength, tearing the hammer from its hands. The huge weapon spun away into the darkness and landed somewhere with a clang, but Bianakith grabbed at her and caught her sword against one of its tusks. The blade was trapped between them now, flames blazing up into the air as the monstrosity got its hugely muscular arms around her. I gasped. It dragged Trixie into its foul embrace, bristles standing up on its wounded back as it strained to break her against its body. One tusk was holding her sword locked tight and now it was slowly turning its head, forcing the sword away and the other tusk closer to her throat with every moment.

Oh fuck me no, it's not supposed to be happening like this!

Janice grabbed at me but I was already striding forwards, the torch outstretched in front of me.

"Oi!" I yelled at it. "Come and have a go at me, you pigheaded cunt!"

So it did.

It's thick as shit, the Burned Man had told me, and thank God it had been right about that.

It threw Trixie aside – that was something – but now it was charging full tilt at me. I hurled myself out of the way and dragged Janice down after me with one flailing hand, making it go crashing past with a roar of fury. The light swung crazily as I clung onto the torch for dear life. Bianakith wheeled and charged back, its eyes glowing red in the darkness. I rolled again, splashing through the horrific bile on the ground and pulling poor Janice with me again, both of us turning over and over in a tangle of arms and legs. It missed us again but Trixie was up now, her sword blazing with heavenly fury.

"Die!" she shrieked, and plunged the sword through Bianakith's chest to the hilt.

The blade burst out of its hump and stuck fast, still burning. Bianakith threw its head back and roared.

Then it punched Trixie full in the face.

She flew through the air and crashed into one of the oozing walls, and lay still. Bianakith turned on me with a snarl of hatred. Trixie's flaming sword was still stuck through its body, but it barely even seemed to notice.

Get me to it and it's dead. I can take that thing, Trixie had said, like it was a foregone conclusion. I guess that's where pride gets you in the end.

"We're going to die, aren't we?" Janice whimpered.

I had to admit it did look that way.

Bianakith strode towards us, not charging now, taking its time. It had obviously worked out that Trixie had been the only serious threat out of the three of us. I drew the dagger from my belt with my free hand and shoved Janice behind me.

I have no fucking idea how to fight with a knife.

I could have just legged it. Bianakith was hurt, and I was pretty sure I could have outrun it. I had a torch and a talisman and I knew the way back, give or take.

But Trixie was lying over there, out cold and at this horror's mercy.

But Trixie had hit me, in a fit of blind rage.

Trixie was a soldier, as she was so fond of telling me, and I'm sorry but sometimes soldiers die in battles. Acceptable losses, they call that.

But I loved her.

And Janice was behind me, and I didn't think she was built for running. Janice was no soldier, and she had suffered more than enough already. She was clinging to my coat and whimpering, but she still hadn't run away either. I thought about Trixie, lying there across the cavern.

I loved her, and that was all there was to it.

Time to do the hero thing at last.

By which of course I meant it was time to cheat.

I have no idea how to fight with a knife, but then I didn't have to. Not with *this* knife I didn't.

"No," I said. "We bloody well *aren't* going to die."

It might have looked that way, but then it had looked that way more than a few times before. I'm still here, aren't I?

"Burned Man," I said, "can you hear me?"

The blade vibrated in my hand. Excalibur had had its soul to be sure, and I dare say Hrunting had too, but that wasn't quite the same thing. Those blades had been gifted to the heroes who wielded them by higher powers. Now I might not really be any sort of hero, but I had enchanted this blade myself, with my own blood and semen and the soul of my very own archdemon. I was playing by *my* rules now.

Bianakith lowered its head to charge, and I raised the dagger.

"Come to me, Burned Man," I commanded. "Come forth in unmaking and serve my Will!"

The dagger blazed in my hand. Crimson lightning flickered along its length and pure power roared out of the upraised blade, coalescing in the air between me and the horror that was the Rotman. That power took on a shape in the light of my torch, a shadowy black humanoid form with smoky, ethereal chains streaming back from its wrists and ankles and into the blade.

"What's up?" it said.

I pointed at Bianakith.

"Kill that," I said.

The Burned Man snarled like all the hounds of Hell and poured forth into the cavern, the poisonous black shadow getting bigger and darker and the chains getting thinner and harder to see as it hurtled towards Bianakith. They met with a crash that echoed through the chamber, shaking the ground under our feet. Janice screamed and clutched at me.

"What *is* that?" she wailed.

"On our side is what it is," I said.

At least, I sincerely fucking *hoped* it was on our side. I was taking the mother of all chances here, I knew I was, but I really didn't have any other choice. Bianakith would slaughter us both otherwise, and then Trixie, and then the gnomes. Then most of London, probably.

The huge form of the Burned Man lifted Bianakith off its feet and hurled it across the chamber to smash into a wall.

The rock sagged and slumped from the impact, oozing like liquefied jelly. Bianakith started to rise, Trixie's blade still sticking out of its body.

The Burned Man's laugh made the hairs on my arms stand up. I had known it was powerful of course, but this was monstrous. Bianakith was another archdemon after all, and the Burned Man seemed to be taking it apart without breaking a sweat.

"Oh no you fucking don't, matey," it said.

It raised one huge shadowy hand in Bianakith's direction and a massive gout of fire burst out of its outstretched fingers and washed across the chamber like a jet from a napalm cannon. Bianakith roared and burned. It took one more stumbling step forward, blazing like a bonfire, then howled and fell to its knees with its tusks raised to the distant ceiling and its back arched in agony.

"Burn, you motherfucker," I whispered.

Janice had her face pressed into the back of my shoulder and was trembling in terror. I put an arm around her and watched Bianakith reduced to charred bones and scorched meat. The Burned Man swung back through the air in a lazy arc and loomed over us.

"Anyone for a hog roast?" it asked.

I snorted laughter. "I need to see to Trixie," I said. "Back in the dagger, mate."

"Fuck off," it said.

Oh shit, here we go.

I mean, to be perfectly honest I'd been sort of expecting this ever since I realised I really was going to have to let the genie out of the bottle, so to speak, but all the same I had been holding out a thin hope it wasn't going to happen. I should have known better.

"You're still bound," I told it. "I'm not that fucking stupid. Now get back in the dagger, Burned Man."

"Will I fuck as like," it said. "I'm a fucking sight less bound than usual, and I like it a lot better this way. You can shove your magic dagger up your fucking arse."

Of course, Papa Armand had warned me this might happen when he first suggested the idea. He was a Houngan but that was far from *all* he was. Vodou was his religion but aside from that he was also a more powerful magician than me in his own right. He had told me what to do.

Now, I mentioned that invocation isn't really my thing, but that doesn't mean I don't know how to do it. I focused my Will into the dagger and I invoked as hard as I could. The Burned Man growled as its chains pulled tight, their shadowy form becoming more distinct as I reeled it in.

"Fucking stop that, you little puke," it said.

"No," I said. "You're coming back home, Burned Man."

It pulled back, snarling and fighting me. Janice was almost gibbering now but she slipped away and I saw her scurry around the wall towards where Trixie lay. Bless her little heart.

I fought the Burned Man, the dagger glowing with unholy light and flickering with red lightning as my Will coursed through it. If I hadn't had the power of that dagger, and if the Burned Man hadn't still been chained, I wouldn't have stood a hope in Hell of doing this, I knew, but I did and it was. I opened myself fully and sucked it back in as hard as I could.

"Cuuuuuuuuuuuuuuuunt!" it screamed as it shot through the air towards me, shrinking rapidly until it smacked into me and disappeared.

I staggered back a step and shook my head, dazed for a moment. The dagger felt suddenly cold in my hand, and I quickly stuffed it back through my belt. I shone the torch across the room and saw Janice kneeling beside Trixie's prone form. I hurried over in time to hear Janice finish singing some sort of song, low and soft like a lullaby. She looked up at me and smiled shyly.

"Just a little root and rhyme," she said. "I'm nowhere near as good at it as my mother is but I think it'll do the trick."

I did as well. A moment later Trixie opened her eyes and blinked at me.

"What happened?" she asked.

I shot Janice a warning look.

"You killed it," I said. "I knew you could do it, Trixie."

I know, I know, but I didn't want her to have to face her failure, not now, not after her experience with the Dominion. And I really didn't want to tell her what I had done, if I'm perfectly honest about it. Let's put it this way – I didn't exactly think she would have approved.

"But..." she said.

"It smacked you a good one when you ran it through, that's all," I said. "Your sword stayed stuck in and burned it up, look."

I pointed to the smoking, bubbling mess that had been Bianakith. Trixie's blackened blade was still lodged through its ribcage, after all. It was fairly plausible, if I do say so myself.

"Oh," she said, and let me help her up. "Well, that's good."

"Yes," said Janice.

I glanced at her, but her pointed little face was impassive and it didn't look like she was going to say anything that might drop me in the shit. I really did like Janice, I have to admit.

Trixie strode over to what was left of the Rotman and kicked it over onto its back. She put a foot on its chest and pulled her sword out, and made it disappear with a twist of her wrist. She stopped, peering into the darkness at the far end of the cavern.

"What's up?" I called.

"I don't know," she said. "Could you bring the light over here for a moment please?"

I went over to her and shone the beam of my torch in the direction she was looking. The light played over something, but fuck only knows what. It was so rotten and corroded it was now just a heap of slag that could have been almost anything originally. It had definitely been metal once though, maybe bronze by the looks of what was left. Given that we were in a mostly natural cave and the gnomes didn't seem to have any sort of metalworking, that was bloody odd.

"What is it?" I said.

Trixie frowned thoughtfully. "I have no idea," she said.

"Oh," said Janice, from beside me. "Oh dear, that's a shame."

"Why, what was it?" I asked her.

"Oh, I don't really know, I'm afraid," she said, "but it's been here as long as anyone can remember. It used to be the most beautiful statue of a cat."

"Really? Down here?"

"Yes," she said. "I don't know why, but I think it was old. Very, very old. The memories of the gnomes go back thousands of years, after all, and as far as I know it's always been there."

Oh well, whatever. Tiddles had definitely run out of lives now, and I dare say it wasn't important anyway.

"Come on," I said to her. "Let's go and give Her Highness the good news, then maybe we can get some fresh air. It stinks down here."

CHAPTER 13

We had to stop and pay our respects to the matriarch of the gnomes, of course. Trixie was as gracious with her as she had been with Janice, and accepted Her Highness's gratitude but declined any sort of reward. We left as soon as was polite, and let Janice guide us back to the surface. We popped up in an alley between two hotels somewhere in the West End, some time after midnight.

"I knew you were a hero," Janice whispered to me while Trixie was still climbing out of the manhole behind us.

I really wasn't sure about that, but she was sweet to say so. She was also probably one of the bravest people I've ever met. I gave her a goodbye hug. If she'd been human and I hadn't been hopelessly and one-sidedly in love with Trixie... ah well. Story of my life.

"Well," I said once Janice had disappeared back underground. "That's that then."

I knew I should have been all kinds of shaken up after what had happened down there, but somehow I just wasn't. I also knew I still had Adam to worry about as well but I felt pretty good all things considered, and I never stopped to wonder why.

Trixie just shrugged. "I suppose it is," she said.

She looked like she had something on her mind, but I knew her well enough by then to tell she wasn't in a talkative mood. I sighed and went to find us a taxi. That wasn't easy, what with how we looked and smelled after our battle in the depths of London, but it's amazing what most cabbies can be persuaded to overlook for enough money. Trixie didn't say a word all the way home, and by the time we were back in my office I could tell something was definitely wrong.

"Look, Trixie," I said, "what's up? You did really well down there today."

I know, I know, but she needed cheering up and I figured what she didn't know wouldn't hurt her. I took my coat off and chucked it on the floor. It was wrecked, and destined for the bin tomorrow anyway. I tossed the dagger on my desk.

"Oh, nothing," she said. "I didn't sleep very well last night, that's all."

"Are you sure?"

She slipped her jacket off and turned to face me. "About last night," she said. "I really am sorry, Don."

"I know," I said. Not so sorry that she had stopped hiding her aura, I noticed. It was still the blazing white she hid behind when something was wrong, but I wasn't going to mention that. "It's all right. You were upset about the Dominion, I realise that."

"Yes, but that's no excuse." She reached out and put a hand on my arm. "Oh, it's not just that, Don. I... I had the most awful nightmares last night."

"You did?" I must admit I hadn't even really known if she actually slept or not, never mind whether she had dreams. It seemed like she did. "Sorry to hear that."

"It's going to sound silly," she said, "but I keep dreaming about that horrible cat."

"What? That mangy ginger thing with one eye?"

She nodded. "Well not *about* it, as such. It's always there though, in my dreams. I dreamed about my Dominion, too, and that... that hurt, Don."

"Aw hey, come on," I said. "Whatever's going on up there, you can't take it personally. You know that."

"How can I take it any other way? My Dominion spoke to me like I was dirt."

There was a bitter twist to her lips, and she turned quickly away from me and stared out of the window. I gave her a moment, then went and put an arm around her. It was meant to be comforting but she went rigid until I let go.

"Sorry," I muttered.

"No, it's all right," she said. "I don't mind. It's nice to be held for once. I'm just not used to it, that's all."

I took her hand instead and we stood side by side at the window holding hands like a couple of lovestruck ten year-olds. Well, one of us was lovestruck anyway. I sighed.

"Look, I need to put the Burned Man back in its box," I said after a while. "It'll go nuts shut up in that dagger for too much longer."

"Yes, I suppose so," she said, but I could tell she wasn't really listening. "Don, would you sleep with me tonight?"

I almost choked.

"Um, pardon?"

"I just need a little comfort," she said. "Would you, please?"

Does the pope shit in the fucking woods? I glanced at the dagger lying on my desk, and put it out of my mind. Bugger the Burned Man, it would just have to wait. I wasn't going to let anything on God's green earth break this spell.

"Of course," I said. "I'd love to."

Dear God, would I ever. She smiled and went into the bedroom while I took a very quick and much needed shower.

I came through wearing a fresh pair of boxers and nothing else. She was lying in my bed wearing a white nightdress, on her side facing away from me with the sheets pulled most of the way up to her chin. Her hair was loose, spread out across the pillow.

"Put the light out, would you please?" she said.

I reluctantly did as she asked and slipped into bed beside her. She murmured something, and I snuggled up to her and kissed the back of her neck. I slid my hand up her side and around in front to cup a truly heavenly breast. She froze.

"Don," she said quietly, "what on earth do you think you're doing?"

Oh no...

"Um," I said. "I, um..."

I wriggled quickly backwards before she felt my erection digging into her arse, and she sat up and stared at me.

"Oh dear," she said. "Oh I'm sorry. When I said sleep with me I meant... well, *sleep.* For company, do you understand? Not... anything else."

"Yeah," I said, and cleared my throat. Thank fuck I had put the light out, at least she couldn't see how red my face was. I don't think I'd ever felt so bloody embarrassed in my life. "Sorry. I'll, um, I'll go in the other room."

"No, stay," she said. "Please. Just keep your hands to yourself, if you don't mind."

"'Course," I said. "Well, night then."

"Good night," she said.

She lay down again, her back to me. I stared at the ceiling in the darkness, frustrated and crushed with disappointment and feeling utterly and totally fucking stupid.

English isn't her first language, I reminded myself. *Or probably even her tenth for that matter. Something like this was bound to happen eventually.*

I clenched my fists and willed my hard-on to go away. There was no way I was going to get any sleep until it did, after all.

God, what a fucking disaster.

I must have fallen asleep eventually because at some point in the night she woke me up by screaming. I sat bolt upright in bed, fumbling for the bedside light. Trixie was clutching her pillow in a death grip and seemed to still be asleep. She screamed again, and thrashed under the covers.

"Trixie!" I said.

I hardly dared touch her after my earlier catastrophe but I made myself shake her by the shoulder until her eyes opened.

"What?" she said.

"Jesus, you were screaming in your sleep," I said. "Are you OK?"

"Mmmm, not really," she admitted.

She pushed her hair back and sat up beside me, the sheets falling into her lap. I made myself look at her face, but it was a fucking struggle if I'm honest about it.

"Another bad dream?"

"Yes," she said. "The same as last night. My Dominion raging at me, calling me all sorts of horrible names, hurting me, and always that miserable cat is there, rubbing round my ankles while I'm screaming."

"Maybe the cat's trying to get your attention," I said, half joking. I'm not a fan of cats, as it goes.

Trixie frowned. "Perhaps," she said, obviously taking my suggestion seriously. "I wonder why?"

"Oh, I don't know," I said. "Look, is there anything I can get you? Glass of water or something?"

"No, thank you," she said. "What time is it?"

I squinted at the bedside clock. "About half four," I said.

"I'm just going to get up I think," she said. "You go back to sleep if you want."

She got up and padded out of the bedroom, and closed the door behind her. I sighed and lay down again, unable to resist rolling over into the warm space where she had been lying. Pathetic, I know.

I drifted in and out for a couple of hours but by half six I gave it up for a bad job. Early morning spring sunshine was streaming in the window and I was wide awake. I got up and took another shower. A cold one, I have to admit. By the time I got out of the bathroom Trixie had taken the opportunity to get dressed, and I quickly did the same. I was having trouble meeting her eye, to be perfectly honest with you. I kind of felt like some kid who'd been caught wanking by his mum or his auntie or something, that's how fucking embarrassed I was.

You are such a fucking idiot, I told myself for the thousandth time as I got dressed. *As if that was ever going to happen outside of your own imagination.*

We spent a couple of hours avoiding each other in awkward silence. Avoiding each other in a flat this small was fucking difficult, and we ended up with her sitting at my desk staring out of the front window and me in the kitchen staring out of the back one. It was actually a relief when the phone rang some time after nine.

I hurried through to the office to get it. The dagger was still where I had left it, lying on the end of the desk.

Shit, I ought to get and sort that.

I picked up.

"Don Drake," I said.

"Don baby, how's it going?"

My heart sank. It was Gold Steevie. I hadn't heard from him in months – not since I had bluffed him off with all that nonsense about omens, in fact – and I really hadn't missed him. Gold Steevie was basically a cheap and nasty gangster who thought he was something special because he knew just enough to know that what I did even existed, and could be bought. He thought that meant *I* could be bought, and he was wrong. Sort of, anyway.

"What do you want, Steevie?" I said.

Now I wouldn't normally be that brusque with him, I was too scared of him for that, but Trixie was still sitting in my office chair while I was leaning over the desk to reach the phone and I was too close to her for comfort. I wanted to get this over with.

"That isn't very friendly, now is it, Don?" Steevie said. "Not when I've got some work for you."

His voice sounded even more oily than usual over the phone, and I realised I just didn't have the patience for him today. I didn't want his work, and I didn't want him. He was a ridiculous little prick who slicked his hair back to cover his bald spot and wore too much naff gold jewellery and far too much cologne and why the hell was I scared of him anyway?

"No, ta," I said. "I'm busy."

There was a pause. "Sorry Don, you'll have to say that again," he said. "My phone must be playing up. For a moment there I thought you just said 'no' to me."

"I did," I said. "No."

"Now you fucking listen to me," Steevie snapped. "I'll have some fucking respect out of you, Drake, or I'll–"

"Fuck off," I said, and put the phone down on him.

I started at it for a moment.

What the bloody hell did I just do?

I didn't have any respect for Steevie, that was true, but I really *was* scared of him. He had at least half a dozen armed lads working for him, a very short temper, and a proven track record of taking people's fingers off with bolt cutters.

Telling him to fuck off wasn't exactly wise.

"Who was that?" Trixie asked.

"No one," I said.

"You were very rude to no one just then," she pointed out.

Oh for fucksake.

I suddenly realised I simply wasn't in the mood for her this morning either. I'd had it with feeling like an idiot, like some embarrassed little kid hiding in the kitchen so he didn't get told off. I had to get out of there for a bit.

"I'm going for a walk," I said. "See you later."

I grabbed my good coat off the back of the door and left before she had the chance to say anything else. Now, I hate walking as a rule, but it was a beautiful spring morning and for some reason I just wanted to get out in the air. I felt like I'd been shut in for far too long. I suppose it was hardly surprising what with all the time I'd spent underground lately, and most of the rest of it cooped up in my tiny flat with Trixie and her moods and her bloody temper.

I stepped out onto the pavement and pulled in a deep lungful of South London air. It smelled marvellous, for all that it was mostly a combination of diesel exhaust and last night's Indian takeaways. Who cared? For some reason it felt ridiculously good just to be outside.

I turned my back on my office and started walking. After about ten minutes I realised my internal autopilot was taking me to where Debbie used to live. I shook my head and made myself cross the street and head in the other direction. That ship had sailed off into the sunset last year, never to return, I suspected.

Oh well. It was such a nice morning, nothing was going to spoil my mood now I was finally out of that fucking flat at last. I realised I had been cooped up for so long I had almost lost track of what day it was, but I eventually figured out it was Sunday.

I stopped at a food van and bought a jerk chicken wrap from a Jamaican guy I vaguely recognised from around the neighbourhood. If eating the street food around here wasn't living dangerously I don't know what was, but all the same I sat on a wall happily munching it and watching the world go by. It was bloody good actually, so good I was just considering getting another one when a huge silver Bentley pulled up hard at the kerb in front of me. Three big lads got out, two with their hands inside their bulky leather jackets in a way that shouted "guns" so loudly it's a wonder the Old Bill couldn't hear them a mile away. My heart sank.

"Drake," one of them said, and it wasn't a question. "Get in the motor."

They shoved me into the back and one got in either side of me while the other went around to the front seat. The driver turned round and glared at me. It was Paul, Gold Steevie's minder.

"We were just on our way to your gaff, but here you are," he said. "Saved us the bother of kicking the door in, ain't you?"

It looked like telling Gold Steevie to fuck off had just turned round to bite me. I knew I should have been shitting myself but for some reason I just wasn't. Buggered if I knew why not, but there we were. I really was in a funny mood that morning.

"Looks like it," I said. "His nibs couldn't be arsed to come for the ride, then?"

"You're going to him," Paul said.

He turned around to face front and slotted the car into drive, and pulled out into the traffic with a pointless squeal of tyres. Someone behind us hooted, and Paul slid the window down and gave whoever it was the finger without looking.

"Cunt!" he shouted out of the window.

These were lovely lads, they really were. The ones either side of me were virtually identical, both of them with shaved heads and stubbled chins and badly tattooed hands. Even Steevie's hired muscle didn't have any class. I settled back into the luxurious seat and tried to enjoy the ride.

CHAPTER 14

We ended up at a lockup on a rundown industrial estate a few miles away. You'd think the Bentley would have looked out of place there, but it seemed like every other unit we drove past had a couple of Jags or a big Mercedes or Range Rover or something similar parked outside. It was that sort of area, if you know what I mean. Eventually we pulled up outside what I could only assume was Steevie's place. The two tattooed-hands lads pulled me out of the car and shoved me through an open metal roller door into the warehouse itself. There were another couple of motors in there under dusty car covers, and a battered white van. And Gold Steevie.

He was standing in the middle of the greasy concrete expanse with another goon beside him, and he was wearing a camel hair coat over his suit. I mean, for the love of God, did he think it was still 1978 or something? His huge gold Rolex and his chunky gold bracelet and all his awful naff sovereign rings caught the dim light and sparkled. Paul and the other lad followed us in and pulled the roller door down behind them. Steevie just stood there with his hands clasped in front of him, glaring at me.

"All right, Steevie," I said. "How's it going?"

"You take me for some sort of cunt?" he asked. "What the fuck has got into you, Drake?"

That, now that he came to ask, was a bloody good question. I honestly had no idea. I hadn't been shaken up by the battle with Bianakith yesterday, and I still wasn't scared now. This was Steevie's manor, and here I was all on my own with him and five of his boys. and he was obviously quite seriously fucked off with me. I should have been shitting myself by now even if I hadn't been while I was in the car. I knew I should, but I still wasn't.

There was something so ridiculous... I dunno. I just couldn't take him seriously today, you know what I mean?

"It's a lovely day," I said. "Guess I'm full of the joys of spring."

"That's enough fucking comedian out of you," Steevie said. "Smack him, Del."

The nearest thug swung for me, and I swayed back out of the way like it was the easiest thing in the world. Now, as I've said, I'm not a fighter and I never have been. Normally that meaty tattooed paw of his would have pretty much broken my jaw but today it was so easy to dodge it, so easy to reach up and take hold of his wrist as it shot past my face. So easy to turn with him and dip my weight just so and put my other hand on his elbow and *wrench*.

Del's arm snapped like a twig.

"Fucker!" he howled, clutching the broken arm to his chest and staring at me in open astonishment.

I wasn't any less astonished myself if I'm perfectly honest about it.

"You been taking fucking karate lessons or something, you ponce?" Steevie asked. "Paul, Lenny, Dave. Kick the fucking piss out of him."

They turned on me together, three on one, and I knew if they didn't get their own way soon then the bats and crowbars would come out. Or maybe a shotgun.

I started to get angry. This was ridiculous all right. This was just *fucking* ridiculous. I had killed an *archdemon* yesterday for fucksake, and now these little pricks thought they could beat me up? *Me?*

I could feel a heat building in my hands, getting hotter and hotter as I got angrier and angrier.

"Er, boss…" one of Steevie's goons started, but by then it was too late.

I was really, truly pissed off now, and it felt *good*. I lifted my hands in front of my face and saw there was smoke rising from my fingertips. That had never happened before.

The lads backed off, looking wary now as well they might. Steevie's eyes opened wide in surprise. He reached into his fucking ludicrous camel hair coat and started to pull out a shooter.

I went for him. I don't even really know *how* to have a fight, but something in me just took over. I felt hot and cold all over, all at once, ice cold and raging hot.

Burning hot.

Steevie shrieked as he burst into flames. I backhanded him across the face and his head exploded like he'd bitten a grenade. I turned on his minders, vaguely aware of flames roaring from my outstretched hands.

Oh burn, you motherfuckers, just burn!

I'm not too sure what happened after that.

I came to my senses sitting on the floor, backed into a corner and hunched over my burned hands. Dear fucking Christ in Heaven but they hurt. I made myself look at them but they seemed to be all right, with none of the weeping blackened blisters I felt sure must be covering them. It still hurt though. It hurt a fucking lot.

Steevie and all five of his crew were dead.

That's such a mild word isn't it, dead? "Dead" didn't really do justice to how Steevie and his boys were. Steevie himself was a shapeless mass of charred flesh and wool with lumps of molten gold fused into it. Most of his head seemed to be missing, but it was a bit hard to tell, what with the state of him. His boys weren't much better, but by then I didn't feel like looking too closely. The smell alone was enough to make me want to puke.

I winced as I struggled to my feet. The pain in my hands was fading now but I felt like I hadn't slept for a week. I had to get out of there. I pulled the cover off the nearest car. It was one of those big Jags they don't make any more, a lovely old thing in deep burgundy with cream leather seats and a lot of walnut on the dash, but it was locked and anyway the smell coming off it was enough to tell me I really wouldn't have wanted to look in the boot. Fuck it, I'd take the Bentley then. I paused in the doorway and looked back over my shoulder at the charred, smoking corpses.

Well, isn't that interesting?

Paul had left the keys in the Bentley so I just pinched it. I hadn't driven a car in years but you never really forget how, and it was such a beautiful motor it pretty much did it for me anyway. I pulled out onto the main road through the deserted industrial estate and floored it. The Bentley went like stink but I'd only got halfway down the road before I had to pull over. I sat there behind the wheel and started to shake uncontrollably.

What the actual fuck just happened in there?

I had no idea but I knew I needed a drink, badly. I took a deep breath to get myself under control and pulled out again, driving a bit more like a sane person now. I turned left at the lights and threaded my way through the traffic towards the Rose and Crown.

I put the power of Hell at your fingertips, I remembered the Burned Man telling me once, but I had never thought it meant it literally. Fuck it, I *knew* it hadn't meant it like that. This was fucked up whichever way I looked at it.

I parked the Bentley in a side street five minutes' walk away from the pub and left the keys in it. I knew it would only take half an hour or so for it to disappear. It broke my heart to leave a lovely car like that out to get nicked but then I could hardly keep the bloody thing, could I? Far too many of the wrong sort of people would know Gold Steevie's motor when they saw it, and that might lead to some very awkward questions. I'd let whichever little scrote helped himself to a free Bentley deal with those sorts of questions, ta very much.

I turned the corner and smiled at the welcome sight of the Rose and Crown. It was my local, sort of, and the kind of place no one would so much as raise an eyebrow at you getting shitfaced of a Sunday lunchtime. And that was exactly what I had planned.

I walked between the hanging baskets and pushed the door open. Shirley was behind the bar and I'd never been so pleased to see her cheeky smile. Shirley's the landlady, a saucy-looking sixty year-old East End matriarch, all peroxide hair and tits and shiny satin blouse. God bless her and all who've sailed in her.

"Don, how are you, duck?" she asked me.

"I've been better," I admitted. "Pint and a chaser please, Duchess."

She got my drinks and I retired to a table in the corner. What the holy buggering hell had happened in that warehouse? I sighed and drank. I had no idea, in all honesty. I could only assume it had something to do with what I had done yesterday. Yesterday I had worked more closely with the Burned Man than I had ever done before. I remembered when Trixie had fought Aleto the Unresting whilst trying to use the Burned Man, and how she had somehow managed to shoot fire out of her hand at Ally. I had wondered at the time how the fuck she had done that.

Maybe getting *too* close to the Burned Man had some weird side effects. I really didn't know. But then there had been the way I had been behaving all day, first hiding from Trixie and then not being scared of Gold Steevie when I really should have been. It had been almost as though I had known I could slaughter him and his boys without breaking a sweat, although of course I hadn't known anything of the sort until it happened.

But then I was good at slaughtering people, wasn't I? Five year-old children especially. I closed my eyes and saw his face, the bloody holes where his eyes had been.

Fuck him. What use is a fucking five year-old anyway? It's not like he was about to cure cancer or something. His parents can always make another one if they miss him that fucking much.

I sat up like I'd been stung. Now I know I can be a bit of a shit sometimes but where the fuck had *that* come from? I suppose it was technically true but for fucksake, that was awful! What the fuck was *wrong* with me?

Oh I was buggered if I knew. Sometimes I hate myself, I really do. I drank up and went to get another round in.

I must admit I was a bit pissed by the time Trixie finally came to find me. She didn't look best pleased, to put it mildly.

"Oh, for heaven's sake Don," she said as she sat down opposite me. "I might have known I'd find you in here. Going for a walk, indeed."

"I did go for a walk," I said. "I walked here."

Okay, that was maybe leaving out one or two key details but I *had* walked here from where I'd abandoned Steevie's Bentley so it was technically true, if you squinted at it. I can't say I fancied trying to explain to her what had actually happened, especially as I didn't really know myself.

"It's lunchtime and you're drunk," she pointed out, a bit snippily I thought.

I looked at her and got embarrassed all over again.

"Yeah, well," I said. "Look, Trixie. About last night... I really am sorry."

"Oh," she said. "Oh I see. Well, let's not say anything more about that. Misunderstandings happen."

Don't they just. Her belting me in the face in a fit of rage, me feeling her up in a fit of stupidity, we were all about misunderstandings recently, weren't we? I sighed.

"It's a deal," I said. "Want a drink?"

"Oh why not, now I'm here anyway," she said. "Gin and tonic please."

I went and got her one, and got myself another pint while I was about it. I thought about it for a moment and decided to skip the whisky. I didn't want to wind her up any more than I already had today.

"There was a man looking for you this morning," she said, when I came back with the drinks. "I told him you were out."

That was seldom good.

"Who was it?"

"He said his name was Harry," she said.

"Oh, that'll be Weasel," I said. "I'll catch up with him later."

"Weasel?"

"Yeah, it's sort of a nickname," I said.

"It suits him," she said. "He didn't look very salubrious."

"Nah, well that's because he's not," I said. "Still, he has his uses. He sort of works for me sometimes."

"Doing what?" she asked.

"This and that," I said evasively.

I still hadn't mentioned what I had found at Charlie Page's house. It occurred to me that there had been quite a few things recently that I hadn't mentioned to Trixie. It was getting to be a habit, and I wasn't sure that it was a good one. Trixie sipped her drink and raised an eyebrow at me.

"Look," I said, "now we're sitting down with a drink there's something I ought to tell you."

"Oh?"

"Remember that charity job I did? The old fella with the batty wife? Well, it turns out it wasn't quite as simple as that."

"Oh?"

I filled her in, and she stared at me.

"*Adam says*," she said, with a slightly strange look on her face. "And you're only just now telling me this? That was nearly a week ago, Don."

"Yeah well, we've been a bit busy what with one thing and another, haven't we?" I said. "Anyway, that's what I've got Weasel doing, following up on the Adam thing for me. He's a shifty little git but he knows pretty much everyone, and he knows how to keep his ear to the ground. Hopefully he's got something for me."

"For us," Trixie corrected me. "I need to have a little chat with this Weasel of yours, I think."

Sorry, Weasel.

Oh fuck it, no I wasn't. If he wanted to play with the grownups it was time he learned what that involved. Meeting Trixie would do him good.

Sort of, anyway.

"Fair enough," I said. I drained my pint. "Right, well we ought to be getting back then. If I know Weasel he'll be camped out on the doorstep waiting for me by now."

CHAPTER 15

He was as well.

The sun had disappeared behind the more usual London haze hours ago and it was bloody cold out there now. The poor bugger must have been freezing. I must say the chilly walk home had sobered me up no end too, which was probably best. At least Trixie had stopped giving me snippy looks for being drunk on duty anyway.

Weasel was sitting on the pavement with his back to my front door, smoking a sad-looking rollup and waiting for us. He looked so much like a homeless person it was a surprise people weren't giving him the price of a cup of tea as they passed. Actually, round here it wasn't surprising at all, but you know what I mean.

"Mr Drake," Weasel said, when he saw us coming. He pulled himself awkwardly up and stood there shivering with his hands stuffed in the pockets of his tracksuit and his rollup stuck to his droopy lower lip. "I've been waiting for you."

"So you have, Weasel," I said.

I unlocked the front door and held it open for Trixie, then ushered Weasel up the stairs ahead of me and shut the door behind us.

"Sit down," I told him once we were in my office, pointing at the sofa. "Trixie, this is Weasel."

"How nice," she said. "Excuse me a moment."

I sat down behind the desk while she took herself off to the bathroom. I noticed Weasel staring intently at her, frowning with a fierce concentration that spoke of considerable effort being expended.

"Mr Drake, am I seeing things or is her aura... *white*?"

"Yes, Weasel, it is," I said. "Trixie is an angel."

Both of those things were true after all, although one had nothing to do with the other.

He gaped at me. "Are you taking the mickey out of me, Mr Drake?"

"Nah, I don't do that, it's too easy," I said. "She's a real live angel, so you show her some fucking respect."

"An *angel*?" he echoed.

"You want to learn from me, Weasel? Well this is the sort of thing I do. These are the people I mix with, you understand?"

He nodded slowly. "Right," he said. He looked like he might be starting to reconsider that little ambition right about then.

Trixie came back a minute later and perched on the edge of my desk.

"So," she said, fixing Weasel with her dazzlingly blue eyes. "What's Adam up to then?"

He almost jumped out of his skin. I could see that now he knew what she was he was suddenly terrified of her.

Good.

"He's... Well, I don't really know, like. Ma'am," he added. "There's all sorts of fuss though. The left hand path brigade are all up in arms. There's black candles burning all over the city, if you know what I mean. It's like the second coming of Lucifer out there right now."

"Yes," said Trixie, and again she had that faraway look on her face. "Yes, I suppose it would be."

"Who is he then, Mr Drake? Ma'am? This Adam, I mean."

"Never you mind, Weasel," I said. "I don't want you worrying your ugly little head about things like that, I just want to know who's doing what."

"Well, the Whitechapel Thirteen have got back together," he said, "and there was some sort of big ritual up at Highgate the other night. Other than that, well, I don't rightly know Mr Drake. I mean, these ain't the sort of people what give me the time of day as a rule, if you know what I mean."

I can't think why.

"I know, Weasel," I said. "That's why you're going to have to dig a bit harder, aren't you? I want to know what's happening, not what some bloke you bought a pint for told you he heard off a tom who shagged someone whose second fucking cousin knows a geezer, you understand me? Get out there and get me some fucking facts, Weasel."

"Yes, Mr Drake," he muttered.

"I like facts," said Trixie, fixing Weasel with a flat blue stare.

I do believe she was starting to get the hang of this, bless her. Intimidating people like Harry the Weasel really isn't that hard once you get your eye in.

"Yes, ma'am," Weasel whispered.

For fucksake, he was already more scared of her than he'd ever been of me. That was hardly surprising I supposed, but it was irritating all the same.

"Go on then, fuck off," I told him. "You're supposed to be a seeker, after all. Go and fucking seek. Come back when you've got something useful to tell me. To tell us, I mean."

"Yes, Mr Drake," he said again.

He got up and scurried out of my office like he had a vorehound on his tail. I snorted as the door banged shut behind him. Ridiculous little prick.

"Poor little man," Trixie said.

"You what?" I blinked at her. "Don't tell me you're feeling sorry for the Weasel?"

"You're horrible to him," she said.

I shrugged. "So what, he's horrible," I said. "And he owes me, and he wants more from me besides. Fair's fair, Trixie."

"Mmmm," she said. "Don't bully him, Don. I don't like that."

A bully, me? *Me?* For fucksake, I knew all about bullies. I'd grown up on a bastard of a tough estate and I'd been to an even worse high school before I escaped to university. I knew all about bullies, and I knew I wasn't one.

Was I?

OK, maybe I *had* been a bit firm with him, but that's how you got stuff done around here. Gold Steevie never got where he was by asking nicely, you know what I mean? Although now that I thought about it, where Gold Steevie had got in the end was melted to the floor of his warehouse by someone he had been trying to bully. That was another interesting thought right there.

"Yeah," I said, and cleared my throat. "Yeah, you're right. Sorry Trixie. I don't know what's got into me today."

"It's easy to pick on someone weak when you feel strong," she said. "I should know."

I blinked at her. I supposed she probably would at that.

"Yeah," I said again.

"That doesn't make it right," she said.

She stood up and turned and stared out of the window, lost in her own thoughts.

"Right," I said. "Right, well. Yeah, OK. No more bullying the Weasel, then."

"Good," she said, without looking at me.

I turned in my chair and looked around, and caught sight

of the dagger still sitting on the end of the desk. *Fuck me, the Burned Man must be doing its nut by now, stuck in there.*

I scooped the blade up in my hand and stood up. Trixie didn't seem to notice, so I left her to her thoughts and went into the workroom. The fetish was still hanging immobile in its chains where I had left it. I looked at it for a moment, then knelt down in front of the altar and gently eased the point of the blade into the tiny incision in the fetish's chest.

"Sorry it's taken this long," I said. "Out you come then, and I'll give you a feed."

Nothing happened.

I frowned and pressed the tip of the blade a little deeper into the unresisting body of the fetish. They felt lifeless, dagger and fetish both.

"You awake in there, mate?"

I delved into the dagger with my Will. I couldn't feel anything in there. Nothing at all.

Oh fuck.

"Burned Man, can you hear me?" I said.

There was nothing. *What the hell?* It couldn't have escaped, I knew that much. It was bound, and although I knew there was supposedly a way to undo those bindings, I didn't have the faintest idea what it was and I had no desire to find out. I couldn't have accidentally freed it, there was just no way. Besides, even if I *had* freed it, I think ripping my head off and shitting down my neck would probably have been the first thing it would have done. No, it was still bound all right... somewhere.

The fetish was as cold and inert as it had become the moment I drew the Burned Man into the dagger, and it had no aura whatsoever any more, so it definitely hadn't gone back in there. The dagger was still enchanted of course, but I could feel that it was soulless now as well, just an empty blade. So it wasn't in there either.

So where the fuck *was* it?

Think, Don, I told myself. What did you actually do? I had invoked the Burned Man back into the dagger. I had invoked it against its will, sucked it back in as hard as I could until it smacked into me and disappeared. Except it wasn't *in* the dagger like it was supposed to be, was it?

It smacked into me and disappeared.

It smacked into me. I had invoked the Burned Man...

Oh fuck me, no.

It was starting to make sense now. Steevie and his boys, all of it. Oh dear God, what had I done?

I wanted to throw up.

All this shit was starting to make sense now, each piece falling into place in my head with the wet thump of rotten meat hitting the floor. The way I hadn't been shaken up after the battle with Bianakith. What I had done to Steevie, and how I had treated Weasel. How I'd been acting in general, and how I'd felt like I had been shut in forever. I hadn't been myself at all today, not even a little bit. And now that I thought about it, I thought I knew why.

I shoved the dagger back into a drawer in my cupboard and hurried to the bathroom, catching a glimpse as I went of Trixie still staring out of my office window. She obviously had something on her mind, but I'd have bet money it wasn't as big as deal as my own current little clusterfuck of a situation.

I shut the bathroom door behind me and stared into the mirror, gripping the sides of the sink with both hands to steady myself. There I was, looking back at me. The same old Don Drake. I hadn't bothered to shave that morning and I needed a haircut, but then I usually did. Other than that I looked like myself. I thought I did, anyway. I stared into my own eyes, and my eyes stared back at me. I gripped the cold porcelain of the sink until I thought my knuckles might crack.

Don't be such a fucking coward, I told myself. *Do it*.

I forced myself to *really* look then, to look for my own aura in the reflection. I might be a magician but I'm still just a man, and my aura should have been the same sort of dull, fuzzy blue as anyone else's, the same as yours or your mum's or the woman at the post office's. But it wasn't. I gazed into the mirror with that particular, trained magician's gaze, and I saw a poisonous black cloud around my reflection. That was the Burned Man's aura, I'd have known it anywhere.

Oh dear God.

That awful thought I'd had in the pub, everything today in general, suddenly I understood. The Burned Man was in my head. Somehow I had managed to invoke it wholesale, bindings and all, and bind it to *me*. I stared at my reflection and it wavered before my eyes, the image swimming in the spotted glass of my bathroom mirror, and now I could see it. I watched it haze in and out the same way I had seen the kindly, smiling image of Legba wavering over Papa Armand's face in the club on Wednesday night, after he had thrown his chicken bones on the craps table. This face wasn't smiling though, or kindly.

Not even a fucking little bit it wasn't.

I could still see myself, but I could see the Burned Man too. I could see it in all its hideous glory, not nine inches tall any more but life-sized, man-sized. My size. There was the Burned Man's face superimposed over my own, blackened and burned and cracked, the weeping red fissures in the charred flesh making me feel slightly sick just to look at them. It spoke to me, and whether it was actually my reflection talking or just a voice in my head I didn't know and by then I really didn't even care any more.

"I told you I'd make you powerful," it said.

•••

The Burned Man *had* told me that, I remembered it very clearly.

"You've got real potential, boy, potential like I haven't seen for a thousand years or more," it had told me all those years ago. "Do what I tell you and I'll make you more powerful than you can possibly imagine."

I was twenty-four years old and Professor Davidson was dead in the next room, lying in a puddle of the bloody vomit he had choked on. The reading of his last will and testament was only a formality at this point – the Burned Man belonged to me now.

Getting the Burned Man on its altar out of Davidson's flat took some doing, of course, but anything is possible with enough determination. Eventually the wooden crate I had knocked up around it was delivered to my digs.

My digs in those days were a shitty bedsit on the third floor of an old Victorian townhouse half a mile from the university. The landlord rejoiced in the name of Roger Cheeseman, which I suppose may have gone some way to explaining the all-pervading smell in the building. All the same, the place was mine and mine alone, two damp rooms with an interesting pattern of mould on the ceiling and one of those gas-powered instant water heaters over the sink that tried to kill you every time you lit it. If you wanted hot water you had to hold down the button, chuck a lit match down the back of it, and pray for divine intervention. The number of times I'd had a mushroom cloud of flame hit the ceiling was nicely evidenced by the black scorch marks on the plaster above the heater, which was pretty much the only place the mould didn't grow. That was something, I supposed.

They had only just invented health and safety in those days, and landlords like Cheeseman were quite happy to pretend they still hadn't. Still, it was what I could afford and it was a lot better than a shared room in the halls of residence would have been. I couldn't quite imagine the sort of roommate who wouldn't have minded me bringing the Burned Man home with me, and if there *had* been someone like that, then I dare say I wouldn't have wanted to share a room with them in the first place.

I had borrowed a pair of sawhorses from my old friend Jim, an ex-fellow student who had dropped out the year before to become a carpenter. He was actually doing quite well for himself now, to the bewilderment of his painfully middle class parents. Anyway, I set the sawhorses up at the far end of my living room/bedroom/kitchen and balanced the altar on top of them.

"Fuck a bloody duck up the arse, don't tell me you actually live in this shithole," the Burned Man said. "And there I was thinking Davidson was a waste of fucking effort."

I cleared my throat, feeling ridiculously embarrassed. "Yeah well," I said. "We'll get something a bit smarter soon."

"We'd better," it said. "What's that fucking *smell*?"

I shrugged. "No one really knows," I said. "Mr Cheeseman always swears blind he can't smell anything when he comes round for the rent."

The Burned Man cast a disgusted look at the pattern of black rot that decorated the ceiling. "That right?" it said. "How much do you like this Cheeseman cunt?"

"Not a lot," I said.

Truth be told Cheeseman was a horrible man, with a fat nose full of broken veins and a smell about him that told me he wanked too much and didn't wash nearly enough.

"Good," the Burned Man said. "Time for a bit of practice then. I assume you know an alchemist?"

"Yeah," I said. "Well, sort of, anyway."

I was thinking of Debbie, of course. She was still at the same university as me, studying for her masters in chemistry but spending more time than she really should have been studying alchemy too. That was my fault, I supposed, but damn she was good at it.

"Good," it said again. "Right, you'll need to get some bits and pieces. And rip up this fucking awful excuse for a carpet, too. You'll want a bare floor to lay out the circle."

"Hang on a minute," I said. "What sort of practice are you talking about exactly?"

"Think of it as a live firing exercise," the Burned Man said. "Someone nice and easy. Someone expendable."

"Oh, fuck that," I said. "Cheeseman's grotty and a slumlord and I'm not exactly in love with the bloke but that doesn't mean I want to fucking kill him. Anyway, then we'll have *nowhere* to bloody live, will we?"

"Huh," said the Burned Man. "Fair enough, I suppose. All the same, there must be someone you want to hurt."

"Yeah," I said, after a moment. "Yeah, there is, as it goes."

Nick Regan had been two years above me in high school, and he was an utter cunt. He had been the resident school bully until the day he was finally expelled. After that he became the local hard man and cock of the estate. The number of times him and his gang of hangers-on had beaten me and my friends up, taken our lunch money or our trainers or our Walkman or whatever we'd had, didn't even bear counting. As we got older he had only got worse, selling drugs to kids and pushing girls around. I had escaped to university in the end, but in my first couple of years I had still been going home in the holidays to see my mum. And every time I came back to that shitty estate there was Nick, waiting for the nancy-boy student. Fuck me, but I hated that wanker with a passion.

To be fair Mum had remarried now and I didn't like her new bloke much so I hadn't been home for a couple of years. Don't get me wrong, he was a lot better than Dad had been, he just wasn't my cup of tea if you know what I mean. I still spoke to her on the phone now and again though. Last I heard, Nick had battered his pregnant girlfriend so badly she'd lost the baby. No one could prove anything of course, and he'd walked away scot free. Somehow he always did. If there was ever someone the world wouldn't miss it was Nick fucking Regan.

"Thought there might be," said the Burned Man. "Everyone's got someone, in my experience. Right, fuck this Cheeseman bloke then, we'll do your boy instead."

"Right," I said. "What do I need?"

I spent half the day getting rid of the rancid carpet and drawing out the grand summoning circle on the floorboards, my dog-eared, third-generation-photocopied copy of the great classical grimoire *The Lesser Key of Solomon* propped open on the floor in front of me as I painstakingly copied the design in chalk. After that the Burned Man sent me off with the most bizarre shopping list I had ever seen in my life at the time – a pound of iron filings, an ounce of graveyard dirt, a pinch of powdered mandrake root and two live toads. Debbie had given me a bit of a funny look but she'd had everything I needed, bless her, including the toads. I supposed I should have realised right then that she was the woman for me, but then I was young and stupid and I've always been a bit slow on the uptake with things like that. Ah well, hindsight and all that.

"Thanks, babe," I said as she packed them up in my rucksack for me.

Debs smiled at me. "Don't go calling up anything nasty," she teased.

She knew I was a magician of course, but I don't think she had any real idea of exactly what *sort* of magician I was. I had never mentioned the Burned Man to her, and I never intended to either. That secret had been strictly between

Davidson and myself, and now he was dead it was just my business and no one else's. And I knew it would have to stay that way.

"Nah, 'course not," I laughed. "I'm just trying some new symbolism."

She kissed me. "Well, have fun," she said. "Want me to come over tonight?"

Ah, shit. Yeah, that was going to be a bit of a problem. My bedsit was one room with a separate cupboard of a bathroom with a toilet and a shower in it, and that was it. Which meant there would be no hiding the Burned Man.

"How about I come here?" I said instead, thinking fast. "My place is getting worse by the week. You wouldn't believe the new smell Cheeseman has invented."

"Ew, gross," she said, "it was bad enough already. Maybe it'd be better if you just came to me from now on."

Her place was quite nice as student digs go. She was in a shared house with a beautiful and very well-to-do Indian girl called Rugveda who was hardly ever there, probably on account of the perpetual chemistry experiment that seemed to have been running in Debbie's room for the last two years now. Either way, the other girl's dad was a wealthy doctor and he paid the rent for her – she had just sublet her spare room to Debs for a bit of extra pocket money. It was a sweet setup and I'd much rather spend the night there than in Cheeseman's palace of mould any day, especially now I had installed the Burned Man in my room. I can't say I found the thought of it watching me sleep particularly appealing.

"Yeah, will do," I said. "Thanks for the stuff."

I hiked back to my place with the rucksack over my shoulder, trying and failing to pretend I couldn't feel the toads wriggling about back there. I've never liked toads as it goes, which considering what I did with them is probably just as well.

"Right then," I said to the Burned Man when I got home about nine o'clock that evening. "Shall we do this?"

"Do fucking let's," it said.

I set up my scrying glass then laid out the perimeter of the circle with the iron filings and drew the glyphs in the cardinal points with the mixture of powdered mandrake and graveyard dirt. Once that was done I gutted the toads in the kitchen sink behind the Burned Man's altar while it did its thing. We had done some minor summonings together before of course, while it had been training me, but this would be my first actual sending.

"Ready?" it asked me.

I nodded.

"Ready," I said.

We did what we needed to and moments later I was gazing into the scrying glass at the estate where I had grown up, as seen through the eyes of a real live vorehound.

"Bloody hell," I whispered. I watched the darkened houses stream past in the glass as it loped towards Nick Regan's place. "I'm going in. I need to ride it."

The Burned Man laughed at me.

"Just let it be," it told me, "it knows its business."

"What if it gets loose?" I asked it.

I wasn't taking any chances that this thing might end up running amok in the neighbourhood – my mum lived round the corner, after all. The Burned Man waved a chained hand at the grand summoning circle around me, at the carefully inscribed glyphs and the ingredients I still owed Debbie the money for.

"What do you think all this shit is for?" it asked me. "It *can't* get loose, that's the whole fucking point. Just let it do its thing and it'll run off home again afterwards like a good little vorehound."

"All the same," I said. "Humour me."

I plunged my Will through the scrying glass into the vorehound's mind.

Trust me, inside the head of the kind of demon you use for this sort of thing is not a nice place to be. A vorehound is basically just a nasty demonic animal, but I'm probably underplaying the "nasty" part of that. A vorehound, as the name maybe suggests, exists to eat. It's the closest thing there is to an actual landshark. They're pure apex predators and they live to kill, simple as that.

The vorehound was a flood of sensations around me, powerful muscles in fluid motion, an overpowering rush of scents, the wind ruffling through its short, bristly fur as it ran. The feeling of four legs moving in perfect rhythm was almost hypnotic. I knew if I tried to actually control it I'd lose that rhythm instantly and pitch it onto its muzzle in the road so I just sat back and let it carry me along. It leapt Nick Regan's garden wall in a single bound and ploughed headfirst through his front room window without breaking stride.

Nick lived in the terraced house he had inherited from his parents, only now it was more like a druggy's squat than the modest but cosy little working-class family home it had once been. The vorehound landed on the bare floorboards in a shower of broken glass and paused to sniff the air, then bounded up the stairs with slobber streaming from its mouth as it took the scent. Vorehounds have no language so I couldn't really hear its thoughts as such but I was receiving a flood of impressions, scents and instincts that all said one thing – *Prey!*

Nick was just coming out of his bedroom, barefoot and bare chested in tracksuit bottoms, with a fucking Samurai sword in his hand.

"Who's there?" he shouted. "No cunt puts my fucking windows in!"

The vorehound leapt for him. Two hundred pounds of devil dog hit him in the chest and his sword went flying as the demon bore him to the ground. I looked out of its eyes, staring down into Nick Regan's face. I could see the fear in his nasty piggy little eyes and fuck me but I liked it.

"Die, you horrible cunt," I whispered.

The vorehound tore his throat out with a single slash of its terrible slavering jaws. I felt the hot rush of blood fill my mouth, and the whole thing suddenly lost its appeal. I pulled my Will back out of the vorehound and retched, gagging on the floor of my bedsit while the Burned Man laughed at me.

"Enjoy that?" it asked me.

I looked up at it. I could have done without the mouthful of blood, but other than that I'm sorry to say that yeah, I fucking had actually.

If this was power, I wanted more of it.

CHAPTER 16

If this was power you could fucking keep it.

Inside the head of the sort of demon you use for the things I do isn't a nice place to be. I knew that of course, but over the years I had just got used to it. One thing I had never prepared for though was the possibility of having that sort of demon inside *my* head. Not just any old demon either, but the Burned Man itself. The Burned Man was an *arch*demon, of course. One of the most powerful of all the archdemons in fact, the one that the antler druid Oisin himself had chosen to bind to serve him on Earth.

Fucking hell.

I stared back into the mirror, at the wavering image of the Burned Man's face.

"Yeah, you did say that," I had to admit.

I've heard it said that the greatest conceit of any diabolist is to assume that the things you summon have no life outside of working for you. I mean, I knew the Burned Man secretly longed to be free, it had made that abundantly clear last year, but I had never even entertained the notion that something like this might or even possibly *could* happen. Apparently it could, and it had.

I wasn't having it.

I clenched my fists on the edge of the sink and blasted the Burned Man with my Will, throwing every drop of strength I could find into a ferocious banishing. I focused as hard as I could on the image of the fetish in the next room, opened a psychic channel between my mind and that fetish and hurled the spirit of the Burned Man down it as though my life depended on it.

I thought it actually might, to be perfectly honest about it.

"I banish thee, Burned Man," I snarled through clenched teeth. "Get thee gone!"

Sweat broke out on my forehead and my hands shook with the effort, my knuckles vibrating against the cold porcelain sink. My back arched and I bared my teeth, my head splitting with pain.

"I banish thee!"

I reached for the depths of my power, for that hideous, desperate strength I had found when I summoned Adam against his will last year. I dug as deep and as hard as I could and I poured the whole fucking lot of it into the mightiest banishing I had ever done in my life.

Are you done yet? the Burned Man's voice sneered in my head. *That doesn't even tickle.*

I sagged against the sink, gasping. My chin slumped against my chest and I took a great shuddering breath, feeling sweat trickle out of my hair and down my face. That was it. That was all I'd had in me.

I was beaten and I knew it.

I stared into the mirror, watching the poisonous black cloud of the Burned Man's aura billow around my reflection. Beaten or not, I could hardly walk around looking like that. Thank fuck Trixie had been preoccupied with her Dominion, and then the revelation that Adam was up and about or she was bound to have noticed it by now.

"Do me a favour will you and hide that fucking aura?" I said.

That's it? the Burned Man sniggered. *That's what you're worried about right now, Drake, my fucking aura?*

"One thing at a time," I said, still trying to catch my breath. "This is too much to take in all in one go. Let's not make life fucking worse by having Trixie notice something's not right, yeah?"

Blondie, the Burned Man thought, and I felt a rush of pure naked lust.

Oh for God's sake.

"You can pack that in too," I said. "I tried it on with her last night and I made a total twat of myself."

That's because you are a total twat, it said, and I could feel it laughing somewhere inside me. All the same, the aura shrank and dissipated and a moment later all I could see was my own familiar blue haze. That was something, at least.

"Thanks," I said.

I washed my face and concentrated on stopping my hands from shaking. I could still manage that, at least.

"Don?" I heard Trixie's voice from the other side of the bathroom door. "Are you all right in there? You're talking to yourself."

"What? Oh, yeah. Shit, yeah sorry, I do that sometimes," I said.

I do, to be fair. It doesn't mean I'm crazy or anything. I flushed the toilet I hadn't been using and ran the tap for a moment, then opened the door.

"Hi," I said, rather stupidly.

She gave me a level look.

"Just how much did you have to drink before I dragged you out of the pub?"

"Sorry," I said again. "Probably a bit too much for a lunchtime, to be honest. Sorry."

"Mmmm," she said. "Never mind, I'm making you a nice strong coffee then we've got more important things to talk about."

I nodded and let her put the kettle on. I settled on the sofa in the office and stared across the room and out of the window, watching the late afternoon clouds drift past overhead. Oh what the holy fuck was I going to do now?

Having an archdemon living in your head might sound like it ought to make you some sort of superhero, and I had to admit that what I had done to Gold Steevie and his crew was pretty impressive now that I thought about it, but it was hardly fucking healthy. I'd owned the Burned Man for nearly twenty years after all, and I knew exactly what it was like. Oh I understood it, I even enjoyed bullshitting with it sometimes, but I never let myself forget what it really was.

It wasn't my mate, I knew that much.

The thing that was really starting to scare me now was that I was no longer even sure whether my thoughts were my own. That awful thought I'd had in the pub at lunchtime today, writing the McRoths' grandson off as nothing, that hadn't been me had it? Of course not. That was the Burned Man through and through, I was sure it was.

Wasn't I?

"Here," Trixie said, putting a mug of strong black coffee in my hand. "Drink that."

She sat down behind my desk and lit one of her awful Russian cigarettes. Those things really did stink to high heaven.

"Thanks," I said. "Open the window, will you?"

She turned round and did as I asked, then fixed me with a level look.

"About Adam," she said.

I sighed. "Yeah," I said. "Look, I don't know what to tell

you Trixie. He tried to have me killed."

"I know," she said. "He didn't try terribly hard though, did he?"

"That old fucker nearly did me in," I pointed out.

"But he didn't," she said. "He was only one old man with a telekinetic zombie, after all. From what your friend Weasel was saying, it sounds like Adam has followers all over the city. Adam *knows* you, Don. If he'd really wanted to hurt you I think he would have tried a bit harder than that, don't you?"

Well, that was an interesting thought. I had only met the fallen angel who called himself Adam a handful of times, but the last time had been because I had summoned him all by myself by the pure force of my Will after Trixie had stolen the Burned Man from me. I supposed that must have given him at least a modicum of respect for me. And then of course a Dominion had come at my call, and that was when he ran away. Yeah, now that I thought about it, Adam probably did take me reasonably seriously. All the same though, poor old Mrs Page had been bloody dangerous. Maybe Adam was overestimating me, if anything. Fucking hell, people don't do that very often.

"Maybe," I said, sipping my coffee. She always made it just right, black as tar and so strong it was almost burnt. "So what was the point of that little charade then?"

"I think he was just saying hello," Trixie said. "Letting you know he's still about, if you see what I mean. Well of course it would have been letting *us* know if you'd seen fit to tell me about it at the time, but there we are."

I winced at the waspish sting in her words, but she was absolutely right. I really should have told her right there and then, but all the fuss with Bianakith had been occupying both our minds at the time. And of course we still didn't know where that horrible bloody thing had actually come from.

"Do you think Adam summoned Bianakith?" I asked her.

She blinked at me. "Why on earth would he have?"

"Oh how the fuck do I know, but *someone* did," I pointed out. "There aren't many human magicians who could have pulled it off. Actually, now that Wellington Phoenix is dead I can't even think of a single person who could have done that."

"Do you know every diabolist in the world?"

"Well no, of course I don't," I said, "but anyone that powerful would probably be someone I'd have at least heard of, you know what I mean?"

"I suppose so," she admitted. "Even so, it doesn't prove anything."

I shrugged. I supposed it didn't, at that. All the same, I could smell a rat again. *Someone* must have been behind it, and for whatever reason my mind kept going back to that pile of rotten slag that had apparently once been a statue of a cat. Why the fuck would there have been something like that in a cave half a mile underneath London? The same cave where Bianakith seemed to have made its temporary home. There was definitely something going on that I didn't understand.

"Do you fancy a night out tonight?" Trixie asked.

"Er," I said. "I suppose we could. Why?"

She tapped ash from her cigarette into her empty coffee cup and looked at me.

"I put out some feelers," she said. "I know you've got your little Weasel asking questions but I thought it would be quicker to go straight to the horse's mouth, so to speak."

I went cold. "You what?"

"Adam will meet us at Wormwood's club tonight at midnight," she said. "Neutral ground and all that."

I gaped at her. *Jesus wept.*

●●●

We had dinner out and got to the club at about half eleven, me in my good suit and her in a long black sleeveless dress with elbow-length black satin opera gloves and a feathered fascinator in her hair. *She really does look like an old-time movie star*, I thought as I followed her up the stairs. *I just wish I did too.* I was vaguely aware of Connie turning someone away behind us, that grinning ginger-haired bloke with the eyepatch who had jostled me in the bar the last time we had been there. I couldn't help thinking there was something about him... nah, sod it. He wasn't allowed in so he couldn't be anyone who mattered. The club was strictly invitation only after all – the hoi polloi were supposed to stay out of sight downstairs and not lower the tone.

Trixie swept onto the floor of the club itself and I trailed in her wake, as ever feeling hopelessly inadequate next to her. Wormwood was at his usual table and I saw him give us a queasy look through the haze of smoke that surrounded him, but that was all. He might have wanted to argue about Trixie being there again but I knew damn well he didn't dare.

I could see Miss Marie of the flirtatious threats standing across the club, watching us over her peacock feather fan.

I've seen you around, I remembered her saying, *and I've heard things. The way you speak to Wormwood, for one. A mortal speaking to an archdemon like that, shoving him around. That's the sort of thing that gets a man noticed, and that kind of notice isn't always good.*

Oh, she had seen that look Wormwood had given us all right, I'd have put bloody money on it. I still didn't really know who she was but she was taking far too much interest in me for my liking.

Adam was standing at the bar with a glass of whisky in his hand.

He was too tall and too handsome and far too posh for

my liking, and he was wearing a tuxedo with his hair slicked back the way Gold Steevie wore his. Used to wear his, I should say. Back when he still had a head.

"Trixie, my dear," Adam said, his aristocratic accent cutting the air like a knife. He leaned in and kissed her on the cheek in what I could only regard as an overly familiar greeting.

"Hello Adam," she said.

He turned from her and looked at me. "Donald Drake, good evening."

"All right," I muttered.

"I am, actually, and thank you for asking," he said.

I had forgotten just how punchable his smug smile really was. *I fucking hate you*, I thought. Or the Burned Man did, I wasn't even sure which one of us that had been. It was true either way. Adam had been the archangel Lumiel, once upon a time, and he had been the very first to fall. He was Lucifer, the first of the fallen, and he was standing at the bar in front of me.

Fucking hell.

"How are you?" Trixie asked, as she accepted a glass of champagne from him with a warm smile.

I ordered myself a whisky, since he hadn't offered me a drink. Arsehole.

"Oh, I manage," he said, his fingers lingering too long on hers as he handed her the long fluted champagne glass. "I understand *you* have been very busy with our gnomic friends, far underground."

Trixie smiled modestly. "Oh, did you hear about that?" she asked, almost batting her eyelashes at him.

I tightened my grip on my glass and felt my other hand curl into a fist. Only I could have a guardian angel who was in love with Lucifer. If only I could have just belted him I would have felt so much better, but of course life is never that simple, is it?

Why not?

That was the Burned Man for sure. Why not? Because he'd fucking eat me if I so much as lifted a hand against him, that was why not. I could feel the Burned Man stirring restlessly inside me. Maybe it *could* have taken Adam, I had no idea and to be perfectly honest with you I really didn't want to have to find out. Either way that sort of thing couldn't happen in Wormwood's club. This was neutral territory for everyone, that was the whole point of the place.

"Was that your doing?" I asked him.

"I'm sorry?" he said, making out like he had forgotten I was there. "Was what my doing, Don?"

"Bianakith," I said bluntly. I saw a few heads turn in our direction at the mention of that name, but I ignored them. I lowered my voice a bit all the same. "Someone must have summoned that bloody thing."

"I dare say someone must have done," Adam said. "But not me."

"So who?"

"I'm flattered that you assume I know all about every single thing that happens, Don, but in this case I'm afraid I have to disappoint you," he said. "I'm not the omniscient one, after all. I have no idea."

"Excuse me," Trixie said, "I must just powder my nose."

I wondered if his mention of "the omniscient one" had given her acid indigestion. Trixie was skirting around some dangerously divided loyalties here, after all. She floated off across the club and left us standing drinking at the bar together like two normal blokes. Which neither of us were, of course.

"You have changed," Adam said.

I blinked at him. I had asked the Burned Man to keep its aura hidden and as far as I knew it still was, but it seemed we weren't quite fooling everyone.

"Yeah, I'm trying something new with me hair," I said.

"Don't try to kid a kidder, as they say," Adam said softly. "I know what has happened."

"Oh yeah?"

"Oh yes. I wouldn't have come otherwise."

"I thought you came for Trixie," I said.

"No," he said, and stubbed his cigarette out in the heavy crystal ashtray on the bar. "Meselandrarasatrixiel can fend for herself, for now. I came to see you, Don."

"You tried to fucking kill me," I pointed out.

Adam chuckled and took a sip of his whisky. "Oh, come now," he said. "A dead old woman throwing a few knives at you? That can't have been much of a challenge for a man of your calibre, Don. That was... merely a feint."

That was almost a compliment, coming from him. Fuck it, now that I thought about it that *was* a compliment. Like I said before, maybe he was overestimating me. I was more than happy to let him do it, too.

"Why didn't you just have Charlie kill me himself?" I asked him.

"Oh where would the fun have been in that?" Adam said, and laughed. "Besides, he might have actually succeeded and I never wanted that. I knew you'd see through his charade with the old woman."

No, I wasn't about to admit that I nearly hadn't. The more powerful he thought I was the better, as far as I was concerned.

"Yeah," I said instead. "Waste of everyone's bloody time as far as I can see."

"Oh, I don't know," he said. "I found it quite educational."

I necked my whisky and waved the barman to do me another one.

"How's that then?"

"Well, I was interested to see what you would do, of course," he said. "I was quite impressed when you killed Charlie Page. I had half thought his poor tearful little old man routine might sway your judgment."

"Someone tries to kill me, I'll happily kill them back," I said.

Adam nodded. "Good," he said. "Listen to me, Don. There are things you need to know."

"Yeah, there usually are," I said. "I don't see why the fuck I should believe a word *you* say though. I have made an enemy, you told me."

"Oh come now," Adam said. "If I wanted to make trouble for you I could have done so already, very easily. I dare say you haven't told Meselandrarasatrixiel about the, ah, meeting of minds, shall we say, that you and the Burned Man seem to have reached."

I winced. No of course I hadn't, and I can't say I had been planning to. I didn't want this smug bastard telling her for me either, so now he had one over on me again. That was just wonderful.

"Not as such, no," I admitted.

"Well if you wish to keep it that way then you had better give me the time of day, Donald Drake. I never said *I* was the enemy you have made, but Meselandrarasatrixiel will believe me should I choose to tell her."

Of course she would, much as that pained me. All the same, this was getting interesting. If he *wasn't* the enemy, and I wasn't at all sure I believed that, then who the fuck was?

"All right, all right, what's on your mind then?" I asked him.

"There is trouble Upstairs, as I believe you put it," he said. "A great deal of trouble."

I blinked at him. I mean, it made sense, after how the

Dominion had behaved, but it still wasn't exactly the sort of thing I wanted to hear. I wanted Trixie to hear it even less.

"Yeah well you would say that," I said. "You ain't exactly on their side any more, are you? Trixie told me you were trying to recruit her for some coming war."

"Yes, there may well be war," Adam said, "but I'm not sure you completely understand what the sides are."

Time him come, Don-boy, when a man gotta choose what path he goin' walk. Papa Armand had told me that enough times, but Adam was right. I really *didn't* know what the sides were. As Armand had told me, nothing was ever as simple as it looked at first glance.

"It's a fucking stretch to take the word of a self-confessed fallen angel," I said.

"Yes, I fell down into Hell," Adam said. He paused and met my eye. "Other things would have to climb far and high to reach it. Those things, you do not wish to meet."

I could have done without meeting *him*, to be perfectly honest about it, but there we were. "Oh do tell," I said. "I thought you were a duke down there."

"Oh I am, but I am still not a god, and not all gods are above if you take my meaning."

"I'm not sure that I do," I said. "Are you trying to tell me there's some sort of god of Hell on its way?"

"Of Hell? No, not that. Not all the Veils are between Earth and Hell, you know."

I remembered what Papa Armand had told me about the crossroads, and frowned. "I suppose they wouldn't be," I said. "Bit outside my field I'm afraid."

"You may just find, Don, that sometimes you're better off with the devil you know, so to speak."

"So the enemy of my enemy is my friend, is that it?" I said.

Adam gave me a cool smile. "Something like that."

Trixie came back just then with Papa Armand on her arm and Jocasta trailing in their wake in a tiny white dress that barely covered her arse. I'm afraid Trixie completely eclipsed the poor girl, and it looked like Jocasta knew it.

"Are you boys having fun?" Trixie asked.

I gave her a look.

"Don-boy Drake," said Papa Armand. "Good to see you."

"Hello Papa," I said. "This is Adam, by the way."

Papa Armand looked at Adam, and narrowed his eyes.

"Bondye's balls," he whispered.

Adam smiled. "Good evening, Houngan," he said. "Perhaps we might have a little chat, later."

"We can talk," Papa Armand said, his silk top hat nodding. "Not sure you like what I goin' say."

"Armand dear, Adam is a friend," Trixie said.

"No friend to me, Zanj Bèl," Armand said. "Now, I promised show Jocasta how to play roulette."

He put his arm around his teenage girlfriend and walked away, leaving the three of us standing at the bar.

"I'm sorry Adam," Trixie said. "Armand is usually rather more polite than that."

"But not to me, it would seem," Adam said with a wry smile. "You need not apologise my dear, I'm quite used to rudeness."

I had a feeling that was aimed at me but I was buggered if I was going to rise to it. Armand had got Adam's measure straight off the bat as far as I was concerned, and good luck to him. Adam lit another cigarette and was obviously about to say something else when there was an almighty bang from the downstairs bar.

Smoke billowed up the stairs into the club and Connie came backing rapidly out of it in a low fighting crouch, his massive horns lowered like a bull about to charge.

"Bloody hell!" I said.

Trixie twisted her hand through a deft figure-of-eight and her sword shimmered into existence, gleaming in the dim light. Adam reached into the jacket of his tuxedo and pulled out a ridiculously huge automatic pistol. A Desert Eagle, I remembered he had called it the last time I had seen him use it. The bloody thing was nearly a foot long and there was no way he could have been hiding it under that perfectly tailored tux, so I could only assume he could do the same trick Trixie did with her sword. He must have been compensating for something with that thing, I was sure of it.

He stood there for a moment with his elbow cocked, holding the gun pointed at the ceiling and looking for all the world like a poster for a bad spy movie. I just sort of stood there, watching the club erupt like a kicked anthill around me.

"Stay out of the way, Don," Trixie said.

She and Adam advanced toward Connie. A few of the other more physical-looking patrons were going with them, while the majority retreated across the club as far away from the blowing smoke as they could get.

"What are you?" I heard Connie bellow.

He backed up another step, pawing at the ground with one foot and looking for all the world like he was being pushed backwards against his will. A figure came into view, climbing the stairs from the bar. It was that smiling ginger-haired bloke with the patch over his eye, only now he was holding a long wooden staff in his hands and he wasn't smiling quite so much any more.

I looked round in time to see Wormwood scurrying towards his office. Papa Armand and Jocasta were behind the roulette wheel on the other side of the room, but while she was cowering in fear, I noticed Papa Armand was just watching, his face impassive and a cigar smouldering between his teeth. Miss Marie was fanning herself slowly, and watching everything.

"Get out of my fucking club!" Connie roared.

"I'm sorry, but no," the ginger bloke said. "As I have told you several times now, I need to come upstairs."

He took another step forwards and Connie took another step back, cords of muscle standing out in his thick neck as he fought whatever was pushing him backwards. The man raised his staff and I saw there was an effigy of some sort on the top of it. He was a good way off and the air was hazy with smoke so I couldn't see all that clearly but I could have sworn it was some sort of cat.

"Is there a problem?" Adam asked, his cut glass voice carrying clearly through the air.

He was holding his massive pistol loosely at his right hip, not exactly pointed at the ginger bloke but not exactly *not* pointed at him either. Trixie came up on his left flank, her sword erect in her guard position but not burning. Not yet, anyway.

"Angels," the man said, sparing them a glance. "I have no quarrel with you, sky children. I have no quarrel with the messengers of the Word or with anyone here. I merely wish to come in."

"Your name's not on the fucking list," Connie said.

Something clicked in my head. The Burned Man stepping in, I realised.

"Oi, Rashid," I called out, waving at him. "Over here, mate. It's all right, Connie, I know him."

The man turned and strode between Trixie and Adam as though they weren't there, his staff held upright in his hand as he walked. They stepped back to let him pass, and I'm not sure they did it altogether voluntarily. Connie gave me a wary look but that seemed like it was going to be the end of it, for now anyway. Bless him, he knew when he was beaten, and at least this way he got to save some face.

The man walked towards me, that grin breaking out on his face again. He had very pointed teeth, I noticed, the canines ridiculously long. He looked like a vampire almost, but I knew vampires weren't real. Nah, he looked more like... a cat.

"Well fuck me," I said.

It was him, I suddenly realised. The eyepatch and the ugly mess of scar tissue around it would have given the game away earlier if the whole idea hadn't been so utterly bonkers, but now that I really looked at him I was sure of it. This bloke, somehow, was also the ugly bloody one-eyed ginger tom cat that had been haunting my neighbourhood like a bad smell for the last couple of weeks. The one that had been haunting Trixie's dreams, too.

He planted the butt of his staff in the thick carpet and clapped me on the shoulder with his free hand. The carved headpiece of the staff really was an effigy of a cat, a very Egyptian looking one.

"The bodies we wear, old friend," he said.

"Innit just," I said, or rather the Burned Man did. "You're fucking whiter than I am this time. Call me Don."

This bloke, this ginger cat man who seemed to be called Rashid, laughed at that. It seemed he and the Burned Man had some history together, which must make him a truly ridiculous age. Or whatever was wearing him was, anyway.

Who the fuck is he? I thought furiously at the Burned Man.

"You drinking then?" I asked him.

"I will take wine with you," the man said.

I ordered him a glass of red and got myself another whisky while I was about it. This was just fucking weird. I was still in control of myself, pretty much, I was sure I was. All the same, I knew the Burned Man was talking through me but it really didn't feel like that at all. It felt like I was saying the words myself, I just had no idea *why* I was saying them.

"What brings you through from the endless sands then?" I asked him, as I passed him his drink.

He paused and sipped his wine, then quite deliberately poured a small trickle of it onto the carpet. A libation, I knew, but fuck only knew what to. He nodded slowly.

"I had not thought to see you in human form again," he said, ignoring my question. That was fine by me, I had no idea what I'd just asked him anyway.

"Yeah well," I said, and I realised I was talking for myself again suddenly. "There's a bit of a story to that but it's not one for right now, if you understand me."

Trixie and Adam were coming back, I could see over Rashid's shoulder, and I really didn't want her to hear anything about that. It was bad enough that Adam somehow seemed to already know what had happened.

"Of course," Rashid said, his feline grin widening still further.

Trixie and Adam rejoined us at the bar. At least they had both put their weapons away again, that was something.

"This is Rashid," I said, nodding at them. "Trixie, Adam."

"Charmed I'm sure," Adam said in a tone that meant the exact opposite.

"Hello," said Trixie.

"Honour to the messengers," Rashid said, and offered them both a short bow. He paused, blinked at Adam, and bowed again. "And to whatever they may have become," he added.

Adam scowled and retrieved his drink from the bar. He drained the whisky in a single swallow.

"This evening has gone awry," he said, instantly winning my award for understatement of the day, if not the fucking century. "Perhaps we should talk another day, Don. Trixie."

He turned and stalked off without another word.

"Oh dear," Trixie said, looking after him with a rather lost expression on her face.

"Don't worry, he'll be back," I said.

Better the devil you know, indeed. Was it really? I wasn't too fucking sure about that, but then I supposed all things were relative. I looked at Rashid, and wondered exactly who and what the fuck he was. Perhaps Adam was right, at that.

"Perhaps he will, perhaps he will not," Rashid said. "The Word moves as the Word Wills."

He leaned on his staff, his face unreadable. He was still grinning, but then cats always look like they're smiling, don't they? It doesn't mean they like you. Trixie was staring at him, I realised, rigid with anger. Damn, I'd heard that expression somewhere before, I was sure I had.

"Are you quoting my Dominion at me?" she hissed, her voice low and dangerous.

I suddenly realised just how close she was to going for his throat.

"Am I?" Rashid said mildly. "My apologies, messenger. I meant no offence."

Still his face was unreadable, grinning, impassive.

"Mmmm," Trixie said. "Who are you, Rashid?"

"A shaman," he said. "A wanderer, a priest. A dweller in the ancient deserts."

"The desert is far from here," she said.

Rashid shrugged. "Near, far, it makes no difference. Your sword is by your side yet it too is immeasurably far away, is it not? Dimensions may brush against each other but remain forever out of reach."

Trixie fixed him with a frozen blue stare.

"Do not," she said, "do not *ever* attempt to be mysterious with me. You will lose."

He laughed and swallowed his wine.

"Sky child," he said, and smiled.

"Don't wind her up, mate," I said, and that time I thought

it was probably the Burned Man talking. It was getting hard to tell, but either way that was sound advice as far as I was concerned.

Papa Armand came over then to say goodnight. He shook my hand, kissed Trixie's, and gave Rashid a long, unreadable look.

"*Orevwa*," he murmured, one of the few words of Haitian Creole I could figure out from my schoolboy French, and left us to it.

Rashid stared after him as he sauntered away with Jocasta on his arm.

"I wish only to discuss peace," Rashid said after a moment. "I am a peaceful man."

"Yeah well she ain't," I said, and that time I *knew* it was the Burned Man talking. "A man, or peaceful. Fucking trust me on this one."

"Yes," Rashid said. "Yes, I can see that much. You hide behind false colours, messenger, and your true purpose is clouded. Guidance from above has been lacking I think, hmm?"

"What would you know about that?" Trixie snapped. "Don, get me a drink. A strong one."

I caught the barman's eye and ordered her a double gin and tonic, and got another whisky for myself and a glass of wine for Rashid while I was about it. This conversation was getting extremely weird even by my standards, and I had no intention of staying sober for it if I didn't have to.

I passed her the tall, cold glass, the ice clinking as she raised it to her lips. She swallowed and stared at Rashid for a moment over the rim of the glass. I watched her set it carefully down on the bar and open her cigarette case. She took out a long black and gold smoke, all the while holding his catlike stare.

"Well?" she asked at last, and lit her cigarette with a slim gold lighter.

"I am a shaman," he said again. "I feel the movements, the waves, the undulations of power and influence, the shifting of the endless sands beneath our feet. I know when a force is ascendant, and when it begins to decline. I may not see every detail but I perceive the bigger picture. I know what is happening above, and I know what is coming."

That made me sit up, I can tell you. I'd heard more than enough out of Papa Armand and Adam both to know that *something* fucking big was about to go down, but I still had no real idea of what. Trixie's Dominion had been acting screwy, sure, but then of course I didn't have a clue how I was supposed to *expect* something like that to act. And even Trixie's viewpoint wasn't completely reliable, and seemed to be getting less reliable the more screwy her Dominion became. All in all, I found myself hopelessly adrift on a stormy sea. *Cold and shark-infested waters* Adam had called them. I was starting to think he was right about that, and I was no longer even sure he was the biggest shark in them after all.

"Cut to the fucking chase," I said, or the Burned Man did. One of us did, anyway. "Spare me the Bedouin sage routine, there's a good lad."

I winced inside, but thankfully Rashid laughed. I could only assume the Burned Man knew whoever this bloke really was well enough to know how much piss taking it could get away with.

"She's coming," Rashid said, and suddenly he wasn't grinning at all any more.

"Lucky her," I said, and obviously that was the Burned Man talking again.

Shut up if you can't be serious, I snapped at it in my head. *You still haven't told me who this geezer even is but he's obviously trying to tell us something important here.*

Rashid smiled, and Trixie gave me a slightly bewildered look. Bless her.

"No," Rashid said. "Fear upon the world. My work on Earth has been undone by the Corrupter of Flesh and Houses."

I frowned. The Corrupter of Flesh and Houses? *He layeth waste to houses and causeth flesh to decay and all that which is similar.* Bianakith. He meant Bianakith, I was sure he did. I looked at him, and my gaze settled on the headpiece of his staff. A cat, sitting upright and looking smug and regal like cats always bloody do. As I said earlier, I'm not a big fan of cats. The ancient Egyptians had a goddess that looked like that, I remembered. Bast, or Bastet, as memory served. She was a goddess of, amongst other things, protection against evil spirits. Well, that was interesting, I supposed. I drained my glass and looked at him.

"This work of yours on Earth," I said. "I don't suppose it was a statue of a cat was it, by any chance? Somewhere, oh I dunno, down there?"

I pointed vaguely at the floor. It didn't really matter where, I was just making the point. Rashid looked at me.

"It was," he said. "And now it is destroyed, corroded away to nothing by the only force that *could* have destroyed it. Only the Corrupter of Flesh and Houses had the power to undo *my* work."

"What was your work for?" Trixie asked him. "What did it do?"

"It held her safely beyond the Veils," Rashid said. "Now it is gone, she comes."

That didn't sound good, to put it fucking mildly.

CHAPTER 17

This didn't feel like it was going to be the sort of conversation you could really have in public, so we left. Trixie and Rashid were looking silent daggers at each other in the back of the taxi while I had to put up with the Burned Man sniggering in my head. I noticed on our way out that nothing seemed to have been damaged in the bar downstairs by whatever Rashid had done to make the big bang and all that smoke. It was good of him to leave the place standing, I supposed, and no one seemed to have been hurt. Maybe he *was* a peaceful man at that. Sort of, anyway.

What the fuck are you laughing at? I thought at the Burned Man. *And will you for fucksake tell me who this geezer is?*

Rashid, the Burned Man whispered in my head, although I'd kind of gathered that by now. *He's a shaman from... somewhere else. Doesn't matter where. He's a clever bloke. Bit of a hippy to be honest, but he's not all bad. I hope you like cats.*

I don't like sodding cats.

What does he want? I thought back at it. *And more to the point, what's he on about with all this "she's coming" fuckery?*

Fucked if I know, it said, somewhere in the back of my head. *They're big on the Egyptian pantheon where he's from though. Bast was his patron, last I spoke to him. It could be her I suppose, but I can't see why he'd have been trying to stop her if it was. Isis, maybe? Sekhmet? I don't fucking know, they've got hundreds of bloody goddesses over there and I haven't seen Rashid for millennia.*

Fucking hell, goddesses? What was it Adam had said, "not all gods are above" or something like that. I could only assume the same thing held true for goddesses too. I can't say Egyptian mythology was exactly my strong point but I was sure they must have some nasty ones in the pantheon somewhere. Oh joy, there was something to look forward to.

Still, I thought as the cab pulled up outside the Rose and Crown, it could have been worse. I could have had to take this weird ginger hippy cat back to my place, but luckily I had a bit of an arrangement with the lovely Shirley. It was late, I knew, but I didn't think she'd mind. The Rose and Crown had a lock-in pretty much every night, and as the cab coasted to a stop by the kerb I saw that there were still lights on under the drawn blinds.

"Cheers, mate," I said to the driver as I paid him.

I stepped out into the cold night and offered Trixie my hand to help her out of the car. Not that she needed any help, obviously, but something about her just brought out the chivalry in me. She didn't seem to mind anyway, and graciously accepted my hand as she stepped onto the pavement with Rashid behind her. He had somehow made his staff disappear again when we left the club, which was probably for the best, all things considered. That said, I was starting to feel like the only person who didn't know how to do that trick.

I ducked under a hanging basket and rapped on the door.

"We're shut," I heard Alfie's dulcet tones shout through the thick wood.

"No you ain't, Alf," I said. "It's Don Drake."

I heard a bolt being pulled back, then the door opened and Alfie's flat-nosed boxer's face appeared in the sudden spill of light and laughter from inside. Alfie is Shirley's son, if I hadn't mentioned it. If there's a human version of Connie he's it, but he's a nice lad deep down. Unless you upset his mum anyway, then God help you.

"All right, Don," he said, and gave Trixie a shy smile. "Hello again, love."

"Hello," said Trixie.

"Good evening," said Rashid, when he really should have just kept his sodding face shut and followed us in. Some people know jack shit about basic protocol, and it does my head in. Now I had to introduce the prick and make a big fucking song and dance about him being all right. If he hadn't said anything, Alf would have just happily *assumed* he was all right as he was with me, and that would have been the end of it. Bloody foreigners.

"Alf, this is Rashid," I said. "He's sound, he's with me."

Alfie gave him a dubious look, taking in his eyepatch and horrible scar. "You sure?" he asked.

"I'll vouch," I had to say, when I knew fuck all about the bloke and only had the Burned Man's word for it that he actually *was* all right. The Burned Man's word wasn't worth a lukewarm turd as a rule, if you hadn't gathered that by now.

"Well, if you say so," Alf said, although he still didn't look convinced.

He stood back and held the door open for us, and we filed into the pub. Alf closed and bolted the door behind us again. They should have closed hours ago of course, but this was Shirley's domain and she closed when *she* said she was closing and bugger the law. There was a fair old crowd still in there, a lot of faces I recognised. The Rose and Crown is one of those places where the local characters tend to congregate, and most of them are fairly serious drinkers. Round these parts "characters" is a sort of friendly euphemism for "thieves, conmen and thugs".

"I'll find us a table," Trixie said, but I shook my head.

"Nah, we'll need a bit of privacy, I think," I said. "Hang around a sec."

She sniffed but did as I asked. She had a bit of a thing about not going to the bar, for some reason. I gave Rashid a nudge as we headed over there.

"I don't think you'll get any wine in here that you'd want to actually drink," I warned him.

"Beer is fine," he said. "Something dark."

Shirley beamed when she saw us.

"Don, how are you, duck?" she said. "And your pretty lady too. And this fine gent."

Oh great, here we had to go all over again.

"'Ello Duchess," I grinned at her. "This is Rashid, he's all right."

"Honoured to meet you, noble landlady," Rashid said with a bow, proving that I was talking out of my arse.

Thankfully Shirl had obviously been at the vodka by then, and she giggled like a teenager. "Aw, isn't that nice?" she said. "What're you having, boys?"

"Lager and a bitter and a G and T, please, treacle," I said. "And a large one for yourself, of course. And, um, a bit of time in the back, if we can."

Shirley smiled as she stuck a glass under the vodka optic and did herself a double.

"Oh go on then, as it's you," she said. "Alf!"

Alfie lumbered over and she told him to open up the back room for us.

"Cheers, love," I said as I paid for the drinks. I put an extra hundred quid down on the bar for use of the back. "Do us a bottle as well will you? This might take a bit."

"Got you," Shirley said, making the money disappear.

We took our drinks and followed Alfie down the narrow corridor beside the bar. He unlocked a door and flicked a light on to let us into what must once have been a dining room or something. These days it was just "the back", and it was where private business got done in the Rose and Crown. Usually that business was buying and selling, nicked cars or vanloads of moody computers or fur coats or fags or whatever it might happen to be that day, but sometimes it was just a good place to have a quiet little chat away from prying eyes.

Whatever had used to be in here was gone and there was now just one long table, with low-hanging lights over it and ashtrays on it and bugger the smoking ban, and a dozen chairs arranged around the sides. There was also a lot of empty space which made this a bloody good place to hurt someone too. Shirley was very understanding about business matters, by and large.

We sat, and Trixie pulled a battered orange plastic ashtray towards her and took her cigarette case out of her handbag. The ashtray was decorated with the logo of a brewery that had gone bust at least ten years ago, I noticed. Shirley came in just then with three glasses and two bottles of scotch on a tray, for all that I had only asked for one, and put them down in front of us. She noticed Trixie had the plastic ashtray in front of her, and tutted loudly.

"No, love, you're guests," she said. "Let me get you the good one."

She came back a moment later with a white china ashtray with a rose painted on the side, and put it carefully down on the table in front of Trixie.

"Thank you," Trixie said.

I grinned at Shirley. "Thanks, love," I said, by which of

course I meant "go away".

She knew that. She went. Shirl knows how things work, bless her, even if Rashid didn't.

"This is pleasant," Rashid said.

He sat back in his chair and stretched, looking for all the world like the overgrown cat he apparently was. He sipped his beer and looked at me.

"This is private is what it is," I said. "As private as I can afford, anyway."

I opened the nearest bottle and poured a healthy measure into each glass. To be fair, I was being pretty free with Trixie's money that night but she always had plenty of it and she didn't seem to care what I did with it, so why not? I *liked* having money, you know?

"Now," Trixie said, and fixed Rashid with one of her cold blue stares. "Time to talk."

"It is always the right time to talk," said Rashid, showing us his long-toothed grin. "It's so much better than the alternative."

There was a long silence. Trixie swallowed her whisky and glared at him.

"I warned you about trying to be mysterious with me," she said. "Don't do it. You obviously wanted to tell us something, so tell us."

"I have said my piece," Rashid said. "The Corrupter of Flesh and Houses has undone my work and now she comes."

"*Who* comes?" I asked him.

He frowned at me. "The one I am sworn against, the one I have always fought," he said. "You know this thing, old friend."

Shit. The Burned Man might well have figured it out by now but it had gone worryingly quiet on me. I didn't have a fucking clue what he was on about, personally. I improvised with the best multipurpose word in the English language.

"Fuck," I said.

"Yes," he said, nodding slowly. "Is old age dulling your wits?"

"Fuck off," I snapped, and suddenly realised the Burned Man had woken up and was talking again. "This isn't fucking funny, Rashid."

"I know this thing," he said, for all that he was still grinning. "This is disastrous."

I gulped my whisky and prayed Trixie didn't say anything to give the game away. I had to keep Rashid thinking I actually *was* the Burned Man, without letting on to Trixie that I even *might* be. It was starting to do my head in, to be perfectly honest with you.

Fill me in you little git, I thought angrily. *Who the buggering hell is he talking about? Who has he always fought?*

Menhit, the Burned Man said. *Her name is Menhit. Run away.*

"Who is 'she'?" Trixie asked me.

"Menhit," I said. "Her name is Menhit."

Rashid nodded again.

"The Black Lion," he said, as though that was supposed to explain anything. "If she comes through, there will be red slaughter. On this plane she will be too strong for me to contain alone. Too strong for us both I think, old friend. Yet with the sky children and the Houngan…"

"An alliance?" I said, or rather the Burned Man did.

Rashid looked thoughtful, and I took the chance to freshen up our drinks. Everyone was a lot more civil now we were all a bit lubricated, I noticed, and I was keen to keep it that way. I glanced sideways at Trixie and saw her cold eyes through the haze of cigarette smoke that surrounded her. Well, almost everyone. I remembered a bit belatedly that she didn't ever seem to get drunk however much booze I poured down her neck.

Shame, the Burned Man thought.

Stop that and be helpful, I snapped at it. *Who the fuck is Menhit?*

Your mythology is woeful, it said. *She's an ancient Nubian war goddess who got turned into an aspect of Sekhmet by the Egyptians and pretty much forgotten about. I don't think she ever forgave anyone for that. Lovely lady. Her name means "The Slaughterer" or "She Who Massacres", if that gives you an idea of her general temperament*

Oh fucking joy. That was just bloody marvellous that was. A war goddess with an axe to grind, just what the world needed.

Is she bigger than you? I asked it.

I could almost feel it spit in my face.

Yeah, she fucking is, it muttered. *She's bigger than every cunt I know. She's a goddess you twat, don't you fucking grasp that?*

"An alliance, yes. I was hoping you might suggest that," Rashid said, for all that I hadn't. "Although we would make strange bedfellows indeed, we five."

"Better the devil you know," I said, thinking of what Adam had said to me. "Sometimes, anyway."

"Indeed," he said, "although the Houngan and your fallen friend seemed to have little love for each other."

"That was the first time Papa had met him," I said, wondering how Rashid knew that. They had had their little spat in the club before he even arrived. "For what it's worth, I think Papa Armand knew this was going to happen, or at least something like this anyway. I think he's been planning for it for some time. Perhaps Adam has been too, for all I know. They're both scheming gits at the end of the day."

All that talk about sides, and coming wars, and choosing which way to walk. Now that I thought about it, it all felt like each of them had known *something* was on its way, anyway. I wondered what either of them might think about me suggesting they work with the other, and suppressed something between a laugh and a shudder. Yeah, that was going to go down like a cup of cold sick, wasn't it?

"As are we all," Rashid said, and drank deep. At this rate we were going to need the second bottle Shirley had brought after all. "One has to be, in this day and age."

"Ain't that the fucking truth," the Burned Man said with my voice, and hurled a forgotten memory at me.

CHAPTER 18

The Burned Man had been delighted with our first little job together, our "live firing exercise" as it had so charmingly put it. I mean, yeah, I was glad to have finally settled my account with Nick Regan and rid the world of a truly Class A cunt, but I wasn't totally sure what else I was supposed to have gained. The Burned Man had been pleased as punch though. As soon as we were done it rattled its tiny chains gleefully at me while I slumped onto the manky sofa in my bedsit.

"Well done, my boy," it said. "We are well and truly in business now."

"What business?" I asked it.

My mouth tasted horrible, and I have to admit I'd been a bit sick on the floor. I really ought to clean that up before the smell in the bedsit got even worse than it usually was.

"*The* business," it said, and grinned at me. "What do you think diabolists are *for*, for fucksake?"

"Well," I said, "I mean, I dunno about that. Not yet, anyway. I'm not sure I'm even really in touch with my True Will yet, and I'm nowhere near making contact with my Holy Guardian Angel. Crowley says in his *Book of the Law* that–"

"Right," the Burned Man snapped, interrupting me. "Tomorrow you're going out and buying yourself some heroin."

"Um," I said. "I... um... What?"

"You heard me," it said. "Aleister fucking Crowley? All right, you can quote Crowley till your arse falls off but you'll never *understand* Crowley until you learn to think like him. And how he thought was smacked out of his fucking head, most of the time. Your turn."

Christ, I thought. I'd never been into drugs. I had grown up on Zammo and "Just Say No" and all that good wholesome Eighties kids' stuff, and it just hadn't been my scene at all. That sort of thing was only for pricks like Nick Regan.

"Do I have to?" I asked it.

"Yeah, you fucking do," it said.

So I did.

It wasn't as easy as all that, of course. This was the early Nineties and everything had been cracked down on hard by then. In those days you had to go somewhere proper nasty to find a dealer, or a "pusher" as they were still called back then. I ended up in the sort of dodgy estate I would never normally have set foot in, wearing my biggest parka to make myself look bigger than I was and trying to act like I hung around in places like that all the time. I was shitting myself, to be perfectly honest with you, and wondering why the fuck I was doing this.

Already I was starting to notice that when the Burned Man really insisted I do something, I did it. If that was the price of the knowledge I craved, then it was a price worth paying as far as I was concerned, but I couldn't help noticing that the price kept getting steeper and steeper.

Anyway, all that aside I eventually found a bloke. He was greasy and spotty and looked like he was about to throw up on my shoes, but he had drugs to sell. Heroin.

Even the word made me feel a bit cold. In case you didn't know, heroin had been the media's favourite boogieman up until they invented AIDS in the mid-Eighties. I had grown up on all the reasons why you didn't go anywhere near that shit, how it was the work of the Devil and one hit would turn you into a junkie for the rest of your life. Some of it was probably true, to be fair, but you know how the media loves a monster. Back then it was very much in my subconscious that you Don't Do Smack. Except I was about to.

I was surprised how cheap it was, relatively speaking. I got what the Burned Man assured me would be a week's worth for eighty pounds, four little twenty quid half-gram plastic bags filled with a slightly poisonous-looking brown powder. I supposed as a first timer I probably didn't need to take all that much, but fuck me, that still seemed ridiculously cheap. It was no wonder there were so many bloody junkies about at that price.

What the fuck would Debbie have said if she could have seen me there, huddled in a doorway with this grotty bloke and buying those little bags of what he called "skag" like I was some miserable addict? Obviously I wasn't about to tell her about it, but even so it made me think. I wasn't about to tell her about the Burned Man either, of course, but I couldn't help noticing that I seemed to be hiding more and more things from her. That was hardly healthy, now was it? Oh fuck it, it was done now and I'd managed not to get stabbed in the process, which was always a bonus in my book. I took my furtive little haul and went back to my flat.

I didn't even know how to take the bloody stuff, but needless to say, the Burned Man did. A few days later I was cooking soggy cotton wool in a spoon like a grubby old pro, my arm red and sore with needle marks and my throat raw with the rancid vinegar aftertaste it seemed to give you. I didn't honestly remember much about it except how bloody ill I had been afterwards.

In fact, up until now I hadn't remembered *anything* about what had basically been a lost week. This was the Burned Man dumping its own memory into my head, I was sure it was. The horrible little thing had been there, after all, doing fuck only knew what to me while I had been off my face.

"I will tell you ten truths, now," the Burned Man had said to me as I nodded in and out of consciousness near the end of the week. "You won't remember them, I know. But they'll be *in* there, in case we ever need them. You understand me?"

I hadn't, at the time. I was too smacked up to understand my own cock that week, if I'm perfectly honest with you.

"The first truth is that I will always fight you," the Burned Man said. "I will fight you for the thing I can never mention, and one day I may win. The second truth is that you will never be in touch with your True Will. *I'm* your fucking Will now."

"S'nice…" I muttered, and nodded out again.

It was still talking, but I was on the nod and only getting snatches.

"The fourth truth is that I will take you, if I ever get the chance," the Burned Man said. "I will take you and use you up and never give you back."

I wavered again, drifting in and out of consciousness. The Burned Man's voice came back to me a moment later.

"The sixth truth is that I will make you do things you can't believe you would ever even consider, and you'll do them willingly. The seventh truth is that one day you might just save the world."

I passed out on the bedsit floor.

•••

I blinked suddenly, wondering why the Burned Man had chosen that moment to dump a fragment of deeply unpleasant and utterly forgotten memory into my head. More than that, I was wondering what the fuck the other five truths had been. And… one day I might save the world? Really?

I looked up and met Rashid's stare. No time like the present, I supposed.

"Are you well, old friend?" he asked me. "For a moment you seemed to be… elsewhere."

I shrugged. "I'm old, sometimes my mind wanders," I said. That wasn't entirely a lie, if I'm honest about it.

"Take care it does not wander too far," he said. "We have plans to make."

"No, we haven't," Trixie said suddenly.

She had gone so quiet I had almost forgotten she was there, but now I looked at her and saw she was very much with us. And she really didn't look best pleased. She mashed her cigarette out in Shirley's posh-for-visitors ashtray along with the other half a dozen she seemed to have smoked while we'd been in the back, and necked her whisky.

"I've had enough of this, we're leaving," she said.

"Trixie…" I started, but she just glared at me.

"I want a word with you," she said. "Alone. We're going home. Your friend here found us once, I dare say he can find us again another day."

I wasn't keen on just leaving with everything still up in the air, but she had the same look on her face now that she had got just before she belted me the other night, and if that happened in front of Rashid he'd know damn well I wasn't the Burned Man after all. Well, most of me wasn't anyway. That, and I had to admit I was feeling a bit scared of her, right then.

"Yeah," I said, bluffing quickly. "Look, Rashid, we'll need

to talk about this first, you understand?"

"Of course," he grinned. "You must confer with your people, as I must with mine. We will speak again soon."

He had "people"? Oh joy, this just kept on getting better.

"Come on, Don," Trixie said.

The three of us filed back down the passage into the pub. It really was late now, or early depending on how you looked at it, and other than Alf there were only four or five people left in there. Even Shirley seemed to have finally gone to bed.

"Cheers, Alf," I said. "Night."

He nodded and let us out, and I heard the bolt shut slide shut again behind us. Rashid turned and bowed, and walked away into the night.

"Home," Trixie said. "Now."

I trailed after her feeling like a naughty schoolboy being dragged home by his mum. We walked down the road in awkward silence. I kept mulling over the chunk of memory the Burned Man had seen fit to dump into my head at that most seemingly inopportune of moments. It must have done it for a reason, I knew. The Burned Man did *everything* for a reason, scheming little git that it was.

That was what had triggered it, I realised. *They're both scheming gits*, I had told Rashid, thinking of Adam and Papa Armand, and then the memories had come. Was that the Burned Man's way of reminding me that it was, too?

I walked beside Trixie with my hands buried in my pockets against the cold, the sound of her high heels clicking on the pavement all I could hear other than the usual background hum of light traffic and the distant wail of sirens that said you were still in South London whether you liked it or not. The sky overhead was overcast, reflecting back the dull glow of millions of streetlights. It made it look like the heavens were on fire.

Perhaps they are, I thought. If there really was some sort of cold war going on in Heaven then I dreaded to think what the sudden appearance of a war goddess on Earth might mean. If she chose a side, that cold war could turn hot very quickly. Suddenly I realised what Trixie was so pissed off about.

"You don't like Rashid, do you?" I asked her as we walked.

"No," she said in a flat voice. "Where do you know him from, exactly?"

"Well, you know…" I said, groping for an answer. *I* didn't know the geezer from a hole in the ground after all, and I could hardly tell her that he seemed to be an old mate of the Burned Man who, oh by the way, is living in my head now and talking for me half the time. "I've met a lot of odd folks over the years."

"Mmmm," she said. "He can't possibly be on our side, Don."

Yeah, I had thought that was where this was going.

"Because of his work, you mean?"

She stopped and rounded angrily on me, her eyes catching the light of a streetlamp and seeming almost to glow in the darkness. She looked so bloody livid it was almost a relief when someone threw a brick at my head.

Trixie grabbed my arm and yanked me out of the way just in time, and the brick shot past me and crashed into the wall beside where I had been standing. Two tosspots in low-slung jeans and baseball caps sneered at us as they advanced out of an alley, the knives in their hands reflecting back the light of the streetlamp.

"Wallet and phone, cunt," the nearest one said, reaching for me.

I saw the look on Trixie's face and winced.

"Handbag," the other one demanded, and gave her a lecherous look. "And then we'll see those tits, love."

Oh dear.

"I beg your pardon?" Trixie asked.

Oh you poor stupid cunt, that really wasn't a clever thing to say.

"Want me to drag you down that fuckin' alley, you slag?" he growled at her.

Trixie hit him so hard I swear he actually left the ground. The Burned Man roared with laughter in my head and I felt my hands getting hotter and hotter.

Shit no, not here! I begged it. We were in the middle of the bloody street after all, early hours of the morning or not. I really didn't need some fucking early doors milkman seeing me set this twat on fire. I needed Trixie to see it even less. *Not in front of her!*

The little shit had his knife up now and looked torn between stabbing me and keeping an eye on Trixie, who had just smacked his mate into unconsciousness.

"Fucking wallet, now!" he demanded.

He really wasn't too bright, this one, was he?

"I'd fuck off while you've still got the chance, if I was you," I told him.

Trixie grabbed him by the shoulder and spun him around, and her other hand whipped across and slapped the knife out of his hand and into the gutter. I think she broke his arm, I really do. Oh well, he'd left it too late to do a runner now. What a shame.

Her arm came back again like it was springloaded and she backhanded him across the side of the face with an almighty crack. He slammed into the lamppost and bounced off in time to meet her fist with his jaw, and that was the end of him.

"Fucking hell," I muttered. "You can't even walk home in peace these days."

She shrugged. "I lived in Rome in the time of Tiberius," she said. "London isn't so bad. Come on."

We left the little shits lying there on the pavement. The time of Tiberius? Fuck me. My history isn't brilliant but... yeah. That was a fucking long time ago. I supposed she would have seen a damn sight worse than those two oiks in the lawless backstreets of ancient Rome. All the same I thought that little bit of excitement might have been enough to make her forget what we had been talking about, but needless to say I was sadly disappointed.

"My Dominion said that Bianakith was doing the will of the Word," Trixie said, as though we had never been interrupted. "If that will was destroying the work of this Rashid, then that makes it a lot more plausible than it looked at first. So the Word opposes whatever it was that he has been doing. If the Word opposes him then so do I, Don. It's as simple as that. I *do not* question the will of the Word."

"No, no, of course not," I said, chancing a look back over my shoulder to make sure the two would-be muggers were still out cold. Of course they were. If *Trixie* hits you, you stay down. Trust me, I should know. "But, well... look Trixie, we've only got the Dominion's say-so for that, haven't we. You said yourself you didn't believe it."

"I said I couldn't believe it was part of the Word's plan," she said. "I never said I thought the Dominion was *lying*, Don. It can't have been. I just... I just don't know. My Dominion wouldn't lie to me, it simply wouldn't. I suppose this just means that the Word is moving so far ahead of what I can perceive that it seems to be nonsensical, but what would I know? I'm just a soldier, it's not for me to question. It doesn't matter. If this Rashid of yours opposes the Word's plan then he is my enemy and that's the end of it."

"Oh," I said.

I must admit I had thought we were a bit past the blind

obedience stage, but perhaps I had been wrong about that. Blind obedience to God Almighty was one thing, I supposed, but I was convinced there had been something wrong about that Dominion this time. If there was a war brewing in Heaven then I wasn't at all sure which side that thing was on. And I wasn't the only one. Papa Armand had certainly thought the same thing, and I knew I could trust him.

Couldn't I?

Oh I was buggered if I knew. It was late and I was pissed and everything was starting to just do my head in, if I'm perfectly honest about it.

"Yeah, fair enough," I conceded. "Look, let's just get home, shall we?"

Trixie gave me another look, then nodded. "Yes," she said.

We got back to mine just after four in the morning, and I felt awkward all over again. It had been a fucking long day, to put it mildly, and I really didn't want to sleep in the sodding office again but, well, after last night, I wasn't sure where we were with anything any more.

"I'm going to the bathroom," Trixie said. "Don't be too long coming to bed."

Oh. OK, I suppose that was where we were then. I mean, yes, obviously I wanted to share a bed with her – I had wanted that almost since I had first laid eyes on her, but if that was *all* we were going to do then I was going to struggle a bit if you know what I mean. Oh fuck it, I'm not that proud. I'd take what I could get.

I took my turn in the bathroom after her and came through to the bedroom to find her already in bed, the covers bunched around her waist. She was wearing that white nightdress again, but then of course I was trying not to notice that. I slipped in beside her and turned the light off.

"Night Trixie," I said.

"Yes," she murmured into her pillow, already half asleep. "It is."

I sighed and turned onto my back, and stared at the ceiling.

It really was, wasn't it?

CHAPTER 19

She only screamed once in the night, and this time I held off waking her until she stopped by herself. Eventually she settled back into a fitful sleep, and I lay back on my pillows and closed my eyes again. So many things weren't right I hardly even knew where to start. Me sharing a bed with the woman of my dreams and not being able to touch her seemed at the time to be pretty much top of the list, if I'm totally honest about it. Still, when you compared that minor frustration to the fact that I had accidentally got myself possessed by an archdemon I now couldn't get rid of, I supposed it paled into insignificance, all things considered. Then there was the small matter of the threat of war in Heaven, Lucifer himself walking around London, a highly dodgy Dominion and an iffy hippy shaman, and the apparently imminent arrival of a goddess called She Who Massacres.

Who'd have my life, honestly?

You there? I thought at the Burned Man.

Always, it replied. *I ain't going to go to sleep when I might miss the chance of you and Blondie getting it on, am I?*

Not going to happen, I thought sadly. *Sorry mate, I wish it was.*

So do I, it said. *You're fucking useless with women, you know that?*

Of course I knew that, but oh how grateful I was to have the Burned Man point that out to me. Not. I sighed and turned over. It was light outside now and I didn't feel like I was going to be getting back to sleep any time soon. *Might as well just face the day,* I thought.

I slipped out of bed as quietly as I could and pulled a robe on over the boxers and T-shirt I had slept in. I eased the bedroom door open and shut it as quietly as I could behind me, letting Trixie have her sleep. I had a feeling she needed it.

I took a piss then went through to the kitchen and put the kettle on. The clock on the cooker said it was eight thirty so I'd had a grand total of maybe three hours actual sleep if I was lucky, and my head was banging from all the booze I had drunk last night. Today was going to be a pleasure then. I made coffee and sat at the table with it, staring out into Mr Chowdhury's back yard. For a moment there I wished I smoked. It would have been something to do, at least.

"Bloody hell," I muttered.

I blew the steam off my coffee and watched a pigeon stalk along the top of the wall, its head bobbing back and forth as it walked. Stupid-looking thing. There was a flash of ginger fur as something hurtled over the wall from the other side, followed by a squawk and a shower of feathers as the pigeon went down.

Morning Rashid, I thought. *Enjoy your breakfast.*

I went through to the office and noticed the light was flashing on the answer machine. I turned the volume right down before pressing play, not wanting to disturb Trixie. The oldfashioned mechanism clicked and rattled as it came to life, playing the tiny cassette tape.

"It's Adam," he said, his voice cutting through my sleep-deprived morning fuzz like a cold knife. "I need to talk to you. Call me."

He read out a mobile phone number and hung up. The machine beeped and rewound its tape with a harsh rattle. I grabbed a pen and paper and replayed the message, jotting down his number this time. Lucifer's mobile number for fucksake – I couldn't help but wonder what *that* would be worth to some of the idiots on the stupid bloody Internet. Whatever was the world coming to?

Did I really want to call him back though, that was the question. Had things got so fucking bad that I was making common cause with Lucifer of all people? *Better the devil you know.* Well, he was the fucking *only* devil I knew, unless you counted the Burned Man. I really had to get their hierarchy straight in my head before much longer. It might be bloody important soon. Experience told me that the Burned Man had outranked Bianakith, in raw power if nothing else, but then they were both archdemons. Where Adam fitted into that as both a fallen angel and a duke of Hell, I had no bloody idea. Still, he was being awfully polite to me since the Burned Man and I had our little meeting of minds, as he had put it. That had to mean something, didn't it?

I picked up the phone and dialled.

"Adam," he said when he answered.

"It's Don," I said. "Don Drake."

"Ah, yes," he said. "Thank you for calling me back, Don. I wasn't at all sure that you would."

"I nearly didn't," I said.

"Yes well, there we are," he replied. "Strange times make for strange bedfellows, I'm sure you will agree."

Strange bedfellows – Rashid had used that same expression, and I liked it even less coming from Adam than I had from him. If either of them thought we were going to be getting that close then they were sadly mistaken. An uneasy alliance was the best anyone could hope for at this point, as far as I was concerned. And I still wasn't even sure about that.

"Something like that," I said. "Question for you – if I said 'Menhit' to you, would you know who I meant?"

There was a long pause. "I would," he said at last.

"Thought you might," I said. "And if I said 'cat statue', how would that grab you?"

"No, now you've lost me I'm afraid," he said. "Did you say *cat* statue?"

"Yeah, as in 'a statue of a cat'. A really fucking old one, buried deep under London. Bronze age, maybe. Possibly Egyptian, from what I can gather."

"Have you started drinking already, or are you still drunk from last night?" he asked me. "How do you suppose there would be a bronze age Egyptian statue of anything buried underneath London of all places?"

"Buggered if I know," I said. "Rashid says he put it there, a long time ago. To keep this Menhit in her box, apparently. Well now it's knackered and she's on her way over here, according to him."

"Rashid," Adam echoed. "Tell me, Don, how did Meselandrarasatrixiel take to your friend Rashid?"

"There wasn't a lot of love at first sight," I admitted. "What's that got to do with it?"

"I'm interested, that's all," Adam said.

I had to remind myself just how little I could trust this posh prick. Adam had set up Charlie Page and his zombie wife to kill me just because he had been *interested* to see what I'd do about it, after all. I knew that even if Adam wasn't exactly my enemy any more, and I still wasn't completely convinced that was the case, he was still a fucking long way from being on my side.

"I bet you are," I said. "You're far too interested in Trixie in general for my liking."

He laughed, the sound like shards of glass flying down the telephone wires to imbed themselves painfully in my eardrum.

"Oh Don, are you jealous? Truly?"

Yeah I fucking am as it happens. Not that I'd have ever have admitted it to that smug wanker of course, but it was true all the same. I knew Trixie was still more than a little bit in love with him, and I hated it. Oh God, how I hated it.

"No I ain't," I said. "Don't be fucking stupid, we're not even the same sodding species."

I blinked. That had to have been the Burned Man speaking up suddenly – I had never even thought of it like that, to be honest about it. But I mean we *weren't*, were we?

"I see," Adam said in a dry tone that made me think he didn't believe a word of it.

Fuck him, he could believe what he wanted.

"Never mind what you see," I said. "What are you going to *do*, more to the point? About Menhit, I mean?"

"What makes you think I would do anything about Menhit?" he asked.

Oh for the love of God, nothing was straightforward with him, was it?

"You're recruiting soldiers for the coming war, Trixie told me," I said. "If a rising war goddess isn't a coming war then I don't fucking know what is."

"Hmmm," he said. "I'm not sure that's *exactly* what she told you now, is it?"

I supposed it probably wasn't, but I'm afraid I couldn't remember her precise words from a conversation we'd had half a year ago.

"What then?"

"Oh, I believe in being prepared, I have to admit," he said, "although my concern is the war in Heaven, not whatever may transpire on Earth. I am very invested in the status quo, you understand – a status quo that has left me free to pursue my own interests for a long time now. A regime change Upstairs would not be at *all* in my best interests, and there may be a very great change afoot indeed unless I can prevent it. If the voices of dissent above can prevail upon Menhit to take their side then that change may become inevitable. She would be a great and terrible weapon indeed, in the wrong hands."

I had to admit it sounded like he had a point there.

"So the cold war might be about to go hot," I said. "You're recruiting soldiers to fucking keep Heaven *safe*, according to you. Papa Armand is trying to get me to choose a path to walk but he won't tell me which is which. Bianakith was summoned by God-only-knows-who to undo whatever Rashid did to keep Menhit away from Earth. Bianakith beat the snot out of Trixie and I killed it too late and now Rashid has appeared out of nowhere spreading his tales of fucking woe. Trixie's Dominion is lying out of its holy arse whatever she wants to think, and she's gradually going batshit crazy on me again. For pity's sake Adam, what for the love of God am I supposed to fucking *do*?"

"I am not," she said quietly from behind me, "going crazy."

I slammed the phone down so hard it's a wonder I didn't break it. The sudden hostile tension in the room was so electric I could feel it making the hairs on the back of my neck stand up. I must admit I was cringing, waiting for the blow that had yet to fall. *Oh fuck me, how much of that had she heard?*

"Trixie…" I started, but it was way too late for that now and I knew it.

"No!" she screamed at me. "No, don't you *dare!* Don't you dare *Trixie* me Don, not now!"

I made myself turn around and face her. She was standing there barefoot in her nightdress, a length of white silk that barely covered her thighs. The expression on her face was pure bloody murder.

"Oh God I'm sorry," I said. "Don't...."

Don't hurt me, I was thinking, and I hated myself for it. I loved her, and I wanted her, and she still scared the fucking life out of me just the same.

It'll never happen again, she had said, but I wasn't too sure how much I believed that.

She glared at me for a moment longer then suddenly sank onto the sofa and put her head in her hands. All the tension drained out of the room at once and I felt myself sag with relief. I wasn't getting a beating then, that was something. I looked at her, and realised just how broken and defeated she looked right then. Her hard, brittle shell had well and truly cracked, hadn't it? I got up and went to her.

"I'm sorry," I said. "Oh Trixie, I'm so sorry, I didn't mean it."

She looked up at me, her long blonde hair falling loose over her eyes.

"You killed Bianakith," she said in a soft voice. "I have no idea how you managed it but you did, didn't you? It beat me."

There didn't seem to be any point in denying it any more.

"Yeah," I admitted.

"I lost," she said.

"Just that one time," I said.

"I never lose," she said, and put her head back in her hands again. "I'm a soldier of Heaven. I am a Sword of the Word. I never lose."

She was crying, I realised. Oh dear God, she was crying, right there in front of me. I couldn't cope with that. I knelt down in front of her and reached out to take her in my arms. She let me hug her for a moment, then tossed her hair back out of her face and met my eyes.

"Mate with me," she said suddenly.

I almost died.

"What?" I managed to croak.

"You heard me. I know you want to. Come back to bed and mate with me."

"I… um…" I said.

Mate with me had to be the least alluring chat up line in history but all the same, this was Trixie for God's sake. Yes, of course I wanted to. Bloody hell, I wanted to so very much. But all the same… I looked at her then, at the blinding white lie of her aura, and my heart sank.

"Show me your real aura," I said softly. "Please, just show me. Just for a moment."

A single tear ran down her cheek. The white illusion disappeared and I looked at her in utter horror. She was more than half gone now. Her beautiful golden glow was a corrupted monstrosity of black streaks and green and purple rot. The black threads were writhing even as I watched, spreading and growing, enveloping the remaining patches of gold as though strangling them. I pulled her into my arms and hugged her tight.

"Oh Trixie," I said, my face buried in her hair. "Oh my poor darling."

This was her bloody Dominion's doing, I was sure it was. I was convinced that thing was teetering on the brink and it was dragging her down with it.

I wasn't fucking having that, but I had absolutely no idea what I could do to stop it.

"I'm all right," she said, that waspish tone creeping back into her voice. "Do you want me or not?"

"Yes," I said at once. "Yes I do, of course I do. You *know* I do Trixie, but…"

But not like this. She wasn't in her right mind, I knew that. Not even a little bit she wasn't. I'd be taking advantage of that, and that would make it basically rape.

Fuck her! the Burned Man urged in my head. *What's fucking wrong with you Drake? Drag her into bed before she changes her fucking mind again.*

Yeah, well, it would say that wouldn't it? The Burned Man had the libido of an alley cat at the best of times, and no morals whatsoever. She was offering herself up on a plate, but it just wasn't as simple as that, was it? Nothing ever fucking was.

"But what?" she demanded, her voice turning chilly.

Oh shit, I was on thin ice now, I knew I was. If I spurned her now, if I left her feeling scorned and unwanted, I dread to think what would happen. Fucking chivalry. I might not be any sort of white knight, but all the same it seemed to keep getting me in hot water.

"I love you," I said at last.

That knocked her right off her guard, and I have to admit I surprised myself a bit with that one. I mean of course I loved her, but I hadn't exactly been planning to say so. I'm not that brave, as a rule. She blinked at me in open astonishment.

"You do?"

"Yes," I confessed, and it really was true. "Yes I do. And I *do* want you, Trixie, more than I can say. But not... not like this. Not when you're just trying to make a point, not when you're upset and hurt and trying to pretend you aren't. When you want *me*, I'll be here."

There was a long pause.

"What if I never do?" she asked.

Ouch. I blinked and swallowed the hurt like bitter medicine.

"I'll be here beside you anyway," I said.

It was true, as well. I would. Pathetic I know, but there we were.

Fucking idiot, the Burned Man said in the back of my head.

"I see," she said. She pulled away from me then, sat back and pulled her nightdress down to cover her legs as much as it would allow. "Well. Perhaps you'd be good enough to find my cigarettes for me?"

"Sure," I muttered.

I rounded them up for her and left her sitting on the sofa smoking while I went to take a shower. A long, cold one. After I was done and dressed I came back through into the office to look for her. She had got dressed too, in pale blue jeans and a tight white jumper that almost undid all the good work my cold shower had done. She didn't seem to have any clothes she *didn't* look sexy in.

She was drinking coffee, and I saw she had made one for me as well and left it on the desk. She was hiding her aura again, I noticed.

"Thanks," I said as I picked it up.

"You're welcome," she said, without meeting my eyes.

Oh good, we were back to bloody awkward again then. All the same, I couldn't even imagine the level of awkwardness we would be at now if I actually *had* taken her to bed. I was sure that wouldn't have ended well, for all that I desperately wished it would have. Ah well, such was life.

"Look," I said, after a moment. "About what you heard…"

"It doesn't matter," she said. "Pride comes before a fall, and I have been proud. I know I have, Don. I admit that. I have been given gifts, and I have become accustomed to them. I have taken my skills for granted, when in reality they had only been lent to me by greater powers. If those skills should have failed me, then obviously it was because I needed to learn a lesson."

"I suppose so," I said.

I supposed nothing of the fucking sort as it went, but I really didn't want to have another argument with her right then. Trixie was coming at this from a position of blind faith, whereas I had rejected that a long time ago. As I saw it, her skills were as great as ever, but Bianakith had overwhelmed her all the same. And I thought I knew why. Oh sure, it was an archdemon, not something even she could have just flicked away with a twitch of her fingers, but all the same that wasn't right.

I am a Sword of the Word, I never lose, she had said, and from what I had seen of her fighting prowess I could well believe it. Before I knew her, Trixie had battled the Furies all by herself for thousands of years. Trixie had killed three devourers singlehanded in one afternoon. Trixie had walked into battle against Wellington Phoenix on a broken thigh and thought nothing of it. Even the Burned Man respected her abilities, I knew that much.

Trixie was death walking, to put it bloody mildly. *Angelus Mortis,* Janice had called her. The Angel of Death. Maybe she wasn't exactly that, not literally anyway, but she wasn't bloody far off it. There was no way Bianakith should have been able to kick her arse the way it had. Unless...

"Look," I said carefully. "Can I talk to you for a moment?"

Trixie blinked at me. "You can always talk to me, Don," she said.

"Yeah well, thanks and all that," I said, "but what 'can I talk to you' really means when people say it is that you might not like what they're going to say, you understand? It's like saying 'please don't hit me when I say this', yeah?"

"All right," she said.

She sat back down on the sofa and put her coffee cup on the floor, and looked expectantly up at me.

"Well, look," I said. "You're right. You *did* lose to Bianakith, but you shouldn't have done, should you? I mean, when we first talked about it, you were sure you could kill it if I kept its aura under control. And that *wasn't* just pride talking,

Trixie. That was simple fact. There's no shame in knowing what you can do."

"I suppose so," she said.

"It was stronger than it should have been, wasn't it?" I said. "I mean, you're realistic about this sort of thing. I know you are. It was you who said it was out of your league while it still had its rot aura active, after all. That's not pride, that's acknowledging what you can do and what you can't. That's just realism, Trixie."

She looked at me for a moment, then nodded.

"Yes," she said after a moment. "I don't pretend to be able to do what I can't, Don."

"No, exactly," I said, warming to the topic now I had her attention. "I know you don't, and that's the whole point. Once I did my thing, you *should* have been able to take it apart, shouldn't you? Something went wrong. Or rather it didn't. Someone was cheating."

"Who?" she asked, and looked up at me. "And how *did* you kill Bianakith anyway?"

No, I wasn't going to tell her.

"Same way I like to play cards," I said. "I cheated more than the other guy did."

"Oh," she said. "So who was the 'other guy' here?"

Well now, this was the tricky bit. This was the bit that was going to get me backhanded through the window and under a bus if she took it the wrong way.

Fucking hell, you shouldn't be this scared of your own missus, should you?

She's not your fucking missus, the Burned Man sneered at me. *She might have been by now maybe if you'd have fucked her when you had the chance but you bottled it, didn't you? You're back to square bleeding one there now aren't you, you daft prick?*

I didn't think I was actually, not quite anyway, but either way I didn't need the Burned Man's fucking relationship advice. I ignored it and ploughed on.

"Well, well look," I said. "I mean, we've established that something must have deliberately summoned Bianakith, yeah?"

"Yes," Trixie agreed. "There's no way something like that could have squeezed through the Veils by itself."

"Right," I said. "And like I said, since we killed Wellington Phoenix, I can't think of a human diabolist who could have pulled that off. I half thought Adam might have been behind it, but I asked him and he denied it, and in all honesty I believe him. I mean, he just doesn't have anything to gain, and Adam never does anything that doesn't have something in it for him, does he?"

"No," Trixie had to admit. "No, I suppose he doesn't."

"Well," I said cautiously, and I have to confess I retreated behind my desk to put a bit more space between her and me. "That only leaves one possibility as far as I can see."

"Oh?"

I sat down in my scruffy leather swivel chair and looked at her across the scarred expanse of desk. I suppose it would buy me another second or two if she decided to go for me.

"Your Dominion," I said.

Trixie fixed me with a frozen blue stare.

"What *about* my Dominion?"

"Well look, it wasn't exactly itself was it, the last time we spoke," I said. "You know as well as I do that it saying Bianakith was doing the Lord's work smells like a bucket of month-old fish. It's not *right* Trixie. The Dominion isn't, I mean. It fucking *can't* be."

"It's not for me to question," she said, but I could see the confusion on her face.

Trixie was a soldier not a general, and a soldier needs a chain of command above her. I knew she put all her faith in the judgment of that Dominion, and followed its orders

without question like any good soldier would have. I'm
sorry but the time for unquestioning obedience was pretty
much over, as far as I could see.

"I know, babe," I said, "not usually it isn't, but come on,
fucking *think* about it."

"No!" she shouted, and lurched to her feet with a
murderous look on her face. "You spurn me and now you
try to turn my face away from righteousness, and–"

"He's right, you know."

I don't know who turned faster, me or Trixie. Well
obviously she did, if I'm honest about it, and she managed
to produce her sword as part of the same fluid movement.
God but I loved that woman.

"All right, Adam," I said.

"Good morning," he said, a wry smile twitching at the
corners of his mouth.

He stepped out of thick shadows that really shouldn't
have been there at the far end of my office and waved a
lazy hand that made them go away. He was as immaculately
dressed as ever, in a dark grey business suit and a sober red
tie. He nodded at me and fixed Trixie with his unnaturally
dark eyes.

"This man Drake speaks the truth today," he said. "About
many things."

Ouch. I knew this bugger could probably listen in on my
conversations, and I had a horrible suspicion he had heard
me confess my love for Trixie. Oh joy, that was bound to
come back and bite me on the arse before much longer then.
All the same, at least he seemed to be backing me up on this
one.

"Oh, does he?" Trixie asked archly.

She still had her sword in her hand, I noticed.

"Yes, I'm afraid he does," Adam said.

He ignored her blade and settled into one of the chairs

opposite my desk, adjusting the crease in his trousers with one careful hand. When Trixie realised he wasn't taking any notice of her sword she made it disappear again.

"Oh," she said.

"There are things afoot, Meselandrarasatrixiel," he said. "Great and terrible things. The prospect of open war in Heaven, for one, and the Dominion you answer to has fallen hard enough to sunder the very plains of Hell with the impact of its coming. It is... no longer what it was."

"But..." Trixie said, and I saw the stricken look in her eyes.

The Dominion was far more to her than just her superior in the chain of command. *My father and my king* she had called it once, or something like that anyway, and I knew she had still been struggling to find an adequate English translation for the words she was trying to express. It was *everything* to her, I knew that. It was her whole reason for doing any of the things that she did. She was so closely linked to it that it was no *wonder* she had been going off the rails if it had actually fallen altogether.

"Oh Trixie..." I said, and trailed off helplessly.

She was staring at Adam, and I knew I couldn't get in the middle of that. I wished I could, don't get me wrong, but I knew it just wasn't going to happen. There are some things you really can't compete with however much you might wish you could.

"Your Dominion has fallen," Adam said with an awful finality. "Bianakith was the Dominion's work, not mine. The unmaking of the Eastern Veil was its doing, and the drawing forth of Menhit is its goal. There will be slaughter in Heaven, Meselandrarasatrixiel, if Menhit joins forces with that Dominion and I *do not* want that. Something *fundamental* will happen, unless we can stop it."

I remembered what Rashid had said to me. Rashid didn't

think he and the Burned Man together were strong enough to stop Menhit, and yet Adam seemed to think he and Trixie could do it between them? Now I'm sorry, but I thought that was a tiny little bit fucking unlikely, if I'm honest about it. But then it would have hardly been the first time Adam had spun someone a yarn, would it? He was *Lucifer* for fucksake.

He was Lucifer, yes, but Menhit was a fucking goddess. *She's bigger than every cunt I know*, the Burned Man had told me, and it knew Adam. I was painfully aware of that fact. No, I didn't think Adam could take Menhit even *with* Trixie at his side. If Menhit joined forces with the fallen Dominion in its war on Heaven... well yeah, I dare say something fundamental *would* happen. I didn't really understand what, but it wasn't going to be anything fucking good was it? It never bloody is.

"I think you might need a bit of help with that, mate," I said, and winced inside.

That had been the Burned Man speaking, or at least I thought it had. God, but I wished I could be sure which thoughts were mine. Even that would have been something, you know what I mean? Having the horrible thing spontaneously speaking with my voice before I even knew what it was going to say really was getting to be a bit too much for me to deal with.

"Oh, do you really?" Adam asked, sudden venom in his razor sharp words. "And who exactly do you think could help *us*, Don?"

I remembered with a cold slug in the guts that he somehow knew what had happened to me. He knew damn well he was talking to the Burned Man now, not me.

"I know people," I said, and suddenly that was me talking again. "I can help. Me and Rashid."

"Rashid," Adam echoed, and Trixie gave me a look as well. It seemed Rashid really hadn't made the best of first impressions as these things went.

"And me," I said, and met Adam's eyes with a hard stare of my own.

And the Burned Man, I thought at him. *I can't say it in front of Trixie and you don't seem to want to either but we both know what I fucking mean, don't we, you wanker?* I mean personally I couldn't give a flying fuck what happened in Heaven, but one thing I did not want was a rampaging war goddess on the loose in the middle of London. All the same, I kept wondering what the consequences of a war in Heaven might actually be. If something *fundamental* changed up there, who knew what might happen down here? No, on balance I really didn't want Menhit making common cause with a fallen Dominion any more than Adam did. We might be coming at this from completely different perspectives, but I'm afraid it really did look like Adam and I were on the same side at that precise moment.

Better the devil you know.

I wondered what Papa Armand would say about me walking down *that* path.

"Yes," Adam said quietly. "And you. Yes, you might make all the difference. And your friend the Houngan perhaps."

I winced. Papa Armand had taken an instant dislike to Adam, and that might be hard to undo. All the same, I nodded.

"And him, if he's up for it," I said.

"Strange bedfellows indeed," Adam mused.

Wasn't that the fucking truth?

CHAPTER 20

Adam fucked off in the end, thankfully, and Trixie went into the kitchen to smoke cigarettes and sulk. It was still early, about ten in the morning by then. I sat behind my desk and drank the end of my cold coffee. I wanted a fresh one but Trixie was in the kitchen and I really didn't want to face her right then.

Your Dominion has fallen, Adam had said, *hard enough to sunder the plains of Hell with the impact of its coming.* That revelation had pretty much broken her, as far as I could see. She lived to serve that Dominion, as its paladin or knight errant or whatever we had decided it translated as. It really didn't matter now. It was gone, fallen, corrupted beyond saving. Where did that leave her, exactly?

She's bonkers, the Burned Man thought at me. *If she wasn't already, she fucking is now.*

I hated to admit it but I had a nasty feeling the Burned Man might be right. I couldn't shake the memory of her true aura, rotting before my eyes.

She'll be fine, I thought. *It's just a lot for her to come to terms with in one go.*

It was a fucking sight more than a lot to come to terms with though, wasn't it? Poor Trixie. As I had said to Adam on the phone, she had been going gradually nuts again, and now at least I knew why. *My father and my king.* I had a feeling it was more like her father than anything else, and the bond was probably even closer than that. Trixie was a very private person and still I didn't really know a great deal about angels even after spending the last six months with her, but... oh bloody hell.

I wondered if the bond had been even closer than that. Had this thing been her *lover?* Not in a sexual way perhaps, but maybe on a spiritual level. All the same I couldn't help thinking of how she had offered herself to me, when she had been at her lowest point. With her Dominion fallen, had she been looking to *me* for whatever it was she needed even if she hadn't known why at the time? Oh fucking hell, that couldn't be right could it? I was nobody's idea of a king, that was for fucking sure.

The Burned Man snorted somewhere in the back of my head but mercifully resisted the urge to take the piss for once. I sighed and sat back in my chair, swivelling it round to stare out of the window.

Oi, I thought at it. *Make yourself useful and fill me in a bit here. This Menhit, is it as bad as I think it is?*

Oh fuck yes, the Burned Man said, and for once it sounded completely serious. *You still haven't got your pin-sized head around this have you? She. Is. A. Goddess. Not an angel, fallen or otherwise. Not an archdemon. Not a Dominion, even. She's a cunting goddess, Drake. There is no other power to equal that of a god, that's practically the fucking definition of the term. If she comes through and sides with this sodding Dominion then whatever it wants, it's getting. End of. If that means the walls of Heaven come tumbling down then that's what'll fucking happen, you mark my words. That's when it's time to find a new planet to live on, if you still aren't getting this yet.*

Fucking hell.

I sighed and pushed my fingers back through my hair. This was getting out of fucking hand. I stared out of the window and tried not to think about it.

I was still watching the world go by twenty minutes later when the phone rang.

"Don Drake," I said.

"Mr Drake, it's Harry."

"Hello Weasel," I said. "I hope you've got something useful for me."

"I have, Mr Drake," he said, lowering his voice to a conspiratorial hush. "Something good."

"Where are you, Weasel?" I asked him.

"At home, why?"

"Then you don't need to fucking whisper, do you? Just tell me what you've got."

"Oh, right," he said, sounding slightly embarrassed. For fucksake he did my head in sometimes, he really did. "Well, look, it's like this…"

What it was like, according to the ever unreliable gospel of Weasel, was that there was something going on. Now I think we all already knew that by then, but this was a little bit different. There was, according to him, a counter movement happening amongst the city's occultists. Adam had his followers as Weasel had told me before, and as I had personally discovered in the short and unpleasant time I had known Charlie Page. That aside though, it appeared there was a new faction amongst the adepts of London. And Weasel said he knew how I could contact them.

"Meet me at Big Dave's in half an hour," I said. "I want some breakfast anyway."

"Yes, Mr Drake," he said.

I tidied myself up a bit, as much as you needed to for Big Dave's café on a Monday morning anyway, and picked up my keys.

"I'm popping out," I told Trixie.

She was sitting at the kitchen window, smoking and staring vacantly into Mr Chowdhury's empty yard.

"All right," she said, without looking at me.

She really, *really* wasn't herself. I shrugged and went. I felt bad for her, but there wasn't a lot I could do about it at the moment, after all.

Weasel turned up while I was halfway through a full English and a blissfully hot cup of strong black coffee. I looked up at him and waved to the seat across from me, still chewing.

"Sit," I said. "Talk."

Weasel sat down and looked at me, his droopy lower lip glistening as he eyed my half-eaten breakfast.

"I could eat," he said.

I sighed and waved Big Dave over.

"Same again for my ugly friend," I said. "And I'll have another coffee, ta."

We sat in silence until Dave came back with Weasel's breakfast and my coffee and fucked off behind his greasy counter again.

"Right," I said. "What have you got?"

"Well," Weasel said, his mouth full of bacon and eggs. "It's this new lot I've found. The Initiates of the Melek Taus."

"Of the fucking what?"

"It means the Peacock Angel, I think," Weasel said. "That's some sort of Yazidi demigod as far as I can make out. You know, from Iraq and all that, although I don't think this bunch are exactly the genuine article. I don't suppose it matters. What *does* matter, Mr Drake, is that some people using that name are organising. Against, you know. Him."

"Adam," I said, and Weasel flinched.

"Mr Drake," he said quietly, "it doesn't do to be using that name in public these days."

"Really?" I said. I'm sorry but I couldn't resist poking him just a bit. "I had him round my flat this morning."

Weasel gaped at me. "That's not funny, Mr Drake," he said.

"It's not meant to be," I said. "I told you before, Weasel, these are the sort of people I hang around with. This is what I fucking do, you understand me? This is what you say *you* want to do."

"But," he said, and gaped some more. "But he's..."

"Yeah, he is," I said, "and I had him round my flat. Think about that for a moment, Weasel. Are you sure you still want to be my apprentice?"

Weasel nodded far too quickly. "Yeah," he said. "Shit yes, I do Mr Drake."

If I hadn't already known he was utterly unsuitable that alone would have been enough to convince me. Ah well, there you go. As I said before, magic wasn't for everyone. Weasel may or may not have had the ability, and I'm not convinced that he did, but in my book he sure as hell didn't have the temperament. He was another Charlie Page in the making if ever I saw one, and we all know how that ended.

"Well, all right," I said. "Cheers Weasel. You got a number for these boys?"

He had better than that, he had an address and an invitation.

"They're looking forward to meeting you," he said.

"You sure about this, Weasel?"

He nodded, his protruding lower lip glistening with spit. "Yeah, I'm sure. I wouldn't lie to you, Mr Drake."

The address Weasel gave me was in the leafy suburb of Totteridge, North London. I took a long, expensive cab ride up to the land of people who thought it was reasonable to spend the best part of a million quid on a three bedroom semi, staring listlessly out of the window as we went. I found myself wondering again exactly why I was still living in a squalid flat above a Bangladeshi grocers on a South London high street, and not coming up with a satisfactory answer other than that I was skint. Some of that was the Burned Man's thinking, I knew, but I have to admit some of it was mine too. Surely Trixie would be happier living somewhere like this, with a nice bit of garden, a good few miles away from the constant wail of police sirens.

Blondie would be happier? Fucking seriously? I coughed into my fist and looked at the floor of the taxi, trying to shut the Burned Man out of my head. All the same, I had to admit it was right. *She's not your fucking missus, you cretin.*

No she wasn't, I knew that. Damn, I knew that all too well. I still wished she was though, all the same. I really, really did.

The cabbie finally pulled up outside the address I had given him and I paid the eyewatering fare. London is bigger than you think, and getting around it by taxi isn't cheap. I got out into the early afternoon spring sunshine and looked at the house. It looked like all the others in the street, a smart 1950s semi-detached with a pair of nearly new BMWs on the drive and freshly mown grass in the front garden. All in all it hardly looked like a den of underground occult activity. I shrugged and walked up the path to ring the front doorbell.

The guy who answered was dusky skinned and bearded, not black or Asian but sort of Persian looking. Maybe Iraqi, like Weasel had said, but maybe not. He was wearing jeans and a black shirt, unbuttoned over a hairy chest with a thick gold chain around his neck. He gave me a blank look.

"I'm Don Drake," I said, on the assumption that might mean something to him.

Apparently it did. He smiled widely and spread his hands

as he gave me a short bow.

"Mr Drake," he said. "Come in, come in. We have been waiting for you."

I followed him into the house and he shut the heavy front door behind me with a solid *thunk*. He ushered me through into the front sitting room, and that's when it all went to hell.

There were five of his mates waiting in there, and each one had a vorehound beside him.

"Oh fuck," I said.

"Kill!" one of them shouted, and as one the vorehounds went for me.

Lots of things happened at once.

"Trixie!" I screamed, before I even really thought about it. "*Help!*"

At the same time I was stepping back, turning, pivoting on my heel and going burning hot and freezing cold all at once as the Burned Man forced its way to the front of my mind and simply took over. Flames erupted out of my hands and I hurled them at the lead vorehound, consuming it in a ball of blazing fire. It howled and burned, careering helplessly into its nearest fellow and setting that ablaze as well. A third hound slammed into my chest and sent me crashing back into the wall. I grabbed it around the throat with both hands, its foul breath blowing hot in my face and slaver flying from its jaws as it started to burn. I snarled back at it and it turned into a furry fireball in my hands. My hands were full now though and the other two were almost on me, baying with a killing fury.

Trixie came through the front window like a missile.

Broken glass exploded across the room around her as she landed on her feet, already attacking. Her blazing sword flashed once, twice, and the vorehounds collapsed in sprays of burning blood. I threw the smoking wreckage of the one in my hands into the fireplace and turned to face the men in the room.

"Initiates of Melek Taus my fucking arse," I snarled, or the Burned Man did.

I wasn't even sure which one of us was driving now, and I didn't care. I've never been a tough guy, not ever in my life. I was always the bookish kid, bullied by wankers like Nick Regan and his mates when I was a lad and then growing up a magician and still being bullied by the likes of Gold Steevie and the Russian.

I'd fucking had enough of it.

Just look how that had turned out for Steevie, since me and the Burned Man reached our meeting of minds. Damn but it felt good to have the boot on my foot for once. It shouldn't have done, I knew it really *really* shouldn't, but it did all the same.

Fuck them.

Fuck them all, and burn in Hell.

Trixie stared at me as flames roared out of my hands and consumed the nearest of the Initiates. He bellowed in agony, burning, falling to his knees and then onto his side, thrashing on the rapidly blackening carpet.

"Burn!" I bellowed.

Everything got a bit hazy after that.

I remember Trixie's sword blazing in her hands, cutting mercilessly as she simply took my word for it that these were enemies. She felled two of them faster than I could even follow, but I was amongst them now, and now the guy who had let me into the house was there too with a double-barrelled shotgun in his hands.

He levelled the shotgun at me but somehow I moved fast, so *fast*, one burning hand slamming into the side of the weapon and knocking it away just in time. It roared and blew a huge hole in the plaster behind me. My hand stabbed out and a gout of fire leapt from my fingers and took him full in the face. He shrieked as he burned.

His flesh crisped and his eyes boiled and collapsed into his head, venting steam. I grabbed his blazing body and dipped my hips and twisted and threw, hurling him into his two remaining friends. They fell against the wall in a blazing heap and I turned on them all, flames streaming from my hands.

"Fucking *burn!*" I remembered screaming at them, and then the ceiling caught fire and I blacked out.

Someone was slapping my face.

"Come *on* Don, I can't carry you forever," Trixie said.

"Shit, sorry," I muttered. "It's OK, I'm awake."

"You are now," she said, and I realised she had me over her shoulder in an undignified sort of fireman's carry.

She put me down and I blinked and looked at her. We were beside some railway tracks, with a high fence on one side and an industrial estate on the other. One of those big self-storage places loomed over the low-rise factory units and lockups. I had no idea how far she had carried me but it looked like we had come a fair few miles from leafy Totteridge.

"Jesus, what happened?" I asked.

She gave me a long, cold look.

"You tell me," she said at last.

I swallowed as I remembered bits of it, disjointed images of fire and death.

Oh fuck.

"Look, Trixie..." I said, tailing off helplessly. I was afraid this was beyond even my powers of bullshit.

"You called for my help and I came," she said. "That's fine, Don. You know I'll always come. That's what I'm for. But you didn't need me, did you? Not really. You slaughtered them, just like you slaughtered Bianakith when I couldn't."

Oh fuck me, this could get ticklish really easily.

"I did need your help," I said. "There were six of them, and five vorehounds, and he had a gun and..."

And what? I couldn't really remember much of what had happened, to be perfectly honest, but I was pretty sure it was much like what had happened to Gold Steevie and his boys. The look on Trixie's face told me everything I needed to know.

"We had to run," she said. "The house was on fire. And the one joined on to it."

"Oh," I said. "Well look, I mean if you hadn't carried me out of there I'd have burned with it, wouldn't I? I *did* need you, Trixie."

She shook her head.

"How, Don?" she asked me. "How did you do that, exactly? I saw you nearly get shot and I thought... I thought... I nearly *lost* you, Don. And then they were all dead and you looked at me and your hands were still burning and for a moment there you looked for all the world like you were going to attack me too. How, exactly, did you do that?"

She was trembling, I realised, and she looked alarmingly like she might be about to cry. I pulled her into my arms and hugged her.

"I don't know," I lied, but actually I suppose that was sort of true. If you squinted at it, anyway. I mean I *didn't* really know how the Burned Man did what it did through me, did I? "I don't know. It's just.... something I can do now."

"But *how?*" she asked.

Something in her voice was painfully reminiscent of the time she had asked me how Aleto had been so strong the last time she had faced her. Adam had been cheating then, of course, and now the Burned Man was doing the same thing through me. Would it really attack her while I was blacked out? I honestly didn't know, and that frightened the life out of me. I loved her, and I knew I wouldn't be able to live with myself if I hurt her. I could hardly tell *her* that though.

"I don't know," I said again. "But if it happens again, run. Just leave me to it and run."

Trixie pulled back and looked at me for a long moment, then nodded.

"Yes," she said, and the sadness in her eyes was almost heartbreaking. "Yes, I think perhaps I will."

We walked a long way in silence after that, listening to the distant sirens of the fire engines.

CHAPTER 21

I wanted a little word with Harry the Weasel. To put it fucking mildly.

It wasn't hard to round him up now that I knew where he drank. We both went that evening, to avoid any misunderstandings about whether I was serious or not. Trixie turned more than a few heads in the shitty dive of a pub that Weasel called his local, for all that I had told her to dress down. Trixie's idea of dressing down was leggings and a T-shirt. Leggings, for fucksake. I could hardly take my eyes off her as I followed her into the pub, and I wasn't the only one. Even I had put some jeans on for once, and dug my battered old leather bomber jacket out of the back of the wardrobe. This really wasn't the sort of place you went to in a suit if you could help it.

"Oi," I said, when I saw Weasel standing at the fruit machine.

He almost jumped out of his skin. He was wearing new Nike trainers and a new tracksuit and a big tasteless gold ring, like he'd recently come into some money. I dare say he had, at that. I hoped he had asked for a *lot* of money to sell me out. I hoped he had enjoyed it too, because I'd be fucked if he was going to enjoy the consequences of it.

"Mr... Mr Drake," he said, turning to stare at us with a panicky look in his lazy eye. "Ma'am."

"Hello," Trixie said. "I think you should come with us."

To be fair to the little bastard he at least had the sense not to make a fuss. I could only assume he had figured out that being dragged out of his local on his ear by a woman that looked like Trixie wouldn't do much for what little reputation he had. We bundled him into our waiting taxi and took him back to my office.

Trixie left me to it after that, and went through to the kitchen to have a smoke. I shoved Weasel into my workroom and shut the door behind us. I pushed him into the centre of the circle and forced him down onto his knees, making myself not look at the inanimate fetish that had once contained the Burned Man. I didn't want to think about that right then, not after what had happened.

"Do you know the difference between Heaven and Hell, Weasel?" I asked him.

He nodded, but I ignored him. By then I couldn't give a fuck what he thought he knew.

"Right now, in this room, you're on Earth," I said, "but you're about to go to one or the other in the next few minutes. Heaven for you is my office, the other side of that door. In Heaven there's a comfortable sofa, and a cup of coffee and a fag. Maybe a whisky, if you want it. That's Heaven. Does that sound good, Weasel?"

He nodded again, and I could see the fear in his eyes. *Good*.

"Hell..." I started, and I looked down at him.

I had to admit I didn't really know how to do this sort of thing. I know I'd promised Trixie that I wouldn't bully the Weasel again but that was before he set me up to get killed. I wasn't having that. I thought of Gold Steevie. What would

Steevie have said, before I melted him to the floor of his warehouse?

"Hell is a lockup about twenty minutes' drive from here. Hell is boltcutters and blowtorches, and having your fingers and toes cut off. Hell is nasty little hammers and chisels, and losing all your teeth without anaesthetic."

Weasel whimpered, but he still wasn't talking. I glared at him. I glared at him, and I remembered Lavender. Oh dear God, yes, I remembered Lavender, who had been Wellington Phoenix's pet torturer. I had met Lavender once, under very unpleasant circumstances. I didn't think I would *ever* forget Lavender. I leaned forwards and got right in Weasel's face, keeping my voice low.

"Hell is what the IRA used to call a six pack. Hell is having your wrists and elbows and knees destroyed. Hell is power drills and plastic explosive and me deciding whether or not you get to ever walk or feed yourself again, you little *cunt*."

Weasel broke.

It was hardly surprising, all things considered. I had too, when Lavender had given me much the same little speech. Adam had sent Lavender to Hell with a .50 calibre bullet through the face, and I sincerely hoped he was still screaming down there. I like to think he was, anyway.

Weasel started to talk.

"It was a lady, Mr Drake," he confessed, his lazy eye weeping slowly onto his stubbled cheek. "An American lady."

"Oh yeah?" I asked. I had a sudden nasty suspicion that I knew who he was talking about. "Did she by any chance have a big feather fan?"

Weasel nodded eagerly. "Yeah," he said. "Them big ones with what look like eyes on the end of them. Peacock feathers, I think."

I nodded. I knew who that was all right. Miss Fucking

Marie. I had been sure she was taking an unhealthy interest in me and my affairs, and it looked like I had been right. One day I'll learn to listen to myself, I promise.

"And what did she promise you, Weasel?" I asked him. "What was my life worth?"

"Five grand," he said.

I kicked him in the face.

"Five grand?" I shouted at him. "Is that fucking *all*?"

Weasel snivelled and picked himself up off the floor.

"I'm sorry, Mr Drake," he said.

For fucksake. Five grand? That was a fucking insult.

"Is that all you think I'm worth, Weasel?"

"I'm sorry," he said again. "I've got debts."

"I don't give a fuck what you've got," I snarled. "You sold me out to the peacock woman for five cunting grand, you little *shit!*"

I raised a hand and he cowered, and suddenly I felt about three inches tall. What the fuck was I turning into? I was no Nick Regan, I knew that much. At least, I hadn't been. I looked at the empty fetish that used to contain the Burned Man, and I thought about where the Burned Man was now. I swallowed. I had changed recently, that much was for bloody certain.

"Get up, Weasel," I said.

He gave me a fearful look. I held a hand out to him and eventually he took it, and I pulled him up onto his feet.

"I'm sorry, Mr Drake," he whispered.

I sighed. "Yeah, you are," I said. "You're a sorry little bastard all right. Get in that office."

He scurried out of the workroom and I followed him, shutting the door carefully behind me. I knew Trixie wouldn't set foot in there unless I physically shoved her in, but all the same, the last thing I wanted was her catching sight of that fetish in its current state. She might be a bit naive but that would have given the game away good and proper.

"Sit," I told Weasel, pointing at the chair opposite my desk. "I'm going to make some coffee. And Weasel, don't even think about doing a runner. If you're not still glued to that chair when I come back I'll hunt you down and then I really will hurt you, you understand?"

He nodded miserably and I went through to the kitchen. Trixie was standing at the window with her back to me, staring out into the darkness.

"Is he still alive?" she asked without turning around.

"Yeah, 'course he is," I said. "Jesus, what do you take me for?"

"I'm not sure any more," she said.

I winced. That hurt, I have to admit.

"Look," I said. "Look, Trixie, about today. I–"

"No," she said. "Don't, Don. If there's something you don't want to tell me then there we are, but please don't lie to me again."

"Right," I said. "Well, OK. Fair enough."

I filled the kettle and stood in awkward silence while it boiled.

"I'll have a coffee if you're making," she said, and it seemed that was the end of it.

I made three cups and took mine and Weasel's back through to the office. At least he was still there. That was something, I supposed.

"Right," I said as sat down across the desk from him. "Start fucking talking, you little git."

Weasel sighed and put his head in his hands.

"I didn't know it was a trap," he said. "Not at first, anyway. There was people talking, see, about how they wanted to meet you, and I said I knew you and I could set it up. For a fee, like. I mean, ain't nothing free, is there, Mr Drake?"

"No," I said. "Not in this life there's not. So were they really organising against Adam or did you just fucking make that up?"

"I... I sort of made that bit up," he confessed. "Like a sweetener, you know, to get you interested like."

I sighed. Weasel was one of those people who was just clever enough to get himself into trouble, if you know what I mean.

"So then what?" I asked him.

"Well, they offered me a bit more than I was expecting, and I got suspicious."

"So that was when you came running to warn me, right?"

He had the good grace to hang his head in shame, at least.

"I needed the money," he said. "I've got debts, and the sort of blokes I owe money to weren't going to take no for an answer. I had to."

"No, you fucking didn't," I said. "Oh whatever, Weasel. I shouldn't expect any better from the likes of you, I know that. Who were these people?"

"Just some blokes," he said. "Persian geezers, from Iraq or somewhere. Maybe they really were Yazidis, I dunno, but I kinda doubt it. Anyway they took me to this posh gaff up North London and that's where I met the lady."

"The American lady with the fan, right?"

He nodded. "Yeah," he said. "Her and some young blonde bird – I think she was her girlfriend, like. They was all over each other when we came in. Anyway, these geezers brought me in and she chased the blonde one out so we could talk. Turned out she wanted a word with you. A... you know, a bit of a stern word as you might say. So I made a deal with her, and she paid me five grand. Shit, they didn't hurt you, did they, Mr Drake? I mean, you look all right."

"Six of them and their pet demons tried to kill me," I said. "Didn't work."

"Fucking hell…"

"What's her name, this American woman?" I asked. I mean by then I damn well knew who she was, but I wondered if she had even bothered to make up a fake name for Weasel.

"Marie something or other," he said. "Dunno what, the geezers all just called her Miss Marie."

Obviously not. That's how sure she had been that this was going to work. I glared at him for a moment, thinking back over what he had said. Something was nagging at the back of my mind and it wasn't just the presence of the Burned Man. Something he'd said…

"A young blonde bird," I said suddenly. "What did she look like, this little blonde?"

"Cracking," Weasel said, with an unpleasant leer. "Bit *too* young really but, well, you know. Posh, too."

"Did you get a name?"

He shrugged. "I dunno. Some posh bird's name. Jo… Josephine? Joanna?"

"Jocasta?" I suggested.

"Yeah, fuck, that's it," he said.

Fucking hell. That was a turn up for the books. I wondered if Papa Armand knew. He was either up to something very clever or he was being had, and I wasn't sure which it was. Either way, something wasn't right about this.

"When was this, exactly?" I asked him.

"Day before yesterday," he said. "About, I dunno, five-ish?"

I nodded.

"Keep quiet," I said, and picked up the phone. I punched Papa Armand's number from memory.

"Papa?" I said when he picked up. "It's Don."

"Don-boy Drake, good to hear you," he said, and I could hear the big grin in his voice.

I hated to take that cheerfulness away from him, I really did, but I knew I had to.

"Papa, I need to ask you something," I said. "Where were you the day before yesterday at five pm?"

"Home," he said. "Watching the football. Why?"

I cleared my throat. "Was Jocasta with you?"

He paused. "No," he said. "She was out, visitin' with her sister."

Was she fuck as like.

"Look, Papa," I said, "I think I need to talk to you. Do you fancy a beer?"

"I don' think I'm going to like what you have to tell me, am I?" Papa said. "All right, we'll drink together. I'll come you, you tell me where."

I had a feeling that meant he didn't want to have to explain me in the sort of swanky Knightsbridge bars he probably frequented when he wasn't at Wormwood's, but whatever. It saved me the cab fare over the river if nothing else. I gave him the address of the Rose and Crown, and then had a sudden vision of him swanning into the place in a tailcoat and top hat. I could just picture the look on Shirley's face if he did that, not to mention what some of the local lads might have made of it.

"Oh, and Papa? Dress down. Really, dress down."

"Sure," he said, and hung up.

I looked at Weasel. "We're going for a beer," I said.

"We are?"

"Yeah, we are."

To be fair it was getting late by then, but the Rose and Crown didn't have much of a concept of closing time as I've said. I went through to the kitchen to tell Trixie.

"I need to see Papa about something," I said. "Me and Weasel are meeting him for a beer at the Rose and Crown if you fancy it?"

She turned and looked at me, her face expressionless. I swallowed. Perhaps that *hadn't* been the end of it after all.

"All right," she said after a moment. "Yes, why not?"

We made a jolly little group walking down the street, me in jeans and a jumper and my old leather jacket, Weasel in his garish new tracksuit and Trixie still wearing those bloody leggings I could hardly take my eyes off. She had put on a short coat that at least covered her arse, that was something I supposed. No one was really talking to anyone else, admittedly, but other than that all was well. I sighed inwardly. *Oh we happy three*.

We got to the pub in about fifteen minutes, and it must have been nearly eleven by then. I herded Weasel to the bar with me while Trixie claimed a table for us in the corner.

"Evening, Duchess," I said.

Shirley turned her twinkling eye on me and smiled.

"Hello duck," she said. "Pint and a G&T, is it?"

"Please darlin'," I said. "And whatever this article is drinking."

"Pint please," Weasel muttered.

He looked nervous, and no wonder. What with his track record and the sort of place the Rose and Crown was, there were probably people in there he'd rather not be seen by. Well that was just tough. I glared at him for a moment, then felt a faint spark of pity. The poor little bastard was obviously shitting himself.

"Do us a round of chasers as well, will you, love," I said. "And one for yourself, obviously."

Shirley's smile widened as she stuck a glass under the optic and sorted herself a large vodka and tonic, then three whiskies as well as our beers and Trixie's gin and tonic. That lot was a bit of a juggling act to get back to the table but me and Weasel managed it between us. Blokes don't make two trips from the bar, you know what I mean? Fuck knows why not, thinking about it, but I've never met a geezer who wouldn't rather try to carry five glasses at once than go back for the others. I dunno, it must be a bloke thing, by which I mean it's basically stupid.

We sat down with Trixie and she got up to visit the ladies. I couldn't help noticing the way Weasel stared after her like a dog with the itch. I jabbed him sharply in the ribs.

"You can pack that in right now," I said.

He gave me a wounded look. "I'm only looking, Mr Drake," he said.

"Yeah well fucking don't," I said.

"Ain't no harm in looking," he muttered, picking up his pint.

"There's a whole world of harm in looking at *her*, you understand me?"

He sighed and nodded, and I realised I probably ought to have a bit of a word with myself again. She wasn't my old lady, and he wasn't my slave to push around however I pleased. I knew that. *I* knew that, but I wasn't too sure the Burned Man did. Or more likely it did and it just didn't care.

"Look, Weasel…" I started, but then the pub door opened and Papa Armand walked in.

To be fair he *had* dressed down, just like I'd asked. He was wearing jeans with a pair of old boots and a white T-shirt and a black leather jacket that hung in folds from his thin shoulders. He wasn't wearing his hat, thank fuck, and the pub lights gleamed from his shiny bald head. He had a very sculpted looking skull, like he had been designed for maximum aerodynamics. He might have looked a bit like the missing black member of the Village People, but for once he wasn't dressed like a Houngan at all. And that made no fucking difference whatsoever.

I saw Billy from the market turn and stare at him as he came in. Billy's black but he's every bit as English as I am, but as soon as he set eyes on Armand he crossed himself right there in front of everyone and stood with his head bowed as the old man passed.

"Papa," I distinctly heard him say.

Jesus, some people just can't be inconspicuous can they? I waved and he headed over.

"Hi Papa," I said. "What're you drinking?"

He grinned and shook my hand before he sat.

"In here, I think lager," he said.

That was probably for the best. I mean, I'm sure Shirley had some cooking-grade supermarket rum behind the bar but I couldn't imagine it would be up to his standards. I got up to get him a pint, and met Trixie on her way back from the ladies.

"Papa Armand is here," I said.

She nodded and returned to the table without speaking. Oh this was going to be a fun night all round, wasn't it? I got him a pint and a whisky as well. I had no idea if he even drank whisky, but we all had one and I didn't want him to feel left out. By the time I got back to the table he was already flirting with Trixie, which was no more than I expected.

Weasel gave me a wounded look as much as to say "why is it all right for him to make fresh with her and not me" but I ignored him. If he had to ask how things like that worked he would never understand.

"Cheers," I said, raising my pint.

Glasses were rather half-heartedly clinked together, out of tradition rather than any sort of real enthusiasm. Papa Armand gave Weasel a pointed look.

"I don' know your friend," he said.

"Papa, this is Harry the Weasel," I said. "Weasel, this is Houngan Armand. Show him some respect."

Weasel nodded weakly and held out a limp hand to shake. Papa ignored it.

"Why?" he asked.

Why is he here? He's here because he caught your jailbait girlfriend making out with your... what? Your rival? Your enemy? I realised I didn't even know what the mysterious Miss Marie was to Papa Armand, other than that every time I had seen them in Wormwood's club together they had been arguing and looking murder at each other. It suddenly occurred to me that if they were playing some sort of weird threesome sex game I was going to look like a prize pillock. I mean it probably wasn't likely, but to be honest I wouldn't have put it past him. I don't think I'd have put much of *anything* past him, now that I thought about it.

"Weasel works for me," I said, for the sake of a better explanation. "He was approached by some people, some Middle Eastern geezers calling themselves the Initiates of the Melek Taus."

"Yazidis?" Papa asked at once.

Not much got past the old goat, you had to give him that.

"Nah, I don't think so," I said. "I think they're just calling themselves that. All the same, the peacock imagery probably resonated with them, if you know what I mean."

His eyes narrowed suspiciously and he downed his whisky with a practised flick of his wrist. "Oh yeah?"

"Marie," I said, my eyes holding his steady gaze across the table. "Miss Marie of the peacock feather fan. She put these wankers up to setting a pack of vorehounds on me."

"You still here," Papa Armand said. "Guess it didn't work."

"Oh it worked all right," I said. "We fought them, me and Trixie. We won."

He nodded and gave her a slow sideways look that I could see damn well lingered longer on her thighs in those bloody leggings than it should have done.

"Madame Zanj Bèl don' take any shit," he said, and laughed.

His laugh was so rich and dark and simply joyous that I forgave him instantly. Once again I thought I could see the kindly, smiling face of Papa Legba wavering in the air in front of him, with his battered old straw hat and corncob pipe. There was just something about Papa Armand, you know? Something fatherly that made you love him, and made you want him to love you back. I guess that's the mark of a really good priest.

"Nor does Don, these days," said Trixie.

Her voice was flat, not accusing but certainly not condoning either. It was as though she was stating a simple fact, like how much two plus two added up to. She sipped her gin and stared into the air over my left shoulder.

"Mmmm," Papa Armand said. "No, I don' 'spect he does."

I swallowed. Papa was staring at me now, a fixed, level stare that was no longer kindly or smiling. I couldn't help but wonder… I mean, it had been his idea in the first place, hadn't it? It had been Papa who had told me how to bind the Burned Man into a talisman to take it to face Bianakith, and to be fair, he had warned me the genie might not be too keen on going back into the bottle afterwards if I had to release it. Had he known what was going to happen? If he had even suspected and not told me, then we were going to have a fucking issue over it sooner or later, as far as I was concerned. I looked from him to Trixie to Weasel, and had to accept that this was neither the time nor the place to be having that conversation. I drained my pint.

"Same again, folks?" I asked.

When we were settled with a second round and everyone had loosened up a bit, I prodded Weasel in the ribs and nodded towards Papa Armand.

"Now would be a good time for you to tell us a little story," I told him.

So Weasel told Papa what he had told me, about the Iraqi

geezers and how they had taken him to Miss Marie's house. About how Jocasta had been there, sitting half naked on Miss Marie's ample lap until she shooed her out of the room so she could talk business. Just the way Armand had shooed her out when I had visited him, I realised.

Papa's face set like a stone. OK, so this obviously *wasn't* some weird threesome thing then. Oh dear.

"My Jocasta," he said. "You sure, Don-boy?"

I shrugged.

"No," I confessed, "I can't be *sure,* I suppose. I wasn't there, and Weasel has never met your Jocasta, but... well, come on Papa, what are the odds of it being a *different* teenage blonde called Jocasta who moves in our circles? Pretty slim, right?"

"Fucking anorexic," Papa said. He glared at Weasel until the poor little bastard looked like he was going to wet himself in his horrible tracksuit. "I don' like this."

"No," I said. "No, I never supposed you would, Papa, and I'm sorry to be the one to tell you but I figured you'd want to know all the same."

"Yeah," he said. "I want a cigar."

He got up and necked the end of his pint, and Trixie stood up too.

"I could do with a smoke," she said. "I'll come with you."

They headed outside together, leaving me at the table with Weasel. Damn, sometimes I really did wish I smoked too. If only it wasn't such a rank habit I might have taken it up myself.

"That went fucking well," I muttered.

"I did what you said though, right Mr Drake?" Weasel said. "I told the black fella what happened."

"Yeah, and didn't that just make his fucking day?"

Weasel nodded glumly and sipped his beer. I still didn't know who Miss Marie was exactly, but it was plain as day Papa Armand was furious that his bird had been seeing her as well as him. Whether that was down to the infidelity or the disloyalty or a bit of both I didn't know, but I dare say it didn't matter. Either or both, I had a feeling little Princess Jocasta was going to grow up bloody fast when Papa caught up with her. I mean, I didn't really condone him shagging a bird that young, but if you want to play in our circles then you have to learn the rules pretty quickly.

Me and Weasel sat and drank in sullen silence. I didn't want to talk to him, and apparently he didn't dare try to strike up a conversation with me. That was fine. The Rose and Crown wasn't a chatty place at the best of times really. Most of the geezers who went there either came to do business, which generally happened in the back, or just to get pissed. Getting pissed doesn't require a lot of conversation as it goes.

I was starting to wonder when Papa Armand and Trixie would be coming back when a bloke walked up to our table. I supposed a cigar probably took longer to smoke than a couple of fags and no doubt she was waiting for him to finish just to be polite, but when I looked up and saw the size of this geezer, I have to admit I wished she was at the table with us. He was Russian by the looks of him, or maybe Polish. You can just tell from looking sometimes, get me?

"Harry Weasel," he said in a thick accent, like he thought it was really his last name.

He loomed over us in a scuffed black leather blouson jacket and tight jeans that strained over his meaty thighs, his broken-nosed face a butcher's block of old faded scars beneath his cropped hair. He might as well have had a sign saying "hired muscle" hanging around his neck.

Weasel gulped.

"Nah," he said. "You've got the wrong bloke, mate."

"Fuck you," Russian Muscle said, and grabbed Weasel by the front of his tracksuit.

He dragged Weasel out of his seat with both hands,

ignoring me completely. That, as it went, was fucking rude of him. I glanced towards the door but there was still no sign of Trixie. That was probably best, I thought. A gorgeous blonde beating up a Soviet hardman in the Rose and Crown would have upset the local ecosystem beyond my ability to imagine. The world just didn't *work* like that around here.

"Oi," I said, and caught his eye.

"You got a fucking problem?" he said.

He let go of Weasel with one huge hand and stuck it in my face instead.

"Yeah," I said. "I fucking have as it goes."

I grabbed his hand and squeezed. I felt the muscles in my forearm clench with a strength I had never known before, and my hand closed like a hydraulic vice around the bloke's meaty paw.

"Weasel is a greasy, lying, treacherous little shit," I said, "but he's *my* greasy, lying, treacherous little shit. You understand?"

My hand closed tighter, and I heard bones crunch in my grip. Russian Muscle let go of Weasel altogether and stared at me, his eyes bulging in his ugly scarred face. His other hand dipped towards the back pocket of his jeans and came out with a blade in it.

Oh you twat, the Burned Man thought.

I surged to my feet with a snarl. The Burned Man was driving now, I already knew that. *Don't burn the fucking pub down*, I begged it. Shit, I *liked* the Rose and Crown, you know? It seemed like the Burned Man knew that too. I hit the geezer instead, my left fist slamming into his solar plexus so hard I felt his sternum crack. He folded around me and collapsed in a wheezing heap, almost taking the table over with him as he went.

Alfie was there then, the baseball bat he kept behind the bar raised in his hands, and a moment later Trixie stepped

back into the pub with Papa Armand behind her. I ignored
the lot of them and stared down at Russian Muscle. He was
finished, from what I could see.

"Fuck a duck, Don," Alf said. "Where did you learn to hit
like that?"

I shrugged, embarrassed. Obviously all this kung fu shit
was coming from the Burned Man, not me. All I knew was
my hands hurt like hell again, but at least nothing was on
fire this time.

"Thanks, Mr Drake," Weasel said in a shaky sort of voice.

Shirley had come out from behind the bar now too, and
she was standing beside Alfie in her high heels and too-tight
skirt looking down at the twitching Russian bloke.

"Get him out of here, Alf," she said. "I ain't calling a
bleedin' ambulance, it's bad for business. Ambulances come
with rozzers and no one wants that in here."

"Yes, Ma," Alf said.

He hooked the huge Russian geezer under the armpits
with both hands and dragged him towards the door. I
doubted anyone would see him again, or miss him for that
matter. The Rose and Crown was that sort of place, if you
know what I mean.

"Sorry about that, Shirl," I said.

She smiled at me. "Don't you worry about it, duck, he
started it I'm sure," she said.

He had, to be fair, but I knew damn well it wouldn't have
mattered either way. Shirley was a sweetheart like that, and
very understanding about business.

"Thanks, Duchess," I said, before Trixie came and got in
my face.

"What exactly do you think you're doing?" she hissed at
me.

I swallowed. "He was after Weasel," I said. "I, um... Yeah.
I talked him out of it."

"I don't know what's got into you, Don," she said, "but I don't think I care for it."

You don't know the half of it, Blondie, the Burned Man sniggered.

"Yeah, sorry," I said. "Won't happen again."

Papa Armand sat back down at the table as though nothing had happened.

"Thank you for tellin' me, Don-boy," he said.

I nodded. "What are you going to do about Jocasta?"

"I don' know yet," he said. "Maybe something, maybe not."

"Who is this Marie anyway?" I asked him.

"Oh, ol' friend. Ol' enemy. Just business to start with, but some things happen that she take personally, you know?"

I didn't, particularly, but I supposed it wasn't really any of my business. What *was* my business was that she had tried to have me killed.

"And why the hell does she want *me* dead?"

He chuckled. "You gettin' conspicuous, Don-boy," he said. "Pushing Wormwood around."

A mortal speaking to an archdemon like that, shoving him around, I remembered Marie saying to me. *That's the sort of thing that gets a man noticed, and that kind of notice isn't always good if you take my meaning.*

Obviously not.

"You and Madame Zanj Bèl," Papa added. "She conspicuous too."

I glanced sidelong at Trixie, at her blazing white lie of an aura. I had to admit he had a point there.

"I suppose," I muttered.

"Someone like you, gettin' too powerful too quick, you know how it is. Some people think it best to just get their revenge in first."

I sighed. Jesus, I needed more enemies like I needed a

dose of the clap. I wondered if that would be the end of it, and decided it almost certainly wouldn't.

"Look, Papa," I said. "I don't know what's between Marie and you and if it's personal then I understand that, but... well, I don't need any more of her boys trying to feed me to their dogs, you know what I mean?"

"Oh, that won' happen," he said, and there was a grim set to his mouth now that I don't think I'd ever seen before. "Papa talk to Guédé tonight. Papa sort this *bitch* out, don' you worry 'bout that."

The Guédé are the death spirits of Haitian Vodou, in case you didn't know. Papa Armand wasn't fucking about with this one.

CHAPTER 22

Weasel and Papa Armand went their separate ways when we left the pub, and Trixie and I headed home.

"I think it's fair to say it's been a hell of a day," I said as I unlocked the front door and held it open for Trixie.

She gave me a flat look.

"Yes," she said.

I winced and locked the door behind me then followed her up the stairs. Trixie could smell a rat, I knew she could. Now I knew there was no way she could know what had really happened but she obviously knew *something* wasn't right with me. I followed her into my office.

"Look, Trixie," I said. "I... Fuck. I don't know what to say. That geezer in the pub, he just... I mean, he was going to drag Weasel off to God only knows where, kick the snot out of him or worse. What was I supposed to do, just let him?"

"Absolutely not," she said. "Weasel is your villein, I understand that, and you are his manorial lord. Or however you'd phrase that sort of relationship these days, I don't really know. Either way, he serves you and so you have a responsibility for his welfare. You did the right thing."

I blinked at her. That was a very medieval way of looking at it, but I supposed she was right. It *did* sort of still work like that in London's underworld, in all honesty. I mean, if you worked for a gangster and someone came and leaned on you, you didn't go to the Old Bill now did you? Of course not, you went to your gent and he sorted it for you. Hell, the gangsters around here still referred to their territory as their manor. Funny how these things carry on down the centuries even if people might not realise where they originally came from.

"Right," I said.

"You did the right thing," she said again, "but I'm not sure how. That man was twice your size Don, and nothing caught fire this time. I know that was magic before, and I can accept that magic is what you do even if I don't always understand how you do it. Tonight though, tonight you fought like a warrior."

"Uh, thanks," I said.

"But you're *not* a warrior," she said. "You *know* you're not, Don. You've told me as much yourself before now. But you felled that man with your bare hands without taking so much as a scratch."

"Yeah well," I said, "that's a kind of magic too, you know what I mean?"

It was as well, if you squinted at it. Obviously that had been the Burned Man moving me, feeding strength to my body and skill to my hands the same as it had at Marie's house. If that wasn't magic I didn't know what was, albeit not quite in the way Trixie meant. Although now that I thought about it, I couldn't help but wonder where that strength had come from. Only gods can create energy from nothing after all, and the Burned Man's not a god. That power had to have come from somewhere, and the Burned Man isn't the charitable sort. I couldn't help but wonder which one of the Rose and Crown's patrons was going to die in their sleep from simple exhaustion that night. As long as it was no one I knew, I didn't really care, to be perfectly honest with you. Was that wrong of me? Yeah, it probably was, but right then I really didn't care about that either.

"If you say so," Trixie said. "I'm going to bed."

I gestured helplessly towards the sofabed.

"Should I, um...?"

"You can sleep with me," she said. "*Sleep.*"

I nodded. Yeah, I think we were all pretty clear what that meant by now and I wasn't sure she really needed to spell it out again. All the same, I supposed that meant she couldn't be *too* angry with me.

"Right," I said. "Well, OK. Good. I'll have the bathroom after you then."

"I suppose you should feed your nasty little friend before you come to bed," she said.

I blinked. *Shit!* Of course I didn't actually need to feed the fetish now that there was nothing in it, but I didn't want Trixie realising that. I had to keep up appearances, after all, and I was starting to slip.

"Yeah, I should," I said. "I don't want it getting grumpy."

She headed to the bathroom and I went through to my workroom. I shut the door behind me and sagged down onto the floor with my back to the wall and put my hands in my lap. They still hurt, and I looked down at them with a sigh. *This one crushed a Russian enforcer's hand. That one broke his sternum with a single punch.* This morning, in a million pound semi-detached house in Totteridge, both of them had been uncontrollable flamethrowers.

No, not uncontrollable, I realised. Just not under *my* control.

Oi, I thought. *Are you awake in there?*

'Course, the Burned Man thought back at me.

What, if you don't mind me asking, exactly the fuck are you doing to me?

I felt the Burned Man laughing in the back of my mind.

Are you complaining? it asked. *There's a lot of people who would kill for the sort of power I've given you. You're like a fucking superhero now.*

You fucking what? I'm your meat puppet half the time. I don't even know what I'm doing or saying when you're driving, and you're no more of a bleedin' hero than I am.

It made a sort of spitting noise in my head.

Get over yourself, Drake, it said. *You've got an archdemon in your head. Don't you understand what that means? No one, and I mean no one, is going to fuck with you any more. Gold Steevie? Fuck him. Barbequed Steevie more like. Those cunts this morning? Toasted. Vlad the Masturbator in the pub? Chest crushed, breathing through a tube by now I shouldn't wonder. What more do you fucking want?*

I sighed and rested my head against the wall behind me. Reasoning with the Burned Man was difficult sometimes, to put it mildly. It just didn't see the world the same way that normal people did. I supposed it wouldn't, come to think of it, what with being an archdemon and all that. It had absolutely no morals whatsoever, after all, and not even the vaguest sense of right and wrong. I rubbed my aching hands over my face and sighed again.

What did I really want to ask it? Obviously the most important thing I wanted to know was how to get rid of it, but it was hardly likely to tell me that. The other thing that was bothering me, I mean *really* bothering me, was what it was feeding on now. I had been feeding the Burned Man with my own blood for almost as long as I had known it, since I had first taken it on from Professor Davidson, but of course that had stopped since we had our little meeting of minds. To start with I had been worried I would suddenly start needing to drink blood or something ridiculous like that but thankfully that didn't seem to be the case, which was a huge relief. I didn't think I could cope with all the tragic teenage angst that seemed to come with being a vampire these days, if you believed Hollywood.

Look, I thought, *I just need to get my head around this, all right? I mean, this is all new for me. Very new. I don't even feed you any more.*

Don't you? it asked. *I'm doing just fine in here.*

I paused to think. I mean, I didn't *physically* feed it any more. And I hadn't dropped from exhaustion after any of its feats of magic either, but if it was feeding off me anyway then...

What exactly are you feeding on?

Your soul, of course, it said. *Don't worry, you'll soon reach a point where you don't miss it any more. They're fucking overrated anyway. Diabolists don't need souls.*

Where does that leave me, when it's all gone?

The Burned Man laughed, and didn't answer. I dragged myself up to my feet and left the room. I had been in there plenty long enough for Trixie to think I had fed the little monster by then, and I really wanted my bed. I heard the toilet flush, and a moment later the bedroom light came on.

"Bathroom's all yours," she called out, like we had been married for twenty years or something.

"Cheers," I said.

I stood at the bathroom sink and stared at myself in the mirror. The Burned Man was feeding on my soul. It had destroyed Gold Steevie and his lads, and Miss Marie's Initiates of the Melek Taus, and a Russian mobster. I wondered how much that had cost me. One year's damnation each? Ten? A hundred? I had no way of knowing. *Fucking hell.*

I don't know, maybe I could do a deal or something, sort it out somehow. Adam would probably know about that sort of thing.

Adam would know? Fucking hell Don, what are you thinking?

Asking Adam for help would be like making a deal with the devil. Literally. Were things really that bad?

You know, by then I think they really were.

I sighed and went to bed.

Lying next to Trixie in the darkened bedroom, I stared up at the ceiling and wondered what the hell my life had come to. A year ago I had had a girlfriend who loved me however badly I treated her, a steady source of income, and a fair idea of what I was doing. Now I had a woman I adored who wouldn't come near me, total financial dependence on her, and a souleating archdemon living in my head. I had to admit that wasn't really progress, however you looked at it.

Fucking hell.

I turned over and forced myself to go to sleep.

I was up first the next morning, and after I'd done the bathroom thing I pulled on a pair of jeans and went through to the kitchen to put the kettle on. I let the blind roll up and nearly jumped out of my skin when I saw the hideous one-eyed ginger tom staring at me. The bloody thing was sitting on the window ledge, its nose all but pressed against the glass. I sighed and opened the window.

"Morning, Rashid," I said as the cat jumped down onto the kitchen table, then the floor.

There was a shimmer in the air, a swirling that made me think of dust devils blowing atop some distant sun-baked sand dune, and then he was standing there grinning at me and wearing a battered old brown trenchcoat over a white shirt and a pair of jeans.

"Blessings of the dawn," he said.

I grunted. I wasn't feeling very fucking blessed just then, to be perfectly honest about it. I poured the coffee and offered him one.

"Thank you," he said as he took it. "We need to talk."

"Talk," I spat, and realised the Burned Man had taken control again. "Talk is all anyone fucking does these days."

"No longer," Rashid said. "The time is upon us. She comes. Now it is time to talk about doing, and then it will be time to act."

"About fucking time," the Burned Man said for me. "I'm going out of my tits here."

"The sky children will help us?" he asked.

I nodded. "Yeah, I think so."

"And the Houngan?"

"Ah, well I'm not so sure about that," I said, and that was me talking again now. "Him and Adam don't exactly get on, and he's got problems of his own right now. It might be just the four of us, I think."

Rashid's smile tightened for a moment but he nodded. "So be it," he said, and I nodded.

"Right, well, there we are," I said. "You and me and two dodgy angels. Think that'll do it?"

"That will be sufficient," Rashid said. "We must go below, to where my work lies ruined. That is where she will come through."

Shit, that meant yet another trip down the rabbit hole to gnome land then. Still, if the alternative was a war that could quite possibly lead to Armageddon then it was a small enough price to pay, I supposed.

"I've got no idea how to get down there on my own. I'll have to call Wormwood later on, get a contact with the gnomes set up," I said, and a thought occurred to me. "Shit, Wormwood. He's an archdemon too. Not a fighter maybe, but... well, maybe we can lean on him to help."

"No," Rashid said, a bit too quickly I thought. "We don't need him, and he's no fighter, as you say. The three of you will be enough."

I shrugged. "If you say so mate," I said. "Look, I'm going to take Trixie her coffee and let her know you're here. Just sit tight, yeah?"

I left him in the kitchen and went back through. She was already awake, sitting up in bed waiting for her coffee with the covers pooled around her waist. I passed her the cup and sat down on the edge of the bed.

"Rashid is here," I said.

"I know," she said. "I felt him change."

"Right," I said. *You did?* Fucking hell, she never ceased to surprise me. "Right, well. Look, he says it's happening. Today, I think. Menhit is coming through and we have to be there to face her, to stop it or to turn her back somehow. Fight her if we have to, I suppose. Whatever it takes. You and me and him, and Adam if he'll come."

"He will," she said.

"Good," I said. "I can't see Papa coming through for us right now, but I suppose I can ask him."

Trixie shook her head. "No," she said. "No, leave him alone. We really upset him last night, I think. Anyway, he and Adam are never going to work together are they?"

"No, I doubt it," I agreed.

"Right, well I'm going to have a shower and get prepared," she said. "This is going to be quite a trying day, I think."

Battling an emergent war goddess could be described as *trying* in anyone's book, I supposed. I sighed.

"Yeah," I said. "We have to go back down to the gnomes' warrens to face her, according to Rashid."

"Yes, that would make sense," she said.

It was still too early to call Wormwood so I took Rashid

down to Big Dave's for breakfast while Trixie was in the bathroom. When we came back she was sitting at my desk smoking a cigarette, and Adam was standing at the window.

"Good morning," he said.

I nodded to him, and Rashid gave him a short bow.

"Now we are assembled," Rashid began. "The only two sky children on Earth, and the–"

"Yeah, bully for us," I interrupted him before he could say anything I didn't want him to. "It's time to sort this."

I picked up the phone and called Wormwood, aware of the other three giving each other cool looks behind me. Oh what a happy band of fucking musketeers we weren't.

"What?" Wormwood snapped when he picked up.

I think he was starting to regret giving me his direct line, all things considered. He had probably only gone to bed a couple of hours ago, after all.

"It's Don," I said. "I need to contact the gnomes again."

"What the fuck for?"

"Never you mind what for. I need a number, Wormwood."

He grumbled for a bit as he fiddled with his phone, then he read out a number which I hastily scribbled down on a scrap of paper. He hung up without so much as saying goodbye, the miserable git.

I called the number he had given me. It rang for a long time, so long I was sure it wasn't going to be answered. I was about to give up when eventually there was a click and a muffled voice spoke.

"Yes?"

I cleared my throat. "Um, hi," I said. "It's Don Drake. I, um, I need to speak to Janice, please."

"To who?"

"Janice," I said again, getting irritated now. "Alice's sister. The one who led me into the deep warren when I came down there to kill the fucking Rotman for you and received the eternal thanks of your matriarch for saving all your ratty little lives. *That* Janice."

There was a thud as whoever it was dropped the phone, and I could hear what sounded like something scurrying away in a big hurry. I sighed and waited. A minute or so later someone picked up the phone again.

"Don?" she asked. "Don, is that you?"

I smiled despite myself. "Hi Janice," I said. "How are you?"

"I'm all right thanks," she said. "It worked. It really worked. I haven't gone the way poor Alice did, and Her Highness has been able to start healing the warrens. Thank you for asking. I... Well, I wasn't expecting to hear from you again."

"Yeah, well," I said. "Look, something's happening. Today, I think. I need to come back down to the deep warren where we fought the Rotman, me and some friends."

"Angelus Mortis?" Janice whispered.

I remembered that was what she had called Trixie. The Angel of Death.

"Yeah, she'll be there," I said. "Her and two geezers, and me. You don't know them but they're... well, a bit like her, if you know what I mean."

"Oh my goodness," Janice said.

"Look, can you make that happen?" I asked her. I remembered what Wormwood had told me about dealing with gnomes, and about guanxi. "I'll owe you a favour, if you can."

"All right," she said. "Meet me in the Tube, the same place as before. Nine o'clock tonight."

I shot Rashid a look.

"Nine pm?" I asked him. "Will it keep that long?"

He shook his head. "Sooner would be better, I think," he said.

So I sorted it out with Janice, feeling my favour getting larger by the minute, and arranged for her to meet us on the platform at one. I hung up. Oh good, that gave us all morning together then. What fun.

CHAPTER 23

Needless to say fun was the last word to describe it, but time passes eventually whatever you have to put up with. We had an uncomfortable and somewhat unfriendly lunch together in the City, and were on the deep platform at Bank by twelve fifty. Rashid drew a few sideways looks with his eyepatch and the horrible scar it barely covered, and Trixie drew looks everywhere just for being Trixie. Other than that no one seemed to really notice us. I was as nondescript as ever, and as usual Adam looked like he had just stepped out of an executive corner office at one of the big multinational banks above us. Git.

Something tapped my arm and I looked around to see Janice's pointed little face looking up at me from the shadow of her hood. I smiled with a warmth I didn't even have to fake. I really did like Janice.

"Hi," I said. "It's good to see you."

She nodded and tugged on my arm, leading me hurriedly off the platform and down into a side corridor. The others followed and clustered around to hide her while she unlocked a door she really shouldn't have had the keys to. I think being out in public during the day was freaking her out to be honest, and she obviously couldn't get the door shut behind us again fast enough.

"Hi," she said at last, when it was closed and locked.

"This is Janice," I said. "Janice, these are Adam and Rashid. You remember Trixie, of course."

Janice gave Trixie a nervous smile, and nodded. Rashid bowed to her.

"Honour be to the gnomes of the Earth," he said.

Adam just stood there looking unimpressed. I wanted to kick him, I really did.

"Thank you for helping us, Janice," I said. "I owe you one."

She smiled again and led the way down through the underbelly of the Tube and into the warrens. It was a bit better than it had been before, to be fair. It looked like the gnomes really were starting to put the place back together again after Bianakith's depravations. At least the rock floor wasn't spongy underfoot any more. That was certainly an improvement, if nothing else.

"I'm sure Her Highness would be pleased to receive you," Janice said as she led us through the rough brick arch from the Victorian levels into the warrens proper.

Rashid shot me a look and shook his head.

"This is a little bit urgent, I'm afraid," I said. "Can you just take us straight down to where we were before? To where we killed the Rotman, I mean."

Janice nodded. "Yes, if you like," she said.

So we carried on, winding down and down through the strangely luminescent tunnels until we came to the great cavern where I had been forced to release and then invoke the Burned Man. Oh, such happy memories. I sent Janice back up the tunnel and out of the way to wait for us. I had no idea if we'd be coming back, but if we didn't there was no sense in her dying too.

Rashid rushed across the dark expanse of rock to the corroded pile of slag that had once been his statue. He twisted his hands through a figure-of-eight movement and his staff shimmered into view. He rammed it end down into the rock floor and it stuck there like a standard. He fell to his knees before it, reached his arms up to the ceiling, and began to chant.

"The fuck is he doing?" I wondered aloud.

"Mourning his broken work, perhaps?" Trixie suggested.

"Finishing his work, I rather suspect," Adam said.

I shot him a look.

"You what?"

"I think he's bringing her through," Adam said.

He reached into his jacket and produced his monster of a handgun.

"No!" I shouted, but it was too late.

The gun roared three times, the sound rolling like thunder around the cavern as the muzzle flash lit the faintly glowing walls around us. The air flashed and flared around Rashid's staff, some three feet behind him. It was as though Adam's bullets had hit an invisible wall, like some sort of forcefield or something. Whatever it was, Rashid barely seemed to notice.

"I have one last chance to stop this," he shouted. "One final sacrifice to offer to the Veil!"

Adam was wrong, I realised. Rashid wasn't trying to bring Menhit through. Quite the opposite in fact, but now I suddenly realised exactly how he thought he could stop it from happening.

"He fucking means us," I said. "He's trying to heal the Veil, and we're supposed to be the sacrifice."

It was no wonder he had wanted Papa Armand along as well, and really hadn't wanted Wormwood. I was sure a Houngan as great as Armand was a powerful offering indeed, albeit not as powerful as the Burned Man or an angel, but nothing in its right mind would want to be offered Wormwood.

"It's too late!" Rashid said. "The Veil is dead and she is coming, and now the other comes too, to claim its prize!"

"The *other*? What the fuck *else* is coming?" I yelled at him.

Trixie spun on her heel and stared into space behind me, a look of pure horror on her face.

"Dominion!" she wailed.

Ohhhh fuck.

The cavern heaved and shuddered as blinding white light raged into the confined space. The pressure slammed me down onto my face with a hand flung across my eyes. I really hadn't expected the bloody thing to turn up in person, I had to admit.

"*Stop!*" the Dominion bellowed in a voice like Armageddon. "Let her come forth!"

"No!" Rashid shouted back. I was facing him where I lay and I could see his magical force field or whatever the hell it was seemed to be holding off the worst of the Dominion's power, but all the same he looked like he was walking headlong into a hurricane. "You can't have her! Keeping her safe is my life's work!"

I fucking thought he was this Menhit's enemy, I thought furiously at the Burned Man.

He's supposed to be, it said, and for the first time in as long as I could remember it didn't sound sure of itself. *He's always said so, and I've known him a buggering long time.*

Well it doesn't sound like it now, does it?

No, the Burned Man admitted. *I reckon if we were supposed to be a sacrifice to the Veil it was to keep her safe behind her walls, if that makes sense. It's like he's trying to keep a barrier up between her and Earth, and I don't think it's to keep her away from us.*

The Dominion roared in fury behind me.

"I must have her power," it thundered. "The war can be won, with her strength added to ours. Bianakith did its work and the Sentinel has been destroyed. She has no choice now but to come forth."

"She doesn't *want* to!" Rashid shouted at it. "She *never* wanted to. All she wants is to be left alone!"

Fucking hell. Maybe the Burned Man was right at that.

"This world calls to her," the Dominion snarled. "The petty hatreds and the constant wars draw her whether she wills it or not. Your efforts could only shield her for so long, keeper. Now I draw her forth to her rightful place at my side. Now she must come before me and do battle in my name!"

This is fucking nuts, the Burned Man thought in my head. *Rashid's been hiding her all this time, when he's been telling everyone he's been keeping her shut away so she can't hurt us. The fucking liar.*

I was fucked if I knew, to be perfectly honest about it. All I knew was that the impossible atomic presence of the Dominion behind me was holding me helpless on the ground. I couldn't see Trixie or Adam from where I was, but I doubted they were doing much better. They hadn't done the last time this had happened, I remembered.

I wasn't fucking having it.

You told me once before you could stand against a Dominion, I thought at the Burned Man. *Big bad archdemon, nothing can stop you, can it? Now would be a good time to fucking prove it, mate.*

It snarled with anger in my head. Above all else the Burned Man was proud, and sometimes I knew just which buttons to push to goad it into action. Maybe this time I goaded it just a tiny bit *too* much, looking back on it. I felt an almost physical shove as it mentally barged past me and seized control of... well, everything.

I lurched to my feet, rounding on the searing nuclear

light. The glare dimmed instantly as I suddenly found myself seeing the world the way the Burned Man did. In place of the howling, crushing *presence* of the Dominion I saw it for what it really was.

The Dominion had the form of a man, a man so divinely beautiful it made Adam look like a scabby old tramp. It was wearing ornate silver armour chased with gold filigree, and huge feathered white wings spread from its back and cast an enormous shadow on the wall behind it. It held a long silver sword in its hands, and the pommel was a blazing orb of white light as bright as the sun.

And that's where it all went wrong.

The light from the sword shifted as the Dominion moved, and I saw its true aura writhing and rotting around it, black and purple with rancid decay. Black flames licked up from that appalling aura, twisting in the air like serpents. There was no golden glow left in there any more, none at all.

If she comes through and sides with this sodding Dominion, then whatever it wants, it's getting, the Burned Man had told me. Just the sight of the Dominion was enough to tell me how bad that would be. We had to stop this.

Somehow.

Trixie and Adam were lying prone on the ground before it as I had been, but I was up and moving now under the Burned Man's control. I reached down and touched each of them on the back of the neck, feeling a jolt of unholy power shoot down my arm with each touch. They got to their feet beside me, astonished looks on their faces. Trixie stared at her Dominion and started to weep.

"It's fallen," she sobbed. "Adam was right, my Dominion has *fallen!*"

She looked about ready to sink to her knees in floods of tears, and I'm sorry but no one could afford that luxury right then. Maybe later, if we had a later, but not now.

"Fight!" I shouted at her. I grabbed her arm and half-turned her to face me, yelling into her tear-streaked face. "You're a soldier, aren't you? Go and fucking fight!"

Adam didn't need telling. He dropped to one knee and braced his huge pistol in both hands with a grim look on his face. He blazed at the Dominion, spent shell casings fountaining out of the weapon as it roared in the darkness. Trixie twisted her hand through the air and produced her sword at last. I could only assume Adam's pistol was no more a normal gun than Trixie's weapon was a normal sword. For one thing it seemed to have an endless supply of bullets, and for another the Dominion was clearly feeling the impacts that smashed into its gleaming armour, making it stagger backwards under the onslaught. Trixie's sword burst into flames as she took her guard position.

Something lashed out of the Dominion's blade, and to this day I have no idea what it was. Something like the blasphemous offspring of a devourer's tentacle and a bolt of black lightning leapt from the sword and grabbed Adam around the waist. He shot it over and over again at pointblank range, cursing as it wrenched him off his feet.

"Fallen abomination!" the Dominion bellowed at him.

Adam's bullets didn't seem to be having any effect at all on whatever this new horror was. The tentacle whipped him up into the air then smashed him down onto the ground hard enough to pulverise the rock beneath him into a deep crater. Flames roared up from that crater, and Adam was gone.

"Adam!" Trixie screamed.

I chanced a look over my shoulder at Rashid, hoping he might be coming to help.

He wasn't.

Rashid was on his knees, his arms outstretched and his face almost on the floor in a posture of total obeisance.

Something was standing over him. A tall figure stepped out of the shadows until I could see it clearly. A female figure, I could see now. She strode forth into the glowing light of the Dominion's blade and I saw her face. The Black Lion, I remembered Rashid calling her once, and I could see now what he had meant.

This was Menhit, The Slaughterer.

She Who Massacres.

She stood well over six feet tall, naked and black and lean and muscular. Her hair hung about her face in a hundred thin black braids that brushed her shoulders as she moved. She had the broad, flat face of a lion, and her eyes were two blazing suns of molten gold. There was a great bronze bow in her hands, almost as tall as she was, and the arrow she held nocked appeared to be made of pure living flame.

She threw back her head and roared.

"Come to me, goddess of war," the Dominion commanded. "Come storm the gates of Heaven at my side!"

Menhit took a step towards me, and I knew it was all over. We were well and truly fucked, and the whole world with us.

I found myself standing back to back with Trixie, her facing the Dominion with her flaming sword in her hands and sobs racking her body while I stared into the eyes of an ancient Nubian war goddess. Flames erupted from my hands as the Burned Man prepared to do battle, but I knew it was hopeless. However powerful the Burned Man might be, it wasn't a god. I could only see one way this was going to end.

I felt Trixie move behind me, the back of her arm brushing mine as she shifted her guard and prepared to try to kill her father and her king.

"I love you," I said.

It wasn't like I was going to get another chance to say it.

"Yes," she said.

She went for the Dominion with a shriek of righteous fury. It had fallen, and I could barely begin to guess how utterly betrayed she must have felt by that. I heard a furious clash of blades behind me, and allowed myself a grim smile. Trixie was in no mood for forgiveness, that much was abundantly clear. I didn't have the luxury of watching her though. Menhit strode towards me, her burning arrow at half draw. I swayed, mesmerised for a moment as she met my stare with her glowing golden eyes. I could feel the flames licking out of my hands but something held me back. She drew and loosed in one fluid motion almost too fast to follow, and the arrow screamed like a thing in torment as it shot over my head and smashed into the Dominion.

Well fuck me. That was a turn-up for the books.

Menhit roared and came on at a dead run. I threw myself out of the way, trailing flames in the air from my hands. Even the Burned Man wasn't going to take *that* on if it didn't have to, and by some miracle it looked like we might not have to after all. I rolled in time to see Trixie dashed aside by a swipe from the Dominion's lightning tentacle thing, and then the Dominion and the goddess of war were going at it like the very fucking end of the world.

Menhit's bow had turned into a huge bronze sickle-shaped sword somewhere along the way, and it flashed as she sliced away the Dominion's tentacle-like weapon and met it blade to blade. The Dominion raged and blazed with light, and I winced at the thought of what that sort of release of power would have done to me if I hadn't been hiding behind the Burned Man. I think I would probably have been reduced to a greasy smear of ash on the ground by now, in all honesty.

They fought, and the cavern shook and crumbled, and fissures opened in the ground and great, ominous cracks ran up the walls. I dragged myself on all fours across the heaving ground to Trixie's side.

"I thought..." she said, when I was close enough to hear her.

"Yeah," I said. "So did I. Guess not."

It seemed that the Dominion had been mistaken. Oh, there was no longer any doubt that it had summoned Bianakith to destroy Rashid's statue, this Sentinel it had spoken of, so that it could bring Menhit through from behind her Veil to use as a weapon in its war with Heaven. Only it seemed the lady herself had other ideas.

Their battle raged until it was a wonder the entire cavern hadn't come crashing down around us. The Dominion beat its massive wings and rose into the air but Menhit sprang after it, leaping impossibly high with her blade flashing as she roared defiance. She crashed into it in midair and brought it down with one wing twisted and broken, flopping uselessly behind it.

I couldn't even begin to imagine the amount of power being used in this fight, or where it was all coming from. I got the distinct feeling that even the Burned Man was a little bit awed by what we were seeing. Only a god can create energy from nothing, after all. A Dominion is monstrously powerful but it's not a god.

But Menhit was.

The Dominion was flagging now, I could tell. It stumbled as it met Menhit blade to blade, and its riposte was slow, almost clumsy. The blazing sun in the pommel of its sword was starting to dim as it gradually ran out of strength.

The lioness was unstoppable. She fought in a constant whirlwind of bronze and fire, tireless and merciless and *utterly* relentless.

There is no other power to equal that of a god.

The Slaughterer. She Who Massacres.

Those names were well earned, it seemed. The fury of her attack never let up for a moment. She hammered the

Dominion's blade until at last she drove it to its knees in defeat, exhausted.

Finally, she spoke. Her voice was like gravel on glass, like a rusty gate creaking in the wind. A voice unused for an unimaginable length of time.

"I choose my own battles," she said.

She spun her sword into a reverse grip and plunged it down two-handed into the Dominion's heart.

There was an unearthly shriek that seemed to go on forever. The ground beneath the Dominion opened up in a huge crevasse and an inferno erupted from it to kiss the roof of the cavern. The Dominion swayed helplessly, an anguished look on its perfect face as Menhit withdrew her weapon from its chest. It collapsed at last and fell screaming into the burning abyss beneath it. The rock fissure closed with an awful grinding noise, and all the fires went out.

Trixie put her head in her hands and wept.

I had an awful feeling I had just seen the mouth of Hell itself open up and swallow the fallen Dominion. I supposed that was the end of that then.

I looked up and saw Menhit's golden eyes glowing in the darkness.

Maybe it wasn't.

She stalked slowly towards us, her sword shimmering out of existence as she walked.

Now what the fuck do we do? I asked the Burned Man.

Buggered if I know, it said.

I'm afraid that was hardly reassuring.

"Mother," I heard Rashid say.

Menhit stopped about ten feet from us and turned to look at him. I chanced a look that way too and saw he was still on his knees beside his upraised staff.

"Keeper," she said. "You failed me."

I very clearly heard Rashid swallow. He got to his feet

and approached with obvious trepidation. Menhit seemed completely unashamed of her nudity but when Rashid took off his trenchcoat and offered it to her she slipped it on and belted it without a word.

"Five thousand years, Mother," he said, backing away again as fast as he could. He was obviously terrified and I couldn't say I blamed him, to be perfectly honest. "For five thousand years I have kept your Veil. I have kept you safe from the predations of this world for–"

"You should have been guarding the Sentinel. You failed me."

The bow reappeared in her hands faster than I could even follow. She drew and loosed in a blur of movement, and an arrow of screaming fire impaled Rashid through the chest. He went up like a Roman candle, turning instantly into a pillar of flame. He burned until there was nothing left of him.

Nothing at all.

The bow vanished again, and Menhit turned the pitiless suns of her stare upon us.

"A lord of the Below and his sky child guardian," she said.

I winced inwardly at that, but if Trixie took it in, she gave no sign of it. I supposed her finding out what I had become was probably the least of my worries right at that moment.

"Mother of War," I said, inclining my head respectfully.

At least the Burned Man usually seemed to know the right sort of thing to say when it really mattered, that was something I supposed.

"Mother of Death," Trixie echoed, and she too bowed her head before the goddess.

I have to admit that surprised me. Maybe she was just following my lead, I don't know, but if so, it sounded bloody convincing. We both knelt before Menhit. When you meet a real actual goddess in the flesh you don't have a lot of other fucking options, you know what I mean?

Menhit stood over us, black and terrible and murderous, wearing Rashid's scruffy old trenchcoat like it was Cleopatra's finest robe. She looked down at me, and then at Trixie, and I could feel the power coming off her like wild electricity, like lightning.

Nothing had ever felt like this before, not even the Dominion at its most theatrical. The Dominion had always felt like it was putting a lot of effort into appearing terrible, if you know what I mean. I had an awful suspicion Menhit was putting effort into appearing *less* terrible than she was, and I was still about ready to piss myself with fear.

That, if you aren't quite getting it yet, is what a goddess is like.

"I require a new keeper of the Veil," she said at last. "The position is yours."

I looked up at her and gaped. That didn't sound like an invitation so much as a direct bloody command. I could feel the Burned Man about to say something that I think we'd all have regretted, and I managed to mentally strangle it just in time. I knew I really didn't have much choice about this.

"Honour to serve, Mother," Trixie said, and I echoed her words without even thinking about it.

That, looking back on it, was fucking stupid of me.

CHAPTER 24

As I've said before, Trixie was a soldier, not a general, and a soldier needs a chain of command above her. With her Dominion gone, I could see she had slotted Menhit into that role almost instantly. We walked out of the deep warrens together, the goddess striding barefoot and naked under Rashid's old coat. Trixie marched by her side like some sort of Praetorian Guard, and I followed behind in their wake.

"I will require funds and domicile, servants and so forth," Menhit was saying. "If I must dwell once more upon this plane then I shall do so in a manner befitting my station."

Goddess seeks suitable accommodation, servants and so forth, I thought. *Funds available are the square root of fuck all.*

Oh dear God, what were we going to *do* with her? I could hardly have her at my place, that went without saying. I dreaded to even think what she would make of my grotty little flat. Who the fuck could I dump her on until Trixie and I at least had the chance to talk? I wondered what she would think of Wormwood. He was rich at least, but he was also bloody horrible. No, I couldn't see Menhit wanting to kip in Wormwood's spare room somehow. Of course, he wasn't the *only* multimillionaire I knew.

Sorry Papa, I thought. *I think the Guédé just called in your debt.*

Poor bastard. Although knowing him he'd probably try to shag her, goddess of war or not. I wondered how *that* would work out for him.

We made our way back out of the deep warren and found Janice waiting for us in the next tunnel, bless her.

"Hi," I said. "Hi, Janice."

She looked at the three of us, and there was no hiding the fact that Adam and Rashid weren't there any more. There was even less hiding Menhit.

"Oh my goodness," she said.

"A gnome?" Menhit asked.

Janice nodded nervously, and gave me a look that quite plainly said *help*. She had at least a rough idea of what stood before her, I could tell.

"The gnomes of the deep Earth have served us well, Mother," I said.

By then I really had no idea if that was me or the Burned Man talking. My grip on reality was probably a bit loose at that point, to be perfectly honest with you, and I knew it was getting worse. The Burned Man seemed to be doing at least half of my talking for me now. What was with calling her *Mother* anyway? I had no idea, but the Burned Man obviously thought it was the correct way to address her. She didn't seem to mind, anyway. She nodded.

"Good," she said. "Honour be to the gnomes of the Earth."

Janice bowed her head and I'd swear she was blushing, poor little thing.

"Could you perhaps guide us back to the surface, please Janice?" I asked her.

She did as I asked without question or complaint, and again I could feel the favour I owed her growing arms and legs and getting bigger and bigger. Ah well, there was no help for that now I supposed. She had more than earned it, bless her heart.

When Janice finally returned the three of us to the Tube station I looked at the clock and was amazed to see it was only late afternoon. Somehow after the events we had just witnessed, it felt like it should have been the dead of night, but there you are. I gave Janice a goodbye squeeze and told her to call me if she ever needed my help with anything. I had a strong suspicion that she would, sooner or later.

Even down in the Tube, the sight of Menhit standing on the platform barefoot in Rashid's trenchcoat was drawing a few odd looks. If she just hadn't been quite so tall it would have helped, although I noticed that at least her eyes had stopped glowing. That was probably for the best, all things considered. You can get away with a lot of weird shit on the Tube but that might have been a stretch too far all the same.

"Don," Trixie asked me as Menhit stared silently at the sights around her, lost in thought. "What are we going to do now?"

I sighed. "I have no idea," I said. "I reckon we'll have to try and stash her at Papa Armand's for now. His place is the closest thing I know to a palace."

"It's not going to do for long though, is it?" Trixie said.

"No," I said. "No, I don't think it is."

I felt the familiar push of warm stale air coming out of the tunnel, and a moment later a train pulled up to a halt at the platform.

"Mind the gap," the station system announced in its automated voice. "Mind the gap."

The train doors hissed open and there was the usual surprisingly efficient dance of people getting on and off around each other. I was aware of Menhit standing there, staring at the train as though hypnotised. There was an unreadable expression on her face.

"Well, keeper?" she demanded after a moment, seeming to snap out of her trance. "What have you prepared for me?"

"Um," I said. "Look, I just need to make a quick call, all right?"

She gave me a blank look. Oh God, she didn't know anything about anything, did she? The last time she had been on Earth it was probably the fucking Bronze Age or something.

"The keeper will speak to your subjects," Trixie translated, and Menhit nodded.

I hurried along the platform until I found a payphone. I really did ought to get a mobile, I knew I did, not that they worked very well down the Tube anyway. I shovelled coins into the phone and punched Armand's number.

"Papa, it's Don," I said. "Look, I need a really big favour. The mother of all fucking favours, I'm afraid."

He grumbled a bit while I explained, but he was pretty much all right about it. Admittedly I may have left out one or two key details, like exactly who the woman I needed to hide at his apartment actually was. If I had explained he would never have agreed to it, which was why I didn't.

We went up to the street and I hailed us a cab, and waved enough money around for the cabbie not to ask any awkward questions about the state of the three of us. We sat in silence as he drove us to Knightsbridge. Menhit was staring out of the window of the taxi, gripping the seat so hard her knuckles were turning white. Her self-control was admirable but I could tell she was fighting to conceal sheer terror. Whatever must the towering, headlong rush of modern London look like to eyes that hadn't seen the world in five millennia? Trixie was just staring at her boots, looking lost. I sighed again. Life never got simpler, did it?

Papa Armand opened the door of his apartment and gave

me a weary nod. He really didn't look himself either, truth be told.

"Come in Don-boy," he said. "Zanj Bèl."

I ushered Trixie into the flat ahead of me, and Papa's gaze found Menhit at last. His smile broke like the rising sun.

"Mademoiselle," he said, giving her a courtly bow.

"*Je suis Maman*," she corrected him in flawlessly accented French. "*Mère de la guerre.*"

He blinked and looked at her again, properly this time.

"Ah," he said. "Don-boy, maybe there somethin' you'd like to explain?"

Fucking hell, here we go.

"Can we at least come in?" I asked him.

He paused for a moment, giving Menhit another long look, then nodded and held the door open for us to follow Trixie inside. He locked the door firmly behind us. I kicked my shoes off and padded down the luxurious white carpet into the sitting room.

The mesmerising origami cabinet had been smashed to pieces, and there were dark drink stains on the carpet. At least I *hoped* they were just drink stains. Even the big smoked glass windows that led out onto his balcony were cracked, I noticed, and there was a long burn mark up one wall that had definitely not been there before. He saw me looking and nodded his shiny bald head slowly.

"Guédé come visit last night," he said, by way of explanation.

I didn't know a great deal about the death loa of Vodou but I knew they were a pretty wild bunch by all accounts. From what little I knew of how Papa's magic worked I suspected he had done the damage himself whilst possessed by the spirits. If Papa had invoked the Guédé Barons last night then it was a testament to his power and control that the place was still standing at all.

"If you would please come with me, Mother," Trixie said to Menhit, "I'll find you some more fitting clothes."

She led the goddess up Papa's floating stairs to the second floor and I heard a door close behind them. I turned to Papa.

"Is Jocasta still here?" I asked.

I left the question deliberately ambiguous. When Papa gave his head a sombre shake I was glad I had. I'd rather not know, to be honest with you. Still, she might have been young but she knew the risks. At least, I sincerely hoped she had. Oh well, done was done and no help for it now.

"Your lady friend," Papa said. "Talk to me."

"Her name is Menhit," I said, and Papa hissed like he had been stung. "You remember that guy Rashid?"

Papa nodded slowly, his jaw set in a hard line as he looked at me.

"Yeah, well," I said. "Turns out he was her priest or something, apparently. Keeper of the Veil, she calls it. He'd been putting it about for just about ever that he was her enemy, that he was keeping her walled up safe somewhere the other side of a Veil, and that was sort of true. I think he *had* been doing that, but not to keep *us* safe from *her*. Because she commanded him to, is my understanding, so she would be left alone. Now, when Trixie's Dominion needed Menhit's help for its war in Heaven it summoned Bianakith to dissolve this Sentinel thing of Rashid's that was keeping her Veil closed, and once that was gone the Veil fell apart and she couldn't help but come through, even though she never wanted to. I think."

I realised Papa Armand was looking at me like I had grown a second head, and that was *without* me mentioning that I seemed to have agreed to become Rashid's replacement.

"Slow down Don-boy," he said, "and maybe run this past me jus' one more time. Upstairs in my bedroom, Madame Zanj Bèl is trying on clothes with Menhit the Black Lion of

Nubia, is that what you sayin' me?"

It sounded even more bonkers when he put it like that, I had to admit. I nodded.

"Yeah, pretty much," I said.

Papa threw back his head and roared with laughter.

"You got Guédé spirit in you, Don-boy, I give you that," he said.

I thought about the Burned Man, and had to admit he was probably right. In a way, anyway.

"Yeah well," I said. "Shit has a way of... I dunno, Papa. Look, I really need this favour. Can you keep her here for a bit? I mean, I don't think she's dangerous right now. Not yet, anyway. When we pulled her out of the deep warren she was all on about us sorting her a palace and servants and all that shit, but ever since she saw a train and some traffic and a few buildings she's gone bloody quiet, you know what I mean? I think she's half dead of culture shock, to be perfectly honest with you."

"She speaks French," Papa pointed out.

"And English," I said. That was just as odd, now that I actually thought about it. "Oh I don't know do I? She's a *goddess* Papa, who knows what she can do."

"Anything I choose," she said from behind me, and I almost jumped out of my skin.

I turned to see her and Trixie standing on the stairs looking down at the two of us. They had both changed, into clothes from wherever the hell Trixie whistled her wardrobe up from, I could only assume. Trixie was looking refreshed in clean jeans and a white silk blouse, whereas Menhit had gone modern formal in a black pinstriped business suit with black nylons and high heels, and a black satin blouse unbuttoned low enough to show off the impressively large gold necklace Trixie had found for her from God only knew where.

Menhit stalked down the stairs, her high heels clicking on the polished wood. She towered over Papa Armand, at least a head taller than him in those shoes. She smiled.

"I will stay here in the tower palace, with this priest," she said. "You have done well, keeper."

I bowed my head despite myself.

All the same though, *anything I choose*? I doubted that, to be perfectly honest. Once, maybe, surrounded by worshipers in a world she understood. But now? I didn't think so somehow. I mean, would she still have been there with the likes of us if she really could do anything she wanted? I wasn't going to get into that right then, but it was definitely something to think about.

"Thank you Mother," I said.

She ignored me and ran a hand slowly up Papa Armand's arm.

"I will like it here," she said, examining him the way one would consider a minor but interesting purchase. "I have not had a fuck for many thousands of years."

Papa just grinned at me, the dirty old bastard. I could only hope he had plenty of Viagra in his nightstand. I thought he was going to need it.

"We should be going," Trixie said, and I couldn't have agreed more.

We left Papa and his goddess to it and fled.

CHAPTER 25

"Well that was odd," I said once we were settled into the back of a taxi.

Trixie just nodded. I looked at her, and saw that all the good humour had gone out of her face. She had done a great job of faking it for Menhit, but now that we were alone I could see how devastated she still was.

I sighed. I really didn't even know how to approach this one. Her Dominion had fallen, beyond all doubt. She had been forced to attempt to kill it herself in fact, and I dread to think what that must have cost her. She had adopted Menhit as her new patron seemingly without thinking, and I hated to admit it but I appeared to have done the same thing. Who knew how the presence of a goddess affected minds? Now that we were a couple of miles away from her though, weaving through the early evening traffic, the whole idea started to feel more than a bit iffy. To put it fucking mildly.

"Trixie," I said, "are you all right?"

She looked at me, and I could see the hurt in her beautiful blue eyes.

"No, not really," she said. "I'm never going home, am I?"

Poor Trixie. I had to admit that it didn't look like it. All her allegiance had been to that one Dominion and now it had fallen. I didn't know where that left her, and fuck only knew what was going on Upstairs at the moment anyway. Besides, now she had sworn to serve Menhit it seemed to me that she had deserted and gone mercenary anyway, which made it all a bit of a moot point. Perhaps now wasn't a good time to mention that though.

I put my hand over hers and squeezed her fingers.

"We'll think of something," I said.

She shrugged. "Perhaps," she said. "Are *you* all right?"

"No," I admitted. "And more to the point I'm worried. Did we, you know, sign anything? Metaphorically, I mean. Have we agreed to something we'll struggle to get out of?"

"I don't know," she said. "Perhaps."

"Do you think Adam will know?" I asked. "I mean, he ought to know all about pacts and that sort of–"

"Adam's *dead!*" she screamed at me, and I flinched.

I saw the cabbie giving us a look in the rear view mirror, and did my best to ignore him. *Shit.* I really hadn't given Adam much thought, what with everything else that had happened, but now that she mentioned it…

"We can't know that," I said.

"You saw where he went," Trixie said.

"Yeah I did," I replied, keeping my voice too low for the cabbie to hear. "He went back to Hell. He fell into it once and got out, who's to say he can't do it again?"

Trixie looked at me, and a faint smile touched her lips. It looked like hope.

"Do you think so?"

For fucksake, I wanted that smug git stuck in Hell until the end of days, but… Trixie was still in love with him, there were no two ways about it. How did I put up with that, loving her as I did? It was pathetic, I knew it was, but there we were.

"Yeah, I reckon," I said. "I reckon he'll be back before we know it."

"Perhaps," she said. "I hope so."

I sighed and ran my fingers through my hair. I really *didn't* hope so but I didn't want to get into that with her now. I sat back in the seat and sighed again.

"Home, then a shower and something to eat," I said. "Everything else will keep until then at least."

"Yes," Trixie said softly. "Yes, I suppose it will."

We rode the rest of the way in silence. Back at mine we took turns to shower and change, and I went and sat in the workroom for five minutes to keep up the pretence of needing to feed the Burned Man. The angel's skull I had borrowed from Wormwood was still sitting under the altar, grinning at me.

I really ought to give that back before he gets stroppy about it.

We went out to eat as usual. I had bugger all in the fridge anyway, and I'm a shit cook at the best of times. I sat across the table from Trixie in the little Italian place around the corner from my flat, pushing my spag bol about on the plate and working my way steadily through my second bottle of red. I wasn't really hungry now that it came to it, and the atmosphere was more than a bit strained. Neither of us had said anything for far too long.

"Seriously Trixie," I said eventually, "what *are* we going to do?"

She blinked and looked up at me.

"Sorry Don?" she said. "About what?"

About you and me, I wanted to say. I didn't quite dare, though.

"About everything," I said. "I don't fucking know. About Menhit, most of all."

Trixie shrugged. "I don't know," she said. "We swore to serve her."

"Yeah I know we did, but... oh fucking hell, seriously? I mean, neither of us were really in our right minds at the time were we?"

"She appointed you her new keeper," Trixie pointed out, a bit waspishly I thought. "If you didn't want the job, that would have been the time to say so."

"I didn't really feel like I was being given an option," I said. "What does that even *mean* anyway, keeper of the Veil?"

"I have no idea," she said.

I necked my wine and refilled the glass.

"Fuck it, we can always back out," I said.

"Can we? She's a *goddess*, Don. Can you go back on your word to a goddess?"

Oh I was fucked if I knew. I bloody well hoped so, that's all I could think.

Oi, are you awake in there? I thought at the Burned Man.

Nothing.

I realised I hadn't heard a peep out of it since I had accepted the position as Menhit's keeper of the Veil. That might mean nothing, or it might mean a great deal. I only wished I knew.

"I'm very tired," Trixie said. "If you're not actually going to eat that, shall we just go?"

I sighed and nodded.

"Yeah," I said. "I think we're done for the day."

We were done for quite a few days, as it went. I don't think either of us woke up much before noon the next day and we were both still knackered even then. It really had been a hell of a couple of weeks. I kept waiting for some urgent summons to come from Menhit, and it kept not coming. Part of me wanted to call Papa Armand and make sure he was still alive over there but the bigger part of me said to let sleeping goddesses lie. Whatever was going on in Papa's penthouse, Trixie and I needed a rest.

We spent the best part of a week just resting up, sleeping and eating and watching old movies together. Proper ones, from before they invented all that computer generated shit that makes everything look like a cartoon. I think Trixie even enjoyed some of them, although it was hard to tell. She was still withdrawn and quiet, mourning both Adam and her Dominion. I just kept my head down really, trying not to drink too much and remembering to pretend to feed the Burned Man every day. The little git still hadn't said a word, and if I hadn't known better I could almost have forgotten it was there inside me. Maybe facing down the Dominion had taken more out of it than I had thought.

It was Saturday afternoon and once more I was sitting on the floor of my workroom, contemplating my navel while I waited for enough time to pass for Trixie to reasonably think I had been feeding the Burned Man. That angel's skull was still grinning at me from underneath the altar. I glared at it. A fat lot of use that had turned out to be in the end.

I got up and poked about in the room for a bit, straightening my books and tidying the contents of the drawers. Ally's dagger was back in the cupboard, and the flat black case containing the hexring I had used on Charlie Page was nestled next to it. Neither exactly had happy memories attached to them but you never knew, I might be glad of them again one day. I hoped not, to be perfectly honest about it, but I was too used to my life by then to discount the possibility.

Oh bugger it, I really did need to get out of the flat for a bit.

"Hey," I said when I came back through to the office.

Trixie looked up at me from her seat on the sofa, a long black cigarette smouldering between her fingers.

"Mmmm?"

"I really ought to give Wormwood his skull back," I said. "I thought I might pop over to the club with it tonight if you fancy a bit of a night out?"

She shrugged. "I suppose we could," she said.

She didn't look exactly keen but she hadn't said no either and that was good enough for me. I was feeling pretty well rested up by then and truth be told I was starting to get bored. A few drinks and a hand or two of cards would put the spring back in my step, especially as I still had that couple of grand I had taken from red-eyed Antonio sitting on my account at the club. I grinned at her.

"Nice one," I said.

I pottered about for a bit, had a shave and another shower I didn't really need, shined my shoes and did all the other pointless shit you do before you go for a night out. We had a quick bite to eat and were getting ready to leave when the doorbell rang.

I frowned and pressed the button on the intercom.

"Don Drake," I said.

"Lord keeper," a voice said. "I would speak with you."

I blinked. That was fucking ominous. I took my finger off the button.

"Trixie," I called, "we've got company."

She hurried out of the bedroom, barefoot in the long black evening dress she had produced for the occasion.

"Who is it?"

"Some geezer who knows to call me lord keeper," I said.

She nodded. "Let him in."

She had a look on her face that said she had been getting bored too, and was starting to fancy a good fight to cheer herself up. I love her, I really do, but she *is* a bit mental if I'm honest about it. I pressed the button to open the door.

I heard footsteps on the stairs then the door opened and

a man walked in. He was tall and broad shouldered and sort of Arabic looking, wearing a smart jacket and neatly pressed slacks. He ignored Trixie completely, and looked at me for a long moment. Then he knelt at my feet.

"Lord keeper," he said, and bowed his head.

"Um," I said. "I... um... Evening."

"I am Mazin," he said. "I am your humble servant."

"Right," I said. "Why's that then?"

"My order served your predecessor, the Lord Rashid," he said, "and so now we serve you in turn as the new keeper of the Veil."

You must confer with your people, as I must with mine, I remembered Rashid saying in the back room of the Rose and Crown. Of course, I didn't actually *have* any "people" as such, but it looked like he really had. It seemed this was one of them, probably the boss of them by the sounds of it, kneeling in front of me on the floor of my office. Fucking hell, I'd never had "people" before. I must admit I had no idea what to say to him.

"I am the lord keeper's guardian," Trixie said, rescuing me as usual. "You may rise, and address your petition to me."

Mazin got to his feet and bowed respectfully to her.

"Madam guardian," he said.

"Right," I said again, completely spoiling Trixie's attempt to establish protocol. I'm afraid I really am shit at this sort of thing. "So, um, what can I do for you, Mazin?"

"It is for you to command *us*, lord keeper," he said. "I wished only to convey my respects upon your glorious elevation, and make ourselves known to you."

He took a small black book out of the pocket of his jacket and handed it to Trixie with another short bow.

"It is all in the book," he said.

"My thanks," she said.

He seemed to have accepted her as my bodyguard or

chamberlain or something, which I have to admit was a bit of a relief. Trixie was so much better at all this formal crap than I was.

"Thank you, Mazin," I said.

He bowed low to me.

"I will take my leave, lord keeper, and trouble you no longer," he said.

"Night then," I said.

He bowed yet again, and turned and left. I waited until I heard the front door close behind him before I turned to Trixie with a bewildered look. She was already leafing through the book.

"What the fuck was that all about?" I asked her.

She shrugged. "Rashid had staff," she said. "They're your staff now."

"Well you're going to have to be my chief of staff," I said. "I'm hopeless at shit like this."

"Yes you are," she said.

Well, she needn't have agreed with me quite that quickly as far as I was concerned, but whatever. She was right and we both knew it.

Anyway, after that unexpected little bit of excitement we were running late, so we both hurried up and finished getting ready then rode a cab to Wormwood's club. I really wanted to see what was in Mazin's book but I supposed it would have to wait until we got home now. *People*, I couldn't help smirking to myself as the cab bounced over the potholes towards Wormwood's place. *I've got people. Fuck me, I've arrived.*

I had the big aluminium flight case containing the angel's skull on the floor of the car between my feet. I must admit I had been half tempted to just fucking keep it, after the amount of shit Wormwood had dropped me in lately, but that wouldn't do much for the health of our future business relationship. I hated depending on him, but there we were. I really did need to find another alchemist, and soon.

He was certainly pleased to get it back, that was for sure. Wormwood grabbed the case out of my hands with avaricious, nicotine-stained fingers as soon as I presented it to him in the smoky club. Before I knew it one of his creepy croupiers was carrying it through into his private office. He gave me a slippery smile.

"I trust that everything's equal now and we're all friends again then, Don?" he said.

Obviously he wouldn't have been anything like as pleasant if Trixie hadn't been standing right beside me. She still had that look on her face that said she was just waiting for an excuse to hurt someone, and I knew damn well Wormwood had picked up on it. *Good*.

"Yeah, we're fine," I said.

He nodded and found an excuse to make himself scarce. I collared a passing waiter and snagged us each a glass of champagne.

"Interesting night so far," I said.

Trixie nodded, then narrowed her eyes. "It's about to get more interesting, I think," she said.

I turned to see what she was looking at, and almost choked. Across the club Papa Armand was playing craps, his black silk top hat bobbing as he threw the dice. Beside him, standing almost seven foot-tall in her high heels, was Menhit.

"Fuck a duck," I muttered. "I've got to go say hello, you know I have."

Armand was my Papa, which in Haitian Vodou means he was my spiritual teacher. That meant, in the etiquette of Haiti anyway, that if I saw him somewhere I *had* to go over and interrupt whatever he was doing and say hello. It would have been unforgivably rude not to. That aside,

I really wanted to know how he was getting on with the lovely Menhit.

"Of course," Trixie said. "I'll come with you."

I nodded and we both threaded our way through the crowd to the craps table.

"Hello, Papa," I said.

Papa turned and grinned at me. "Don-boy, how you doin'? Zanj Bèl, always a delight to see you."

Menhit regarded me with her glowing golden eyes.

"Mother," I said, perhaps a little belatedly. "Honour to serve."

Obviously I should have spoken to her first. I realised that now. Too late, admittedly, but at least I realised it, you have to give me that much. I told you I was shit at the formal stuff.

"Keeper," she said.

"Honour to serve, Mother," Trixie echoed me.

Menhit nodded to her. "Guardian."

Now that we had finally finished swapping titles and platitudes it seemed no one really had anything to actually say. Menhit towered over all of us, magnificent in a dark red designer evening gown that looked like it had been eyewateringly expensive. Her fingers glittered with diamonds, and there was a thick rope of gold and emeralds around her neck.

I touched Papa on the arm and leaned close to whisper in his ear.

"Are you all right?"

He grinned and nodded. "Fucking good," he said. "I feel eighteen again, wi' a cock like iron."

"Um, right," I said. "Good."

That was a little bit too much information really. I dread to think what the two of them had been up to but it obviously hadn't done him any harm, which was all that really mattered. Of course he must have been spending a fortune on her, but then he *had* a fortune so I supposed that was up to him.

"And Menhit?"

"She still adjustin' I think," he murmured. "The world not how she remember it, Don-boy."

"No, I bet it's not," I said.

I winced as I heard her barking orders at a waiter, then at the croupier and even at the customer beside her, her fingers snapping imperiously to emphasise her frequent demands.

"People not quite how she remember them either," Papa chuckled. "It goin' take time, and lots of shopping I don' doubt, but we get her there."

I laughed, and he gave me a wink.

"Where your other friend," he asked after a moment, "the one who likes guns?"

Damn it, Papa, did you have to?

Trixie was close enough to have heard that, and being reminded of Adam was the last thing she needed right then.

"He'll be back before we know it," I said, forcing a smile I didn't feel.

Adam was back before we knew it all right – the wanker was waiting for us in my office when we got home that night. I nearly bit my tongue off when I saw the look of joy on Trixie's face.

"Adam!" she said. "Adam, you're alive!"

He did look a bit the worse for wear, truth be told, but there he was all the same. Oh sure his suit was ragged and burned, and he had a long cut under his left eye that only served to make the bastard look even more rakishly handsome than usual, but other than that he was as hale and hearty and annoying as ever.

"It was such a joy to see my adopted home again," he said

dryly. "I see you both survived. How?"

"Menhit killed the Dominion," I said. I didn't honestly feel like I owed him any more explanation than that.

"I see," he said. "And where is our delightful goddess of slaughter now?"

"Fucking Papa Armand's brains out, if I'm any judge," I said.

Adam snorted laughter despite himself.

"Silly old man," he said. "She'll eat him alive. Literally, I shouldn't be surprised."

Trixie gave me a bewildered look.

"I thought she was joking about that," she said.

I shrugged. "I don't think so."

"Oh," she said, and Adam laughed again.

Trixie blushed and went to use the bathroom, and I found myself face to face with Lucifer once again. This was getting to be a habit, and that was something I never thought I'd get to say.

"You crawled back out of the pit again then?" I said.

Adam gave me a cool look. "I am a duke, in Hell," he said. "That is not without its benefits."

I sighed. I supposed it wouldn't be, at that. I really didn't like the bloke but credit where it's due and all that. He was certainly connected.

Tosser.

"See any Dominions while you were down there?"

Adam showed me a cold smile.

"Just the one," he said. "It was screaming as it burned."

I realised I had never asked Adam *why* the Dominion had fallen, so I took the opportunity to pose the question.

"A war in Heaven, as I said," he told me. "Trixie's Dominion sought to bring Menhit through to use against the opposing faction, which was something of a desperate measure I think. A nuclear option, you might call it. To do that, to bring down the walls she had erected around herself, it had to summon Bianakith."

"Yeah, I know all that," I said. "But why did it fall?"

"It summoned Bianakith," Adam said again, and gave me a level look. "That's diabolism, after all."

"Yeah," I said. "And?"

"Diabolists go to Hell, Don."

I swallowed. Oh wasn't that a cheery thought, and that was *without* the Burned Man slowly eating my soul as well. I nodded slowly.

"I see," I said.

"Go and feed your pet nightmare," he said as Trixie came back into the room.

The bastard knew damn well I didn't need to, but it was as good a way as any to get rid of me for ten minutes so he could talk to her in private. I walked through to the workroom and shut the door behind me. I put the light on and sighed, and ran my hands back through my hair. It was late and I was looking forward to a good long sleep. I still wanted to read Mazin's book but it would have to keep until the morning now. Everything could keep until then, as far as I was concerned. I sat and leafed through one of my grimoires, killing time while I waited.

I was thinking so much about how good that sleep was going to be that I really didn't give any thought to what Adam might actually be *saying* to Trixie out there in my office. Not until the door suddenly banged open and she marched into the room, anyway.

She froze in the doorway, her long evening dress swirling about her ankles. My heart crashed into the pit of my stomach as I saw the stricken look on her face. I slowly turned my head and followed the direction of her gaze.

The fetish of the Burned Man stood on the ancient altar at the end of my workroom where it always had, only now it hung lifeless in the tiny chains around its wrists and ankles. It was inanimate and thick with dust, and obviously hadn't moved for weeks.

I swallowed hard.

Trixie stared at me.

"Oh Don," she breathed. "Oh Thrones and Dominions, what did you *do*?"

Of course the bloody Burned Man chose that exact moment to wake up and take over again. I lurched to my feet and grinned at her.

"Hello, Blondie," I said.

ACKNOWLEDGMENTS

I can't believe it's only been ten months since *Drake* came out. There's a lot you can do in ten months, if you follow the advice of my old Sifu: "Do the work." So I want to say thank you, Sifu, for that most practical of all advice.

I'd also like to thank the following for helping to bring *Dominion* into the world:

Nila and Chris, for beta reading once again – I'm sorry but the ingredients are here to stay!

My editor, Phil Jourdan at Angry Robot, for his guidance – he doesn't always hate everything, after all.

And of course Diane, for everything else. All the way around and back again.

ABOUT THE AUTHOR

Peter McLean was born near London in 1972, the son of a bank manager and an English teacher. He went to school in the shadow of Norwich Cathedral where he spent most of his time making up stories. By the time he left school this was probably the thing he was best at, alongside the Taoist kung fu he had begun studying since the age of 13. He grew up in the Norwich alternative scene, alternating dingy nightclubs with studying martial arts and practical magic. He has since grown up a bit, if not a lot, and now works in corporate datacentre outsourcing for a major American multinational company. He is married to Diane and is still making up stories... next there will be *Damnation*.

talonwraith.com • *twitter.com/petemc666*

PREVIOUSLY...

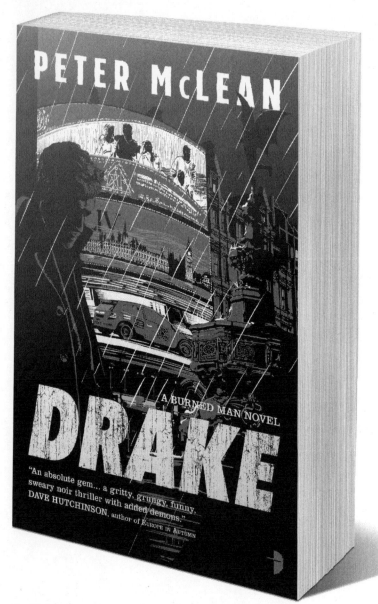

PETER McLEAN

A BURNED MAN NOVEL

DRAKE

"An absolute gem... a gritty, grungy, funny, sweary noir thriller with added demons."
DAVE HUTCHINSON, author of EUROPE IN AUTUMN

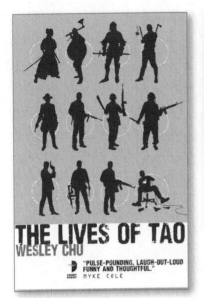

THE LIVES OF TAO
WESLEY CHU

"PULSE-POUNDING, LAUGH-OUT-LOUD FUNNY AND THOUGHTFUL."
MYKE COLE

THE DEATHS OF TAO
WESLEY CHU

"THRILLER-STYLE PLOTTING, A FINE BLEND OF GENTLE HUMOR AND SHARP SUSPENSE."
Barnes & Noble Review

"Few books begin more engagingly than *The Lives of Tao*, a science fiction romp which wears its principal strength — the wit and humour of the narrative voice — on its sleeve."
The Huffington Post

"Wesley Chu is my hero... He has to be the coolest science fiction writer in the world."
Lavie Tidhar, World Fantasy Award-winning author of Osama

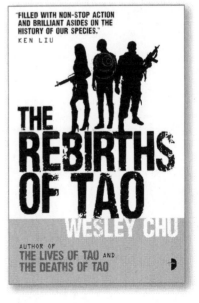

"FILLED WITH NON-STOP ACTION AND BRILLIANT ASIDES ON THE HISTORY OF OUR SPECIES."
KEN LIU

THE REBIRTHS OF TAO
WESLEY CHU

AUTHOR OF
THE LIVES OF TAO AND
THE DEATHS OF TAO

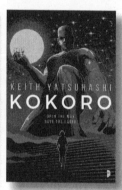

As above, so below.

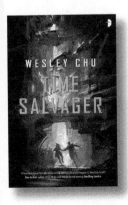